"Philippa—" he began in a ragged voice.

She didn't give him a chance to beg, to explain, to persuade. "You have gravely overstepped the boundaries of polite society."

"I didn't do it alone," St. Just responded, his eyes hot, gleaming dark with unslaked need.

"How dare you try to implicate me in your base conduct?" Philippa flamed. "Let me remind you that this is not some decadent European court filled with women who are dying of lust for your attentions."

He had the audacity to give another throaty laugh. "You're just angry because you liked it."

* * *

The Viscount Claims His Bride
Harlequin® Historical #929—January 2009

Author Note

I had such a good time writing Philippa and Valerian's story! I am a fan of reunited loves. But I also thoroughly enjoyed researching the plot surrounding them. This was a perfect opportunity to explore some interesting angles on Cornwall. Here are some:

The mining industry: The fuse Valerian considers investing in was real! It was patented at that time by the gentleman named in the story. Mining was also the perfect backdrop for Lucien's evil attempt to establish a mining cartel (mining cartels did come to pass about twenty years later).

Trist House in Veryan: Trist House was indeed owned at that time by a man who did redo the landscaping and remodel the folly where Philippa and Valerian have a very hot kiss. Quarry rock is authentic, too. Philippa and Valerian also see a monkey puzzle tree there. Research suggests that Trist House was one of the first places in Britain to attempt to grow the monkey puzzle tree, otherwise known as a Chilean pine.

The Balkans: I am a history buff, and I absolutely loved creating Valerian's experience in Negush. The Phanariot-led uprising did occur. I liked the Phanariot backdrop so much that I'm bringing it back with Lilya and Beldon's story in a forthcoming novel.

Enjoy this book. I hope you find it to be an entertaining, passionate and informative story.

Readers can stay in touch on my Web site, www.bronwynscott.com, or at my blog, www.bronwynswriting.blogspot.com.
I love hearing from my readers.

BRONWYN SCOTT

THE VISCOUNT CLAIMS HIS BRIDE

HARLEQUIN®

TORONTO • NEW YORK • LONDON
AMSTERDAM • PARIS • SYDNEY • HAMBURG
STOCKHOLM • ATHENS • TOKYO • MILAN • MADRID
PRAGUE • WARSAW • BUDAPEST • AUCKLAND

Recycling programs
for this product may
not exist in your area.

ISBN-13: 978-0-373-29529-6
ISBN-10:   0-373-29529-4

THE VISCOUNT CLAIMS HIS BRIDE

Copyright © 2009 by Nikki Poppen

First North American Publication 2009

www.eHarlequin.com

Printed in U.S.A.

DON'T MISS THESE OTHER
NOVELS AVAILABLE NOW:

#927 TEXAS RANGER, RUNAWAY HEIRESS—Carol Finch

Texas Ranger Hudson Stone must find Gabrielle Price. He believes
her to be a spoiled debutante, but Bri enflames his desires—
and the wealthy, forbidden beauty is strictly off-limits!
Romance in the rugged canyons of Texas….

#928 MARRYING THE CAPTAIN—Carla Kelly

Captain Oliver Worthy is a confirmed bachelor—so falling
in love with Eleanor Massie is about the last thing he intends!
But in the turbulence of a national emergency,
Eleanor is everything he needs....
The captain finds the woman of his dreams!

#930 HIGH SEAS STOWAWAY—Amanda McCabe

Meeting Balthazar Grattiano years after their first fateful
encounter, Bianca Simonetti finds he has sailed the seas, battled
pirates and is captain of his own ship. Bianca is shocked that her
old infatuation has deepened to an irresistible sexual attraction….
Enemies become lovers….

Prologue

London, June 1820

Valerian Inglemoore, the Viscount St Just, had a secret, a dreadful secret that caused him to tremble in guilt and self-loathing as he stood alone on Lady Rutherford's veranda, gazing at the paper lantern-lit garden beyond the balustrade, but not really seeing it.

His secret was all consuming, too consuming to spare a glance for the elegant town garden with its fountains and well-laid paths that wound through knot gardens and small privet hedges.

Under normal circumstances, the garden would have been quite enticing. But tonight, his secret was nearly too much to bear. He was twenty-one and he was in love with Philippa Stratten, Baron Pendennys's daughter, and she was in love with him. She was to meet him here tonight.

But nothing would ever come of it.

That was the secret.

Tonight, he was breaking it off with her, at her father's request. Tonight, he had to convince her after two months of stolen kisses and clandestine meetings that his affections were nothing more than a young man's fleeting fancy. He didn't know how he'd manage. He loved her so much.

After tonight, he'd never take her in his arms, never feel her run her fingers through his hair, as if it were the rarest silk. The last two months had been heaven. He'd danced with her at her début in April and every night since. They'd made a habit of heated kisses in curtained alcoves, and taking long walks in gardens during Venetian breakfasts and afternoon teas. It had been simple enough to manipulate time alone with her. He was an avid botanist as well as a horseman. It was plausible enough to say they were going off to look at a certain variety of flower or to see a new colt in the stables.

Oh, yes, they'd fallen madly in love with each other. One could almost say it was love at first sight except that he had known Philippa for years. She was his best friend Beldon's sister. The threesome had spent school holidays roaming the Cornish coast together. He'd known since his first visit home with Beldon that his heart could belong to no other.

Behind him, the Rutherfords' ballroom played host to three hundred of London's finest dancing away the night in their silks and satins, champagne never more than a footman's tray away. But he cared not a whit. His heart was breaking.

'Valerian.' A familiar, dear voice spoke his name

in the darkness. He drew a final breath, praying for the strength to give her up. It would be for her own good, although she'd never believe it.

He turned towards the sound of her voice, letting her beauty overwhelm him as it always did. The effect was no less devastating tonight. This evening, her beauty was at its zenith, shown to perfection in the pale blue fabric of her gown. In the moonlight, the fabric appeared to shimmer when she moved. A soft summer breeze drew the thin fabric of her gown against her body, reminding Valerian of the fine figure beneath the filmy layers of summer chiffon.

'Val.' She whispered his name in response, moving towards him, her hands outstretched. 'I could hardly wait.' She wore a gentle smile on her lips, a soft look for him alone in the blue depths of her eyes. It was intoxicating to think the excitement that simmered beneath the surface of that gentle smile and soft look were all for him.

He savoured it. After tonight, he would not feel such joy again.

She slipped her gloved hands into his, expecting him to take her in his arms as he usually did. He swallowed hard against the temptation. He'd come out here to do his duty to her family, a family which had loved and harboured him since his adolescence. They'd asked him to give her up for sake of their finances and her future. It was a difficult task at best. Her merest touch, her slightest affection, made it Herculean.

The embrace did not come. He could not give it to her as much as he desired to take her in his arms and feel her against him. To do so would be to fail the family in the only thing they'd ever asked of him. As a man of honour, he owed them more.

She looked up into his face, reading him aright, unconsciously warning him to better school his features if he was to carry off his task believably. 'Aren't you happy to see me?' Philippa began.

'Of course I am happy to see you. I am always happy to see a dear friend,' Valerian said, hoping Philippa didn't hear the unspoken lie. He'd always seen her as much more than a friend.

'Then kiss me. I've waited all day for you, for this moment.' She flirted, trying to press up against him, to make him take her in his arms.

He was too skilled for her untutored efforts. 'Philippa, stop. We have to talk.'

'Here?' She glanced around curiously, disappointment evident on her features. Valerian wondered what she'd been expecting that this location was not suitable. Certainly, she wasn't expecting what he had to tell her. Her father, Baron Pendennys, had indicated that Beldon and Philippa were completely in the dark about the family's situation.

The balcony was mostly empty, but there were a few couples strolling about. It wasn't nearly as private as he'd hoped. Valerian shook his head. 'No, not here. Come walk in the garden with me.'

They found a bench settled among rhododendrons in full bloom and sat. Valerian kept her hand. He nodded towards a bower of roses across the pathway. 'The roses are lovely. I hear Lady Rutherford has imported a special yellow rose from Turkey.'

He was stalling and he knew it, putting off the news as long as he could, storing up every memory of her—beautiful, innocent Philippa, believing in the purity of his love when he'd come to prove her beliefs ill founded and her heart played falsely. It would be years before she would understand this was a sham designed to protect her family.

'What is it, Val? You didn't come out here to show me roses,' Philippa coaxed.

'I spoke to your father earlier this evening.'

Her face lit with joy. A little cry of delight escaped her lips. She clapped a gloved hand over her mouth. He replayed the words in his head the way she would hear them. He knew he'd mis-stepped. She thought he had come to propose. He must be more careful, more convincing.

Valerian shook his head in warning. 'No, Philippa, it is not what you think. Your father has told me of your betrothal to the Duke of Cambourne. He accepted an offer for your hand this afternoon.'

Philippa furrowed her brow, disbelief and confusion warring across her face. His words had achieved their goal. This pronouncement was so far from what she'd expected she couldn't even be angry. She couldn't get angry with him until she put the pieces together. The poor girl hadn't even known Cambourne was interested, although the betting book at White's had been full of wagers over when the widower Duke would make his move. The men about town had privately acknowledged Cambourne's interest in the Season's finest débutante weeks ago. Valerian had hoped to wait out the storm. He might have succeeded if the Baron's need for funds hadn't been so desperate.

'Cambourne? You must be mistaken, Val.' She was all naïve logic, standing up and shaking out her skirts, convinced she only had to march into the ballroom and explain the situation to her father. 'He loves you. Nothing would please him more than to welcome you into our family. He would want this for me, for us.'

'Wait, Philippa.' Valerian kept his voice even and cold, not betraying the emotion threatening beneath his hardening veneer. 'I came out here to encourage you to accept Cambourne's offer.'

'What do you mean? You want me to marry Cambourne?' Philippa exclaimed, horrified. 'He's old enough to be my father! I don't love him. Beyond a few dances, I hardly know the man at all.' Her infamous temper started to show now that the initial shock had passed. Valerian did not relish being on the receiving end of her sharp tongue.

'You have the rest of your life to get to know him, Philippa.' Valerian dismissed her argument with callous disregard. 'He's an excellent catch for you, if you think about it.' Valerian made a show of ticking the other man's merits off on his gloved fingers. 'He's from our part of the world. You'll still be close to home and your family. He's wealthy. He loves horses as you do. He's not a cruel or unattractive man. You could find happiness with him. He will offer you stability and security.'

'But not love,' Philippa fired back. 'Here you are, laying out his assets like a business merger. But the only one I care about is love. He can't possibly love me. He doesn't know me. You know me, Val. If those criteria are so important to my father, then why won't you suit? You live in our part of the world, you love horses, you're kind and attractive, you have money. Under those conditions, I don't see why your offer isn't as good. What was wrong with you, Val? Let me talk to my father. We'll be engaged by midnight. You'll see.'

Valerian looked into the azure depths of her beseeching eyes. It was deuced awkward playing the jilt. If he was successful, she'd walk out of the garden thinking he was unaffected by the turn of events. She'd never know he'd carried a ring in his pocket for the last two weeks, hoping against hope that Cambourne's suit would come to naught.

The ring was still there, in the left pocket of his evening coat. And there it would remain. He strongly doubted he'd ever give it to another. It was slow torture to outline Cambourne's merits to her, to offer her reassurances that all would be well when in fact he didn't think he'd ever be well again. His stomach was churning.

'What was wrong with me?' Valerian echoed with feigned flippancy 'For starters, I don't want to be engaged by midnight. Secondly, I didn't ask.'

More lies. He had asked anyway, even knowing the situation. Her father had explained plainly that the young viscount didn't have enough money—at least not until he was twenty-seven and came into his inheritance. But Baron Pendennys couldn't wait that long. It had hurt enormously to realise his dreams had been sold for golden guineas. He would be a wealthy man for ever living without the one thing his money couldn't buy.

'What? You never asked?' Her eyes filled with tears, her voice full of disbelief. 'I don't understand.'

God, she was beautiful. Valerian fought the urge to pull her against him. She stood so close it would hardly be an effort to do so. He could smell the light fragrance of her lemon-scented soap rising from her skin, the lavender rinse of her clean hair.

She sat down hard on the stone bench, grasping at the logic of it all. 'I thought you loved me. I thought you wanted to marry me.'

Valerian fought the urge to follow her down, and take her hands in comfort. He had to stop touching her or she'd know it was all a lie.

'Keep your voice down. We don't want to draw attention,' Valerian scolded, covertly casting his gaze about the area. 'The last thing we need now when it's all over is to be compromised.' He'd meant it to be a set-down. She seized on it as the answer to their troubles.

'That's it!' Philippa said wildly. 'If you compromise me, Father will have to let us marry and Cambourne will have a gracious out. Everyone would understand he couldn't marry me then.'

Valerian felt himself rouse at the very idea. It would be easy enough to compromise her, but he loved her too much not to warn her of the consequences—consequences she couldn't fathom through the lens of her innocence, but with three years of town bronze on him, Valerian could.

'Philippa, no one in London would receive us. We'd live a life of exile and I could not doom you to that. I could not doom myself to that,' he added selfishly.

Philippa could not be fooled, and her face tilted, perplexed by the incongruous statement. 'Do such things matter to you? I thought if you had your horses and your gardens and me, it would be enough.' She rose and moved into his embrace, her head finding its way to his shoulder.

Valerian let her, although he held himself stiff, his arms wooden at his side. He was tired of fighting on all fronts. It was inevitable now. He was down to last things. He would not see Philippa after tonight. He'd decided already that he could not go back to his home in Cornwall and watch her become the wife of a neighbour. It would drive him insane to know she and her husband lived only a day's ride away. He'd known when he met her tonight what he had to do. He'd known she would try to argue against her father's choice. He'd known he would have to resist her entreaties no matter what form they took. He had not known how painful it would be.

In her desperation, Philippa was arguing with all the tools at her disposal, even her body as she was doing now. Early on in their relationship, he'd revelled in teaching her about a man's body. There was something heady about tutoring one's beloved in the sensual arts. He'd never dreamed he would not be the one to teach her the ultimate love lesson. He fought back the wave of nausea sweeping his form.

Philippa raised her head from his shoulder, a lock of her long hair falling from its loose coiffure.

Valerian involuntarily reached out to brush the russet strand back from her face. How many times had he made that gesture in the past months?

'If you won't marry me or compromise me, at least give me one night of passion. Let me be with you, as we intended to be together,' she whispered.

Just hearing her utter the words completed his growing erection. A small moan of regret escaped his lips as he shut his eyes, gathering his strength. With her head on his shoulder, thankfully she could not see the torture on his face, although he knew she could feel his desire straining against her stomach. God knew how much he wanted her. He made no attempt to hide his arousal. She knew how she affected him and he her. But he was a man of honour. He'd promised to let her go.

'That's a very unwise suggestion, Philippa,' he heard himself saying in a steady voice that sounded as if it came from another man who watched the vignette unfolding with great uninterest.

'Please, Val,' Philippa cried, clutching his hands. 'I love you and you love me, I know you do. I can feel it.'

He had to end this scene soon. She was on the verge of breaking and his restraint was failing. If this went on much longer, his reserve would crack and they would spend the rest of their lives paying for the foolishness of a few mad minutes. He would not do that to her.

'Don't beg. I can't stand to see you grovel,' he said in a low voice close to her ear. Then he released her and stepped back, preparing to say the most difficult words he'd ever uttered, but he had to make her believe them. 'I do love you, but perhaps not in the same way you love me. I am sorry if you've mis-understood my intentions when we started our little experiment in *l'amour*. We are finished now, you and I. Whatever we had is done, a fair-weather fling. That is how it is for a man.'

He could feel the nervous tic jump in his cheek as a silent curtain fell between them. A tickling bead of sweat ran its slow race down his back as he waited on her next words. His heart warred with his mind. His mind wanted her to see the practical logic of ending their *affaire* and accept his hurtful fabrication. His heart wanted her to see the words for the farce they were.

He watched coldness steal over Philippa's face as her features changed from desperation back to anger. An unchecked fury raged in the depths of her eyes as her mind raced towards the conclusions he'd wanted her to draw. When she spoke, he could hear her voice tremble with emotions.

'A fair-weather fling? This was all a game to you? Everything was a lie?' she cried as the truth spread across her face, like clouds across the sun, as she began to acknowledge the import of his words. He wished he didn't know her so well as to guess her thoughts. In her pale face he saw her doubt and pain. He knew that she believed that every knowing look, hot kiss and searing touch had been little more than seductive perjury of the worst kind. He'd played his part well. She believed those gestures had meant nothing at all to him while they had meant everything to her.

'I thought you were a man of honour, Valerian.' Her voice trembled. Her heart was breaking.

Valerian tightened the reins on his resolve. 'I am a man of honour. That's why I feel I need to call a halt before our sweet interlude goes any further.'

'Interlude?' Philippa was incredulous. 'You make it sound as if our *affaire* is nothing more than an intermission at the theatre! Something to occupy your time between activities!'

Valerian held himself stiffly, ready to deliver the *coup de grace*, the last stroke. 'I am to leave tomorrow to join my uncle on the Continent, something of a belated Grand Tour now that peace has been restored.'

'Valerian, this is not like you. You're playing a cruel game.' There was reproach in her voice for both of them. Reproach for his despicable behaviour and self-chiding for her rashness. She was wrong, of course, he loved her very much, but there was no honourable way out of the situation. Perhaps it was best if she believed the worst, that his love was a fraud, that she was an extended exercise in dalliance. Valerian said nothing in his own defence. Instead, he gave her a neat bow. 'I'll leave you here. I can see you need a moment to collect yourself before returning to the ball,' he said with polite coldness and turned to leave.

Philippa called to him one last time. Her anger was perilously close to giving way to tears as she spoke in a strangled whisper. 'Tell me you loved me, that it wasn't all false coin.'

Valerian stopped, but did not look back. Like Orpheus, it would be his undoing. 'Miss Stratten, I cannot.' He comforted himself with the fact that it was the truth. He was too choked with emotion to utter the words she wanted to hear. Worse, he knew the reason for his silence would be misconstrued as heartlessness. In reality, to say the words would be to give her false hope. If she thought there was any window of opportunity for her case, she'd not give in. Philippa was tenacious. He was counting on that tenacity to help her through this crisis and build a new life for herself.

Valerian closed his eyes as loss swept through him. It was better that the words went unsaid, no matter what cruel conclusions she might draw. His logic was cold comfort when Philippa spoke again, her emotions mastered, her quiet parting words piercing him like a venom arrow to the heart. 'I will not forget this, Valerian.'

Miserable and heartsick, Valerian squared his shoulders, intending to find Philippa's father and tell him the deed was done. He'd no longer stand in the way of the family's financial stability. He'd tell Beldon to take Philippa home. Then he'd leave—it was the only truth he'd told tonight.

In the other pocket of his evening coat was his uncle's letter, inviting Valerian to join his uncle's family on the Continent where he served as one of Britain's premier diplomats. The letter had come yesterday in response to Valerian's own inquiries. Valerian knew he could not stay in England and watch Philippa's new life unfold. Instead, he would go and serve England against whatever threats arose and try to exorcise the memory of Philippa Stratten from his hot blood.

Chapter One

⁓⁓⁓⁓⁓

30 December 1829

An icy wind blew steadily through the poorly sealed post chaise, keeping its two occupants chilled in spite of their caped greatcoats and the hot bricks they'd installed at the posting inn. But it had been the best they could do at the time. The west country was not known for its luxuries. The newly returned Viscount St Just didn't mind. He'd been in far less comfortable situations over the past nine years and he was simply glad to be home.

'What are you smiling about?' Beldon Stratten, the young Baron Pendennys, groused, stamping his feet in a futile attempt to generate some body heat.

'Am I smiling?' Valerian asked. 'I was unaware of it.'

'You've been smiling since the inn at St Austell. I can't imagine what about.'

Beldon was right. There wasn't much to smile

about. Their journey had become a comedy of errors. Nothing had gone right since they'd left London after celebrating the Christmas holidays in town. They'd hoped to sail down the Cornish coast to St Just-in-Roseland, Valerian's home on the peninsula, and avoid the roads. But foul weather on the Channel had scotched those plans. So they'd set out on horseback, hoping to make better time than a lumbering coach. Valerian had a yen to be settled in his home by New Year. But weather again played them false, turning too cold for safe passage on horseback. They'd abandoned the horses at St Austell and hired the only post chaise available.

It went unspoken between them that they'd get no farther than Truro today. If they wanted to try for St Just-in-Roseland by New Year, it would have to wait until tomorrow.

'Do you believe in serendipity, Val?' Beldon asked, stretching his long legs out across the small space between the seats.

Valerian looked at him queerly. 'I am not exactly sure what you mean.'

'You know, making valuable discoveries by accident.'

'Ah, coincidence,' Valerian corrected. 'You think it is merely a fortuitous happening that I ran into you in London.'

'Definitely luck since you'd sent no word ahead of your return.' There was a censorious note in Beldon's voice. Valerian did not miss it. He had not said goodbye to Beldon properly when he'd left London so abruptly years ago and he had not written over the long years with the exception of one short letter early on. It was a credit to the depth of their friendship that Beldon had felt his absence so keenly and forgiven him so readily.

Beldon's tone softened. 'Perhaps you will explain to me some day why you all but vanished into your uncle's household overnight. I am your friend. I would understand, whatever your reasons. We all missed you, even Philippa. I think she had always admired you from afar.'

Valerian started at that. Had Philippa kept their secret all these years? He'd expected her to blurt it all out. He'd imagined her crying on Beldon's shoulder in the garden that last night, sobbing out how her heart had been broken by her brother's cad of a best friend.

He'd known this moment was inevitable. Hearing her name would be just the first of many such moments. He knew in his heart that was why he hadn't written ahead to Beldon to tell him of his return. Of course, he hadn't known until the last moment that he would be assigned to the team of negotiators sent to London to pound out a peace treaty to end the latest conflict between the Turks and Russia. Even when he'd known with a certainty he'd be coming back, he still hadn't sent advance notice of his return. It was a stalling mechanism and a desperate one at that, designed to put off any encounter with Philippa until the very last.

His tenure on the Continent had not outlasted his own broken heart. He had stayed on in Europe as long as he could, volunteering for myriad diplomatic assignments that lingered in the wake of the Napoleonic Wars. Napoleon's efforts had left their mark on old and new regimes alike and Valerian had quickly learned that there was always someone to fight.

Treaties may have been signed, but Europe, particularly the Balkans, was not at peace. There was still plenty for Britain to worry over as countries fought to define themselves and empires sought to expand in the power vacuum left by Napoleon's defeat.

Valerian had watched modern history play out before his very eyes as Britain and the rest of Europe fought to corner the fledgling Balkan markets.

After years of pointless victories and disappointments, Valerian found he had no stomach for a fight motivated by greed and avarice, thinly cloaked in a facade of ideals, and he could not stay away from home indefinitely. He had gardens and an estate to manage. He could not rely on his steward for ever.

While a broken-hearted young man of twenty-one could be forgiven for impetuously leaving his inheritance, a grown man of thirty years, who knew his duty, could not continue to shirk it. Yet it was difficult turning for home when he knew it would mean facing Philippa and Cambourne. But duty and honour beckoned, two ideals he had always held dear even when his country hadn't.

'How is your sister?' Valerian inquired, hoping to sound casual.

Beldon nodded. 'She's doing well. I see her often. You just missed her in London. She spent the holidays with a friend in Richmond before heading out here. If I had known you were coming, I could have persuaded her to stay in town.' Beldon paused, seeming to consider his next words before speaking them. 'It's hard to believe she's twenty-seven and already through her first husband. Here I am at thirty and I haven't been married, not even close. It makes me feel "behind" somehow.'

Valerian felt his body tense. 'Through her first husband?'

'Yes, didn't you know? It was in all the papers, quite a newsworthy death.'

'I wasn't exactly holed up in Vienna the entire time,' Valerian said wryly, thinking of the rugged Balkan territories he'd journeyed through with their mountains and sparse populations. There were places in Europe the mails didn't reach, places with names like Voden and Negush. Places that didn't appear on a map unless you were a Turkish Pasha charged with keeping the Christian millet in line.

'Cambourne died three years ago in a mining accident. There was a cave-in while he was touring one of his tin mines. It was a freak incident. A shaft support gave way. The miners pulled him out, but he died of his injuries three days later at home.'

Philippa was a widow. The implications were not lost on him. Valerian's emotions ricocheted from a morbid elation that Philippa was free to a sadness that she'd had to bear the loss of a husband, set adrift in society as a dowager so early in life.

'I hope Cambourne left her well provided for,' he said quietly, knowing that the Pendennys's fortunes had rested so completely on Cambourne's welfare. Valerian didn't like to think that her marriage had come to naught.

'Absolutely. He had a cousin who inherited the title and the other estates, but Philippa has all she needs or wants. Of course, the principal estate went to his heir, but Philippa has the house in Cornwall where they spent their marriage. To my mind, she got the better end of the deal. Coppercrest is a much more hospitable dwelling. Even Cambourne himself preferred it.

'"The heir" isn't much on going up to town, so Philippa has free run of the town house. Cambourne also bequeathed her a substantial interest in the mines and the associate businesses. He owned a tin smelter and a small gunpowder works.'

Valerian only half-listened to Beldon's itemization of Philippa's situation. The first line had caught most of his attention—a cousin had inherited. Ah, there were no children. Another delicate question answered. Valerian wondered if Beldon had shared that information on purpose or if it had been accidental.

Beldon chuckled softly. 'I forget that you haven't seen her recently. She's much changed since you saw her last. She's not a budding débutante any more. She's a sophisticated woman now, as comfortable in town among the leading hostesses and politicians as she is in the country, tramping over the cliffs and riding neck-for-nothing at the hunt. When she's in town, her house teems with politicos. Everyone seeks her endorsement and asks her opinion. She's a leading supporter of mine reform these days, and with justifiable reason.'

Valerian smiled thoughtfully in the gathering gloom. The grey afternoon was turning towards evening. Truro couldn't be more than a few miles in the offing. Beldon's revelations were enough to fill the time. Valerian turned his mind inwards, pondering all Beldon had shared.

Philippa was free. In a fairy-tale world, he would have a second chance. But his world was far from a fairy tale. They had parted badly nine years ago. Philippa's final words to him were still achingly clear. And now there was all he had done during those years to contend with as well. His years in the Balkans had left him with another set of nightmares, another set of people he'd failed in their hour of need. Those failures hung like an invisible millstone about his neck, even when he was able to subdue the more physical reminders of his futile efforts.

He'd been surprised in London to know how much people had heard about his antics on the Continent. Of course, no one had known the depth of such shenanigans, but they knew the gist. He'd led a flamboyant lifestyle in Vienna during his brief time there, playing the role of a womanising diplomat. It had been the perfect foil for something darker that took him to the sinister underbelly of the rebellions popping up across Europe. He'd been nothing short of an expert spy and negotiator, engaging in the kind of diplomacy that *never* made the broadsheets.

'We'll stop tonight at Lucien Canton's place just outside Truro. It'll be much better than an inn. He has an excellent cook and an even better cellar,' Beldon broke into Valerian's ruminations.

Valerian nodded, only half-engaged in the conversation. 'It won't be an imposition, I hope?' He didn't remember this friend of Beldon's from their early days as young bucks on the town. 'I don't believe I know him.'

'He's Viscount Montfort's son and heir. He was close to Cambourne before his death. Since then, he's been Philippa's strong right hand.'

Valerian couldn't quite read Beldon's expression. It didn't seem that Beldon was precisely elated about the man's association with his sister, but had resigned himself to it. Beldon's conversation was moving on. 'It will be a party before the party, the three of us together again like old times. With luck, Philippa is there already. Lucien asked her to act as hostess for his New Year's gala since she's the best hostess in the neighbourhood and his sister couldn't come down from London to do it.'

Now Valerian was fully engaged. 'Philippa will be there?' Regardless of Beldon's assurances that Lucien Canton was a grand chap, Valerian doubted he'd like the man very much. He was inclined to dislike any man who had a claim on Philippa's attentions and this Lucien clearly did. No one played hostess for someone they didn't know well. They must be good friends indeed and perhaps something more.

Beldon grinned and leaned forwards in his growing excitement. 'Yes. She will be beyond surprised to see you.'

She would indeed, Valerian reflected wryly, although he and Beldon would likely disagree about her reaction to that surprise.

Philippa Lytton, the widowed duchess of Cambourne, glided down the curved staircase of Lucien Canton's Truro manor at half-past six, consciously aware that she would be the last one to the drawing room and that she'd be the only female present. What had started out as a small *en famille* supper with Canton and the bachelor vicar from down the road had turned into a supper party with three unexpected guests.

One of them was her brother, Beldon, who had arrived unannounced just two hours ago and a guest he'd brought with him. Beldon's arrival was understandable given the terrible weather and the fact that she was already in residence. The third guest's presence was less clearly explained. Lucien knew him only through the acquaintances of others. He was a Mister Danforth, a well-to-do shipping merchant from Liverpool who hoped to start a provincial bank. He was not someone they would normally associate with. He was a rich Cit who'd made most of his money during the war, making his fortune somewhat speculative as to the legitimacy of its origins. But the underpopulated wilds of Cornwall in mid-winter and his tenuous connection to Lucien made it difficult to turn him away.

Philippa stopped at the foot of the stairs to draw a deep breath and square her shoulders. She stole a glance in the hallway mirror as a final check. She looked fine with her hair piled high and threaded with pearls. The heavy satin folds of her skirts fell neatly to her ankles into a deep Van-dyked hem. She liked the quiet shushing of the satin skirt as she walked.

Indeed, she loved this gown for its textures and feel as much as she loved it for its look. The cream skirt was set off by the deep blue velvet of the round bodice that fell low over her shoulders and into a plunging vee in the back. She fiddled with the simple choker of blue Kashmir sapphires that set off the expanse between her neck and the delicate cream-lace trim of her bodice.

She looked well. Not that she wanted to attract any attention. She wasn't dressing for a man's approval, not even Lucien's, although he'd readily give it. Being in high looks boosted her confidence, a security blanket of sorts. In a room dominated by the male species, one could never have too much confidence if one was going to hold one's own.

She stepped into the wide doorway of the drawing room, her eyes quickly assessing the gathering. Lucien stood at the carved-oak fireplace mantel, dressed in dark evening clothes, looking slender and elegant with his usual immaculate perfection. He was doing his host's duty by chatting with the unworthy Mr Danforth. Across the room in a little grouping of chairs situated beneath an expansive Gainsborough landscape sat her brother, the vicar and apparently the guest her brother had brought with him. The guest's back was to her, affording her only a glimpse of broad shoulders and dark hair, sleek in the evening light of candles.

Beldon saw her first. He gestured that she should

join them, saving her from joining Lucien and his odious guest at the fireplace. Philippa smiled warmly at her brother and moved towards the group. She was always glad to see Beldon. They had been close as children and become even closer with her marriage to Cambourne. He'd supported her as she had learned to navigate London society and after when she had to re-learn the treacherous paths of society as a new widow.

He and the little cohort under the Gainsborough rose as she approached. 'Beldon, I am so happy to see you! We weren't expecting you, but it's delightful all the same.' She gave him a sisterly kiss on the cheek, having to reach up only slightly to do so. They were nearly of a same height, both of them tall and built for grace. Anyone seeing them side by side would not doubt their similar genetic origins. Both had sharp blue eyes and russet hair the colour of chestnuts, each strikingly attractive in their own way.

The vicar leaned forward to take Philippa's hand in greeting. 'I am pleased to see you again, your Grace.'

'And I you, Vicar. How are your plans for a miner's school coming? I believe you had plans drawn up when we spoke last.'

'Very well, thank you. It is kind of you to remember.' The vicar beamed. 'I hope we'll have time to talk about its progress later tonight. I would love your opinion on a few things.' He gently inclined his head to indicate the third gentleman in the group.

The vicar was right. It would be unseemly to jump into conversation before all the introductions were made. Philippa turned her attention to the stranger immediately, small talk coming easily to her lips. But the man to her right was no stranger at all and the small talk died a quick death.

Chapter Two

Valerian Inglemoore was the last man she'd expected to see in Lucien Canton's drawing room. Philippa mustered all her aplomb. 'Viscount, this is indeed a surprise.'

Surprise didn't even begin to cover it. What was he doing in Truro? How long had he been back? A thousand questions rioted through her mind. She mentally tried to tamp them down, telling herself she didn't care about such information. But it was like fighting the Hydra. The more she tried to squelch the rising tide of questions, the more questions came forward—worse questions because they didn't deal with the basic information of who, what and when, but with more intimate concerns—had he thought of her at all during his absence? Had he realised what he'd termed a mere dalliance was something far stronger? Did he have feelings for her yet? Did she, in spite of her efforts to deny it? Her pulse was certainly racing as if she did, as if she'd forgotten why she'd foresworn any connection to him years ago.

'It is a surprise for me as well, and a pleasant one at that, I might add.' Valerian bent over her gloved hand with an elegant bow. *'Enchanté, Duchesse.'*

The warmth of his touch sent a powerful *frisson* up her arm, so sharp she had to control herself not to snatch her hand back as if burnt. She told herself the reaction was due to the strength of his grip. The reaction had nothing to do with still being attracted to him. She had hardened her heart against Valerian Inglemoore years ago and rightly so.

Time had proved her choice a good one and her escape from his seductive clutches a lucky one. Reports from Europe during his sojourn abroad reached her circles, portraying him as a splendid diplomat with a talent for seduction. From captain's wives to Continental princesses, no woman was safe from the dashing viscount's wiles and no woman wanted to be. He'd become a much sought-after commodity.

It was easy to see why. She was doubly glad she'd given him up years ago. He was far too handsome for his own good now that he'd come into the fullness of his adulthood. Anyone less wise than she would be easily distracted by the silky sleekness of his dark hair. She knew from experience how simple it was to spend an evening thinking about running hands through those ebony skeins.

If the hair didn't distract one thoroughly enough, there was the trap of his piercing jade eyes, the angular planes of his chiselled face, the sensual promise of his lips, the caress of knowing hands, firm and confident as they learned the contours of one's body and the pledge of his own body, all muscles and hot strength beneath superbly tailored clothes. Ah, yes, Valerian Inglemoore was a walking minefield of passion—promising pleasure but delivering heartache to the unsuspecting miss. It was good she knew better. That was one trap she would not fall into again.

Valerian gave her a slight nod, a smug smile playing on his lips. She felt herself blush. He'd caught her looking. She hadn't meant for that to happen.

The butler entered and intoned the announcement for dinner. Philippa felt herself breathe again. She started towards Lucien, eager to escape the scrutiny of Valerian's gaze. A warm hand on her arm stayed her.

'Would you do me the honour of allowing me to escort you into dinner?' Valerian asked, his voice low next to her ear, his message just for her.

Philippa shot a look at Lucien, but he would be of no use to her. He'd already acquiesced to the situation, a hard look in his eyes that belied the friendly tenor of his words. 'You've got her then, St Just? I remember now that the three of you grew up together.' It was said pleasantly enough, but Philippa didn't miss the tightness of Lucien's smile or the covert scrutiny in his eyes.

Valerian seated her at the foot of the table and put himself promptly on her right, leaving Beldon and the vicar to juggle Mr Danforth between them.

Philippa couldn't decide if she preferred Valerian next to her or next to Lucien. Both positions offered their own forms of temptation. She could either have him next to her and struggle with his physical nearness or spend the entire evening fighting the distraction of his handsome visage down the table. But it hardly mattered, she reprimanded herself. He didn't affect her either way. Her current reaction was merely the shock of seeing him again without warning.

She wished she could read Valerian better. It would be a small measure of comfort if he was struggling to adapt as well. Did she have any effect on him at all? All at once, she vividly recalled the hardness of his erection, the feel of him pulsing through his trousers in their youth, how he'd taught her to caress him. Was he hard now? Or entirely immune? No matter that he'd once claimed only the shallowest of feelings for her, he'd roused to her none the less.

She had to stop! Philippa reached for her wine glass and took a generous sip. These were unseemly thoughts. They were base in nature and had no place at the dinner table, especially coming from a woman who had spent the years putting the memory of his kisses behind her.

The footmen removed the soup and served up the fish course. Conversation lagged as they performed their duties. Once the course was settled, Lucien picked up the threads of small talk. 'St Just, are you home for good or has the Continent enchanted you?'

Valerian patted his mouth with a fine linen napkin before speaking. 'I am home for the duration and proud to say it. I terminated my affiliation with the diplomatic corps while I was in London over Christmas. I can now devote my time to my estate, my much neglected gardens and my nursery.'

The statement was ambiguous. Anyone knowing Valerian as she did would wonder if he meant his flower nurseries or perhaps a nursery of another sort. No one was ill bred enough to ask for an explanation, but apparently such probing was not beyond the pale for Mr Danforth, who hadn't known Valerian for more than the time it had taken to eat the soup.

With a smug masculine tone to his voice, Danforth said, 'You mean to marry and beget an heir. Very good thinking. I hear you've quite a fortune. You'll need an heir to look after things.'

At the head of the table, Lucien nearly sprayed a mouthful of wine at the tactless comment. It was practically an art form to make such a *faux pas* as mentioning 'begetting' *and* money in the same poor comment.

Valerian met the rude comment evenly. 'In fact, I do mean to marry as soon as possible. Enough time has been wasted, I think. I find myself eager to embrace matrimony. With the right woman, of course.'

'Naturally,' Danforth agreed, oblivious to the social *faux pas* he'd committed. 'A wife must have certain qualities. She must be pretty, biddable, malleable, open to a husband's training and all that. No man wants to spend his life leg-shackled to an opinion-spouting shrew, no matter what her dowry.'

Philippa stiffened at Danforth's belittling remarks. 'I think finding a wife is altogether different than shopping for a brood mare, Mr Danforth. At least it is for those of us who hold marriage as something more than servitude.'

Beldon coughed and the vicar looked nonplussed. There was more she'd liked to have said to the sputtering Danforth, but Valerian's hand pressed heavily on her thigh beneath the damask cloth in warning. She fought back a smile. Was he remembering her infamous temper?

Valerian smoothly intervened with the honed skill of a diplomat. 'For myself, Mr Danforth, I am looking for different qualities in a wife. I prefer a more mature woman, a woman who can speak for herself, who can hold her own in an argument. In short, a woman of independence.'

Danforth bristled. 'Yes, I've heard that about you.' His beady gaze met Valerian's directly in a surprising show of spine.

Everyone at the table stopped eating. Philippa wondered how Valerian would confront his 'reputation', as it were. Would he deny it? Part of her wished he would.

Valerian smiled. It was not a friendly smile, but a wolfish one that suggested he was not, nor ever would be, the prey. 'Then you will have also heard that I am not afraid of a woman's opinions, that I am not a man who will cower behind old-fashioned thought and conventions when it comes to the suppression of the fairer sex. Much would be missed in our world if we neglected half the population. Take, for example, the excellent champagne our host is serving from his excellent cellar tomorrow night.'

Valerian turned to Canton. 'Pendennys mentioned you'd be offering a Veuve Clicquot, an outstanding champagne thanks to the revolutionary efforts of

Clicquot's widow. Did you know, Danforth, that she is responsible for inventing the *remuage* process? We have a woman to thank for clear champagne. Without her efforts, we'd have nothing more than a cloudy, fizzy novelty.' Valerian raised his glass. 'Here's to Madame Clicquot.'

In a few short sentences Valerian had eloquently smoothed over Danforth's uncomfortable claims and moved the conversation into the safer realm of wine. Danforth did not venture out to play with verbal fire again.

Dinner went smoothly after that if Philippa did not count the unnerving sensation of Valerian's body in such close proximity to her own. In all the numerous dinner parties she'd attended, she had not ever noticed the intimate closeness she was now exceedingly aware of with Valerian next to her. His knee touched hers; she dropped her napkin and his hand brushed her skirt as he bent to retrieve it, beating the footman to the task.

By the time dessert was served, Philippa's nerves were jangled beyond reason. She stood as soon as it was politely possible. 'Gentlemen, excuse me. I'll leave you to your port and cigars.'

Lucien rose and protested. 'Please stay, my dear. You are welcome to stay.' He directed the comment at her, but his hazel stare was directed at Valerian. The look in his gaze was sharp and penetrating, meant to send a message.

So he had noticed Valerian's casual touches, Philippa thought, and he'd found them as unsettling as she did, but for altogether different reasons. She could feel Valerian's eyes read every message, spoken or not. She had no desire to stay in the dining room and become a prize to be fought over. 'Really, I would prefer to retire and give you gentlemen some privacy,' she insisted, not waiting for permission to leave the room.

Philippa collected a shawl from her bedroom and then made good her escape to a quiet veranda where she could let the cold air do its work. She needed a clear head. Valerian was back and he would have to be contended with. His presumptuous behaviour at dinner suggested he wasn't the least bit penitent about breaking her young girl's heart, nor was he disinclined to live down the rumours regarding his profligate behaviour abroad.

Certainly, she didn't want to be petty. What had happened between them had occurred years ago. They were both adults now. She should put the past behind her. He obviously had if his behaviour at dinner was any indication. He apparently thought she might welcome his advances. But he would have to take her for a fool if he thought she would disregard his well-taught lessons after one flirtatious encounter.

Would she disregard his harsh lesson in love? The thought that she might re-think her position on Valerian was startling. In her mind, she'd often played out an imaginary encounter. In that encounter, she'd been an aloof lady with grand manners, icily polite to a fault and he would know that his attentions had come too late.

Funny how in her imaginings she always assumed he'd care what had become of her. Maybe that was because she could not fathom how he'd gone from a dedicated suitor with words of undying devotion on his lips to that of a cold jilt in the span of a day. Undisputably, he'd broken her heart, but she'd never quite convinced herself it was for the reasons he'd cited. None the less, in the end, the results had been the same.

Valerian would drive her mad! Perhaps it was time to think more seriously about Lucien Canton's offer. There had been no formal proposal, but much was implied in their long-standing relationship. She did expect a proposal soon. Perhaps Valerian was the impetus she needed for getting on with her life.

Lucien was exactly the kind of man she needed and he'd spent the years since Cambourne's death proving it. He'd overseen the difficult tangle of financial matters and entailments until she'd learned to manage them on her own. He'd been the one to ride out to the mines and keep the Cambourne industries running while she was in mourning. Besides herself, no one knew the extensive Cambourne holdings better than Lucien. He was competent, handsome, well mannered, comfortable to be with. He was reliable and steady, a constant companion.

'Philippa.'

All thoughts of Lucien vanished. She didn't need to turn to know it was Valerian. 'I came out here to be alone.'

'Then we have something in common. I came out here to be alone with you, too.' Valerian took up a position next to her at the railing, leaning on his elbows. 'I wanted to talk to you. There are things I want to explain.'

Philippa shifted her body to face him. 'I don't think that's a good idea unless you want to start explaining why your hand spent most of dinner on my thigh. We are finished. You made that clear nine years ago.'

Valerian would not be put off by her harsh words. It was disappointing, but not unexpected that he could not be handled like the ballroom beaux. A set-down from her usually sent them scrambling for apologies.

Instead of begging forgiveness, Valerian laughed softly in the darkness, a beautiful, sensual sound that promised indecent pleasures. One would have thought she'd spoken love words to him instead of a scolding.

'You are more sharp-tongued than I remember.' He paused to look at her, his voice lowering. 'And more beautiful. You've done well for yourself.'

If he refused to be scolded, then she would refuse to be taken in by his flattery. 'St Just, if you intended that as a compliment, your skill is diminished greatly. I am insulted by the idea that my beauty has done well for me as if my looks were an industry designed to turn a profit. My looks have bought me a few houses and financial security. While those are not unpleasing things, the price for them has been my personal happiness. To think that my looks have done well for me is to be misled by the shallow mind you apparently possess. You show yourself poorly by believing I would settle for so little.'

There, such a scalding set-down should drive even him from the veranda. But Philippa was supremely dissatisfied with the results.

Valerian's face broke into a wide grin, showing all his white teeth. His voice was low and private, laughter lurking beneath the surface. 'I am glad to see that along with selling your hand in marriage, your parents didn't succeed in selling your soul.' He chuckled, enjoying his humour.

'You've a black sense of humour, St Just.'

Valerian reached for her hand where it rested on the railing, caressing it idly with his fingertips. 'My dear, when have I ever been St Just to you? Call me Valerian as my friends do, as you once did.'

Philippa snatched her hand away. How dare he come out here to insult her and then expect that he could take liberties? 'Let me set you straight. I am not your "dear" or your friend. Nine years ago, I paid the price for what passes as friendship with you. I shall not make that mistake again. I have a new life now and there's no room for you in it.' It was important that she define the rules first before he had a chance to worm himself into her good graces. He could be charming and she must be wary of letting her guard down, of letting him pretend to be her friend.

His face flushed at her words. She did not think the flush was from her candour, but rather from a rising anger. Valerian gripped her by the arms, his soft sensuality of moments ago replaced by a hard envy. 'A life that includes Lucien Canton? What is Lucien Canton to you? Is he your lover?'

'Take your hands off me. I don't answer to you.' Philippa looked him squarely in the eye. Something dangerous and erotic lurked in their emerald depths. In an unfair moment she thought Lucien's hazel eyes merely pretended towards greenness.

He ignored her request. He crowded her against the hard iron of the railing. Somewhere in the far recesses of her mind she thought she should have minded the invasion. But his hot envy had transmuted into molten seduction.

'Your body answers to me, Philippa. My hands were made for you and you alone. No one has ever felt like you do, Philippa. I've not forgotten how your skin feels like rose petals.' He pushed back the shawl from her arms and trailed the back of his hands down their length, removing the long gloves as he went until her arms were completely exposed.

'I have not forgotten what it is to span the width of your back with my hand and pull you against me.' Warm skin met warm skin where the plunging vee of her gown bared her back and she trembled against her will.

'And you've not forgotten either,' Valerian whispered against her mouth, his lips moving to seal hers, his hands moving to crush her against him, one hand finding the firm mound of breast beneath the velvet bodice. He palmed it, caressed it reverently until she cried out in his mouth from unwanted pleasure.

It was all coming back to her in a rush, how he felt against her, how he could make her body come alive, how she loved the exquisite sensations he could coax from her. How could she have forgotten *this*?

Philippa burned. Every part of her body was on fire. Heat licked at her from the inside out. Pressure built at her core until she wanted to scream. Valerian was the sum of her world in that moment. He was everywhere—his hands on her body, his scent in her nostrils—and she didn't want him to stop. She wanted this moment to go on for eternity. She hated herself for it.

She pulled away with the greatest of efforts, panting and desperate. Valerian looked dismayed at her retreat. That was some gratification. 'Have a care, St Just. Lucien will not tolerate playing the cuckold.' She gave a slight nod to the empty room beyond the French doors, where Beldon and Lucien had just arrived. She hoped she didn't look as dishevelled as she felt.

'Philippa—' he began in a ragged voice.

She didn't give him a chance to beg, to explain, to persuade. 'You have gravely overstepped the boundaries of polite society.'

'I didn't do it alone,' St Just responded, his eyes hot, gleaming dark with unslaked need.

'How dare you try to implicate me in your base conduct?' Philippa flamed. 'Let me remind you that this is not some decadent European court filled with women who are dying of lust for your attentions.'

'You're just angry because you liked it.' He had the audacity to give another throaty laugh.

Philippa's nerves were stretched to breaking. She raised her right hand and slapped him hard across the face.

'What was that for?' Valerian put a hand to his red cheek, stunned.

Philippa inhaled deeply, squaring her shoulders. 'That was "welcome home."'

Chapter Three

Welcome home indeed, Valerian thought sourly, watching Philippa disappear inside. Through the glass panes of the French doors he could see her sit down at the polished cherry-wood pianoforte and arrange her skirts.

Lucien Canton slid on to the bench next to her, ready to turn pages, acting the devoted suitor to perfection. From the looks of him, the man did everything to perfection. He was immaculately turned out and not just his clothes, Valerian had noted. Canton's nails were trimmed and buffed to a healthy sheen, his face freshly shaved. Valerian looked at his own nails, just as neatly kept. He too was fastidious in his personal habits. He had learned quickly in his time abroad that women responded to two things, cleanliness and sincerity, both of which were in short supply in many parts of the world. But from all appearances through the window pane, Canton possessed both qualities in abundance. Through the panes, Philippa smiled and laughed at something Canton had said.

Primal envy sparked in Valerian. He didn't want Philippa laughing with Canton. He wanted her laughing with him. He hadn't come home expecting to woo her. He hadn't even known wooing her would be a possibility until Beldon had mentioned Cambourne's death in the coach. But now that the chance to win her back was present, he could see no other course of action.

He'd meant what he'd said at dinner about taking a wife and starting a family—as long as that wife was Philippa. He still desired her and she still responded to him, if that ill-conceived interlude here on the balcony was any indication. He only had to convince her of that. She'd had nine years to nurse her grudge and she'd always been far too stubborn. The sting of her slap suggested the job in front of him would not be an easy one. The passion of her body's response to his said the task would not be without its rewards. She might have struck him, but he was not convinced she'd slapped him out of anger about his advances. Given her response to him, she'd struck him out of anger over her own behaviour. He was merely a convenient target.

However, he was willing to acknowledge that it had been the height of foolhardiness to seek her out alone, knowing that his emotions were ruling his better judgement. The thrill of seeing her again, of feeling her presence next to him at dinner, of watching her deal with Danforth, combined with the surge of jealously that coursed through him at seeing

Canton lay claim to her, was too potent a mixture to swallow without consequence.

He'd meant to confess his feelings to her, to declare his devotion and even to explain away the events of their last evening together as the poor decisions of youth. He'd got nowhere with his agenda. Instead, he'd no doubt affirmed all the sordid rumours that had trickled back to London about him. Within moments they'd been sparring and then, his blood hot, he'd taken her in his arms and silenced her the only way he knew how. But his reckless kiss had been more consistent with the behaviour he wanted to refute than the man he wanted to convince Philippa he was, and had always been, in spite of actions to the very persuasive contrary.

The only thing more senseless than kissing Philippa was standing out here in the cold, allowing Canton to hold Philippa's attention uncontested. Valerian pushed open the door and went inside. The battle was joined.

Lucien spied his return to the company as Philippa finished playing a pretty country piece. The small group clapped politely. 'Let us play our duet for them,' Lucien suggested to Philippa, sorting through the sheets of music until he found the one he was looking for. He gave Valerian a challenging look that could not be mistaken for anything other than what it was—a silent dare. Valerian returned the stare with a short nod of acknowledgement.

They executed the duet flawlessly. Valerian had known Philippa was a dab hand at the pianoforte, but Lucien was the stronger of the two players. He wondered if Canton knew he played as well. The piece flowed seamlessly, the four hands following each other to Lucien's trademark perfection.

Amid the brief applause at the end, Canton tossed him a smug look of satisfaction. Philippa caught him at it and gave Canton a hard look. Valerian was hard pressed to smother a laugh. Lucien didn't know Philippa well if he thought such masculine antics would go unpunished. She would make Canton pay and, he noted ruefully when her quick stare censured him as well, he would pay too.

'Anyone else care to play?' Lucien asked, once more the congenial host. Valerian doubted any of the other guests were aware of the currents flowing between the little triangle. It was tempting to play, but it was also petty. Valerian opted to refrain, but Philippa had different ideas. She caught his eye. 'Viscount St Just is quite accomplished if I remember correctly. Do you still play, St Just?'

'Yes, I do. It would be an honour to perform on such a fine instrument.' Valerian took the bench and flexed his hands experimentally.

'I have some music…' Canton began.

'I won't need any music,' Valerian said shortly and launched into a complicated scherzo that left the audience mesmerised.

'Magnificent! You've been training,' Beldon enthused afterwards. 'I'd forgotten how good you were.'

'Thank you,' Valerian said, rising from the bench. He tossed a covert glance towards Canton, making sure the man understood he'd picked up the gauntlet.

The tea tray arrived, but no one lingered overlong.

There would be much to do on the morrow to be ready for the evening's festivities. As everyone retired, Valerian stopped off at the library to select a book to read. A few minutes later there were muffled footsteps on the Axminster carpet. He didn't need to turn around to know the newcomer was Lucien Canton. He'd expected as much. The problem with perfection was that it was often predictable.

'I thought you and I should talk, St Just. Have a seat.' Canton sat down and motioned to the chair across from him.

'You have an extensive collection of books,' Valerian said glibly.

Canton waved away the attempt at small talk. 'I am not here to trade banalities with you. I came to make sure you understood how things stand between myself and Lady Cambourne.' His eyes glittered like hard gems.

Valerian steepled his hands. 'I understand from Pendennys that she is acting as hostess in your sister's stead,' he said, deliberately misinterpreting the implications of Canton's message. If the man wanted to stake his claim, he'd have to do it directly. He would not get away with subtlety.

'She is more than my hostess. We have discussed the possibility of a more permanent arrangement between us. I mean to propose marriage to her and I have every reason to believe that my suit would be met favourably.'

'Why are you telling me, a mere stranger, this?'

'You know very well why—you didn't take her into dinner for the sake of old friendships renewed and all that. I did not know the depth of your former relationship was quite so, ah, developed. It is clearly much more than a friendship. No one looks at an old friend the way you looked at her tonight.'

'And how is that?' He'd been more transparent than he thought, or perhaps Canton was simply more astute.

'Like a starving man looks at a feast,' Canton said acidly.

Valerian raised his eyebrows, ready to strike. 'Is that cliché the best you can do?' He liked Canton less and less by the moment and not all of it had to do with envy. All his instincts said Canton had ulterior motives regarding Philippa. A man in love and certain of his affections being returned would not feel a need to stake such a blatant claim. Canton's next statement confirmed Valerian's suspicions.

'I know you didn't go to the drawing room to study the Gainsborough when you left the dining room,' Canton said, referring to the facile lie Valerian had used to excuse himself and to follow Philippa. 'My footman reported the two of you were out on the balcony, intimately engaged.'

'Spying on your guests? That's quite an admirable trait,' Valerian said drily. 'I wonder how the Duchess would feel if she knew you had her followed. Do you do it regularly?' He rose, book in hand. 'I've had enough of this gentlemanly conversation. Goodnight, Canton.'

Lucien rose with him. 'I mean to have her, St Just. She's mine. I'm the one who has been here through the years when she was in mourning. You can't waltz into my home after a nine-year absence and undo in the span of a few short hours what I've worked years to accomplish.'

Valerian stopped at the door, his hand forcefully gripping the knob as he reined in his temper. He'd faced down Mehemet Ali, the renowned Egyptian naval commander. By God, he would not suffer the threats of a viscount's top-lofty heir whose only pretension to greatness was his father's title. 'You're wrong, Canton. If a stolen kiss and a dinner among others are all it takes to "undo" your hard work, it was never "done" in the first place.'

He strode purposefully up the stairs to his chambers, fitting pieces together in his mind. He knew now what he didn't like about Lucien Canton beyond the simple fact that he coveted Philippa: Lucien Canton was dangerous.

Behind his polished perfection was a lethal streak. He'd seen men like Canton during his years abroad in the highest levels of covert intelligence and diplomacy, catapulted into such positions because of their cunning and arch-shrewdness. To these men, attainment of their goal was everything. Nothing was too sacred to escape sacrifice. There was something Lucien Canton wanted and Philippa was a vital link in his ability to get it. He speculated that Lucien Canton would be willing to do more than marry to secure it as well.

The man had portrayed no signs of lover-like affections, but had instead acted like a man in possession of a great treasure around which he must place guards and fences. It didn't take a large amount of speculation, even knowing as little as he did about the state of Philippa's inheritance from Cambourne, to surmise Canton had his eye on some aspect of her estate.

Beldon had asked him in the coach if he believed in serendipity. Absolutely not. He had not survived the dark side of diplomacy by luck. He'd survived because he believed a man made his own chances. From the looks of things, Lucien Canton believed that too. That made the man more dangerous than he might have been otherwise.

He wondered if Philippa knew Canton didn't love her, but what she owned. If not, he'd be sure to call it to her attention by showing her the depths of his own passion for her. It looked like he wouldn't make Roseland Hall by New Year after all.

31 December

The dancers whirled about Valerian in a dervish of luxurious winter velvets and satins to a rowdy country dance played by the five-piece orchestra seated above the crowd in the small balcony at the top of the ballroom, designed for just such a purpose. The guests were in high spirits as midnight approached. Philippa had done a splendid job playing hostess, making sure everyone had partners for dancing. No one went unnoticed, from the plainest of girls to the quietest of matrons.

He and Beldon had done their parts to ensure her success in that pursuit. They'd danced with the matrons and charmed the local wallflowers until they blossomed.

But for the most part, Valerian had spent the evening listening to the rhythm of Cornwall. What did people think about these days? What was the life-blood of the Cornish economy? Where did people think their future lay? The answer repeatedly came back to mining.

It was not surprising. Mining had been an ongoing consideration in the region for literally centuries. Valerian's own family had mining interests upon which the family fortunes were built. He knew the Duke of Cambourne had invested heavily in tin and copper mines as well as the ancillary businesses that accompanied the industry of mining: smelting, furnace parts and mining equipment.

What *did* surprise him was the growing competition. Mining had not yet reached its apex, but the foundations for managing those future interests were being laid now. Mining had become a full blown industry and much more highly politicised than it had been before.

Valerian had caught snatches of conversations regarding mining-related legislation. House of Commons members, home from the Michaelmas session of Parliament, and members of the House of Lords, debated the need for safety laws that ensured a quality of life for the miners and their families.

More intriguing to Valerian were the conversations he overheard regarding the merits of importing metal ores from British settlements in Chile and Argentina. The capitalists of the group argued importing would certainly help meet growing industrial need, while other, cooler, heads argued for caution;

glutting the market with copper and tin would drive the price down, which in turn would affect the domestic market's ability to turn a profit.

Canton sided with the capitalists, avidly arguing for aggressive expansion in South American mining. Valerian's earlier suspicions about Canton coveting the assets brought to him through marriage to Philippa were finding substantiation in Canton's avaricious stance on the economics of mining. Valerian made a mental note to ask Beldon about the extent of Philippa's mining assets.

'Fifteen minutes until midnight!' The cry went up from the orchestra conductor, who urged everyone to find a partner for the 'last waltz of the year'. There was an excited flurry on the dance floor as people laughingly paired up.

Valerian strode purposefully towards the group Philippa stood with. Other than acting as a willing dance partner for her wallflowers, Valerian had stayed apart from her. He preferred to study her movements and behaviour from afar—a certain kind of exquisite torture he'd imposed on himself as punishment for the prior evening. In hindsight, he acknowledged that he had not handled himself well on the balcony. He'd rushed his fences without knowing his quarry.

Tonight, she sparkled among an already glittering crowd. The deep gold of her gown was an elegant foil for the mass of burnished hair piled on her head and coiffed in strands of gold, woven through the coils like other women wove pearls. Her long neck was shown to advantage with the upsweep of her hair and Valerian was seized with the urge to kiss her nape as he came up behind her. He settled for putting his hands on her shoulders as if he were settling an imaginary cloak about her. He bent close to her ear, saying, 'I believe this dance is mine.'

It was a proprietary overture on his part and he knew it well. Most women thrilled to such a seductive, possessive claim. Odds were that Philippa wouldn't. But neither would she be able to politely refuse without looking like a shrew in front of the others.

Whatever scold she had in store for him would be worth the feel of her in his arms. Waltzing was something they'd done often and well in the old days.

'Viscount,' Philippa said, recovering from having been caught unaware by his gambit, 'I thought you'd forgotten. You've left it until the last minute.' She gave a smile, forced to cover for his presumptions.

'My apologies.' Valerian swept her a gallant bow and escorted her to the dance floor, knowing he wouldn't get off that easily. He had no sooner fitted his hand against her back when she showed her displeasure.

'Don't ever handle me like that again,' she began.

'I am afraid it would be rather difficult to dance without touching you,' Valerian said obtusely.

'That's not what I meant and you know it. You put me in a position where I could not refuse you without looking rag-mannered. Moreover, you insinuated claims on my attentions that you do not have.'

'Haven't I?' He couldn't resist the temptation to flirt with her.

The music started up before she could fire another insult at his head. Valerian swept her out into the centre of the floor, effortlessly creating space for them in the crowd. He was confident her pique wouldn't last long. Philippa could not resist the lure of the waltz. It had always been her favourite dance.

He had waltzed women across dance floors from the Black Sea to St Mark's Square in Venice, but no partner could rival the beauty of Philippa in his arms. Her long legs matched his stride with ease; her body answered the subtle guidance of his hand. She was all fluid grace as they moved through the turn at the top of the ballroom, her anger at him erased in the exhilaration of the dance.

They turned swiftly and tightly, giving him a reason to bring her up close to him instead of holding her at arm's length. She gasped at the change in contact, then threw back her head and gave an honest laugh. 'You waltz scandalously, St Just. Is this how they do it in Vienna?'

'It's how *I* do it.' He wondered how long he could keep her like this. The sight of her smile was breathtaking. In that moment, the smile was all for him. It was not her hostess smile, or her duchess smile, just *her* smile. A smile he'd known for years. It was the smile she'd given him when they raced neck or nothing, the smile she'd given him when they'd danced at her début, the smile she'd given him the first time he'd kissed her, deeply, thoroughly, and she'd recognised him as a man of powerful urges.

He laughed back and whirled them about at a

faster pace, heedless of convention. The dancing halted promptly at midnight in order for the ballroom to cheer in the New Year. Both of them were laughing and breathless. Valerian had his arm about her waist, keeping her close at his side, enjoying her unhampered good humour.

All her masks were off and she was Philippa Stratten beside him once more. His masks were off too. He was simply a young man again, in the throes of a first and true love, untouched by the rougher edges of life. A giddy elation fired his blood at the final stroke of midnight. As the raucous cheers went up, he recklessly pulled her to him and kissed her full on the mouth. Her arms wound around his neck and her head tipped back to take his kiss completely. There was an unequalled sweetness in knowing she felt the fire, too, and had given herself over to it. In that moment Valerian swore a silent resolution to himself in the fashion of old English tradition. By this time next year, he would have her. He'd already lived too long without her.

The orchestra struck up a tune for another waltz before the guests headed in for the New Year's supper. Valerian swung her into the dance without asking. She protested with a laugh, 'We've already danced once tonight.'

'That was last year,' Valerian parried easily, his elation only partially dampened by the stare of an infuriated Lucien Canton, who watched them from the sidelines, rage emanating from every pore of his impeccably groomed form.

* * *

Lucien viewed the pair waltzing with abandon and a disgusting amount of apparent ease in each other's arms. They were beautiful to watch as long as one wasn't also watching one's opportunity to marry one of them decreasing exponentially. Valerian Inglemoore was most definitely an unlooked-for complication in the progress of his plans. He had meant to propose to Philippa in the spring when he could do it in high style in London among the haut monde. Watching her with the newly returned viscount, Lucien knew without doubt he couldn't wait that long.

He had to strike *before* the iron was hot, as it were. Most people who knew him believed him to be a keen judge of human nature. Lucien knew his accuracy in guessing people's motivations and desires was partly his own intuition, but also partly because he spied on everyone in his milieu. The duchess was not exempt.

His spies indicated that the viscount was besotted with her, stealing away from the dinner table last night to steal kisses on the veranda. It was no balm to Lucien's concern that his spy also reported Philippa had slapped the bastard across the face. At the moment she might be conflicted over her response to the return of her curious friend, but hate ran a close parallel to love. From what Lucien had seen, if he waited until spring, the lovely and pivotal duchess would no longer be interested or available.

Without the Cambourne mines, his hopes to corner the tin market and establish an elite, profitable tin cartel, with holdings in Britain and South America, would become an idle dream. And without access to the Cambourne finances, he'd be hard pressed to cover some of his investments. It didn't take any amount of genius to know that if St Just claimed Philippa's affections, Lucien's own friendship with her would come to a quick end. St Just was not the type of man who'd allow his wife to keep a close male friend.

Lucien's hard gaze followed St Just into the last turn of the waltz. He'd ordered murder done before to get what he wanted. He wouldn't hesitate to see it done again.

Chapter Four

'He made you look the whore last night,' Lucien bit out crisply over breakfast late the next morning in the library.

Well, there it was. Philippa had expected as much when she'd received the note requesting they privately break their fast together, away from the other guests. Lucien was a stickler for propriety. Not one of his more desirable traits. Apparently, he was covetous too. She'd not had reason to notice that before. But no one had ever posed a threat to his claims on her time.

Philippa buttered her toast calmly, unbothered by Lucien's pique. 'You can hardly be jealous because I danced with an old friend.' That wasn't to say she was pleased with her behaviour the night before. She had indeed let her guard down with Valerian, a behaviour she did not indulge in with anyone. But Valerian's enthusiasm had been contagious and in his arms she'd felt the responsibilities of her world lift for a moment.

'Old friend? The word is too tame,' Lucien scoffed, reaching for his coffee. 'I've never danced with the sister of an old friend the way he waltzed with you. He desires you, Philippa. One cannot *not* notice. He makes no effort to hide it. Such behaviour is better suited for a brothel than a ballroom.' Lucien set his cup down and looked at her squarely. 'St Just needs to understand in specific terms that his attentions are not welcome, even if they were encouraged in the past.'

Philippa met his stern gaze evenly, bridling at his insinuations about her virtue. She was the Dowager Duchess of Cambourne. She would not be commanded in such a high-handed fashion. She chose to ignore Lucien's subtle probe into her past. Whatever had transpired between she and Valerian was their business alone. Lucien could speculate all he wanted. She hadn't even told Beldon.

'Are you suggesting I am forbidden to see him?' This possessiveness was exactly the kind of behaviour she'd been trying to avoid in a relationship with any male acquaintance of her circle since Cambourne's death. She didn't need to take direction from well-meaning men who thought she couldn't manage the reins of her estate or social life on her own. In Lucien, she'd thought she'd found a liberated man who would tolerate her independence.

It had been the basis of her attraction to him. Lucien had been a welcome friend during a difficult transition period for her. He'd been a loyal escort and adviser when she'd begun rebuilding her social circle after Cambourne's death. She'd believed they complemented one another well and had a comfortable companionship between matched intellects and interests.

She'd helped him too in a myriad of ways, like acting the hostess when his busy sister wasn't available. It had been the least she could do in return for the assistance he'd given her throughout the years.

'What right do you have to make such a demand of me?' Philippa flicked him a tight glance.

Lucien's eyes flashed. 'What right? We have been together for years.'

'We are hardly married, Lucien,' Philippa warned. They'd not explicitly talked in such terms before, although it would be unfair to say the issue had not arisen in other ways in the last year.

'Perhaps we should be. Married, that is,' Lucien said coldly.

'Is that a proposal? Your lack of enthusiasm makes it rather hard to tell,' Philippa shot back. Damn Valerian for this, Philippa thought hotly. Lucien's proposal, if one could call it that, was all his doing. He had to come rushing in and wreck everything with hot kisses and knowing caresses, making her remember the possibilities.

Philippa put down her napkin and rose, leaving her toast untouched, but it didn't matter. Her stomach couldn't tolerate a bite of food now. 'I regret to inform you that I have no intention of accepting a proposal articulated with such lacklustre ardour. It bodes ill for the marriage.' She tinged her voice with exaggerated ennui. The sooner she was out of the room the better. She hoped she made the door before she gave full vent to her temper.

Lucien rose, the glacial calm that usually accompanied his demeanour, melting at her comment. 'My displays of "ardor" have been quite acceptable to you right up until St Just began stealing kisses on the balcony right under my nose.'

Philippa stiffened. How could he have known? But to accuse him of spying on her would mean admitting he had the right of it. She turned to face Lucien before sweeping into the hallway. 'You've shown yourself in a poor light this morning, Lucien. Jealousy does not become you.'

Wrapped in a heavy wool cloak against the damp weather, Philippa stormed out to the gardens. No one else was about in such inclement weather. She was glad for it. She would make terrible company. She would be hard pressed to behave politely when all her thoughts were focused on less than polite behaviour.

Valerian and Lucien were worse than two stallions in season fighting over a mare and now Lucien had proposed, no doubt prompted by his sense of honour and apparently the belief that she needed protection from the likes of Valerian. In the three years of their association, Lucien had never once pressed her for a discreet affair. There had been nothing beyond a few private, dry kisses, a gentleman's touch on the dance floor or helping her in and out of carriages. *Nothing at all to compare with Valerian's very public seduction.*

Lucien's kisses were preludes to nothing. They inspired no wish to lose control, to cross over the boundaries of propriety. Valerian's kisses lit a raging fire in her, forced her to abandon her grip on control. Valerian's kisses were an invitation to decadence.

The very thought of Valerian's audacious assumptions brought colour to her wind-whipped cheeks. Lucien was right. Valerian made no secret of his sensual habits. The differences between the two men could not be more clearly illustrated if she drew a line in the dirt. On one side there was Lucien with his icy good looks and restrained passions to match his rigid sense of honour. On the other, there was Valerian, all devil-dark hair and hot eyes, flouting honour and convention at every turn. If the disparities were so obvious, why did she hesitate?

The answer gnawed at her. She was no longer sure Lucien's companionship would be enough for either of them. She was hard pressed to believe Lucien was happy with the dry affection that passed between them. Certainly, he must wish for more. Surely there must be another reason why he'd forgo physical pleasure. She wished she knew what he'd gain to make the sacrifice worthwhile. She could understand if he openly declared he needed to marry for money. But she did not appreciate hidden motivations. They were usually dark and dangerous and wrapped in lies.

Valerian leaned on his cue stick in the billiards room, pretending to watch Beldon take a shot. In reality, his gaze was fixed on a point just beyond Beldon's shoulder, through the window. Philippa was walking in the garden, alone. He'd been disappointed to learn she and Canton were taking breakfast privately when he'd come downstairs late in the morning. He could imagine what they'd talked about. Canton was none too pleased with him.

Beldon cleared his throat. 'Val, it's your turn.'

'So it is,' Valerian returned, but his interest in the game had waned. 'Beldon, would you mind if we finished our game later? I suddenly remember some pressing business I need to see to.'

Valerian didn't stay long enough to let Beldon quiz him on his sudden business. He slowed his pace only when he neared Philippa. It wouldn't do to appear the over-eager swain. She needn't know he'd interrupted his billiards game to rush after her the moment he'd glimpsed her.

She looked lovely, her colour high and her hair less than perfect from the wind. Desire surged in him, raw and elemental like the weather. She turned and spotted him at the gate.

'Nice day for a walk,' Valerian offered drily, striding towards her.

'I found the house a bit stifling,' Philippa said shortly, bending to study a dormant plant.

'The house or our Mr Canton?' Valerian pried shamelessly. 'I heard the two of you were closeted together over breakfast. I hope he wasn't angry about last night.' The last was a lie.

'You are too bold, St Just.' Philippa straightened, her eyes flashing as they studied him. He liked the feel of her gaze on him. Let her look and see that he desired her.

'But yes, Lucien has asked that I make our relationship clear to you.'

'So to speed my departure,' Valerian mused aloud uncharitably.

'Be fair, St Just. Lucien has done nothing to earn your enmity besides stand my friend.'

Valerian studied her. 'Is he your friend? I did not know him from before. He must be a new friend.'

'Why, of course he's a friend and he's perfectly acceptable. He's the oldest son of a viscount with excellent prospects of his own. He's not a new friend, not to me anyway. I've known him since John…' she hesitated here and then corrected herself '…Cambourne's death. He was with John the day of the accident and he's been with me ever since.' Her sharp tone had softened at the mention of her husband.

Valerian matched it with a quiet tone of his own. 'Beldon mentioned the accident briefly. Cambourne lived a while afterwards,' he prompted, liking the quiet intimacy that had sprung up between them.

Philippa turned bittersweet eyes on him, her gaze far away with her memories. 'Lucien got him home and arranged for a physician, even though he was hurt himself. We stayed by John's side for the next few days.' She shook her head. 'The doctor had known immediately that there would be no recovery. I was afraid to leave him out of fear that he would slip away the moment I was gone.'

Valerian took Philippa's hand, stroking her knuckles with his thumb, pleased that she hadn't snatched it away. A queer pang jabbed at him. He was both grateful that Philippa had cared for her husband and yet envious that those affections had been given to another. 'You cared for the duke, then?' he asked curiously, wanting to know the nature of the relationship she'd shared with Cambourne.

'I grew fond of him. He was a good mentor to me and he denied me nothing. He let me use his wealth and his name to build a model school for miners' children in the village. It's the one the vicar is modelling his own school after. He was a good and tolerant man. I sincerely missed him when he was gone.'

'But Lucien was there,' Valerian prodded.

'Yes. He helped with all the details of transferring the estates to me and to John's heir. That can be tedious work and Beldon was so busy settling the Pendennys estate in those days it was a relief not to burden him with my worries as well.' Philippa sighed.

The bastard knows how much she's worth to the farthing. He's had an intimate look at her holdings. The thought was unworthy, but it was the first one that came to mind. How convenient everything was for the man. That raised an alarm for Valerian. He no more believed in 'conveniences' than he believed in Beldon's blasted 'serendipity'. A man made his own luck. Lucien Canton appeared to have manufactured quite a lot of it.

Valerian's talk with Philippa in the garden did not go unremarked. Mandeville Danforth let the length of curtain drop in front of the library windows. 'Look at them, close as courters. He's holding her hand, damn it. Canton, how could you let him upset things so quickly and so thoroughly? He's turning her head.'

Lucien pierced the man with a cold stare. 'I didn't know he was coming. He and her brother arrived unannounced, much like yourself,' he said pointedly. 'How was I to know that he was more than her brother's best friend?'

'You could tell the minute he saw her,' Danforth groused.

'We *all* could tell. It's amazing the house didn't spontaneously combust. But by then it was too late. I could hardly expel him from the house. We have to be careful with Pendennys. We need his blunt. Where he invests, others will follow. Giving his friend the cold shoulder won't help our cause, especially with Pendennys still sitting on the proverbial fence where the bank is concerned.'

Danforth huffed in concession to Lucien's wisdom. 'Winning the Dowager Duchess of Cambourne's affections would be enough to bring her brother into the fold. It's a bad time for a kink in the works. Did you read your father's letter? I hope it was important enough for me to hare down here from London.'

Lucien felt some inward satisfaction that Danforth didn't know the contents of the letter. The man was getting above himself to think he could scold a viscount's son. He had not missed Danforth's barb about the need to win Philippa's affections. But Danforth was wrong to assume his only role in this scheme was to play the suitor and woo Lady Cambourne.

While the thought of finally having Philippa in his bed after all this time was pleasant enough, he'd invested the last three years of his life for a far more lucrative gambit than a roll in the ducal bed. He had an empire at stake.

Lucien gave Danforth a cold smile. 'My father writes that the London investors are in place. We may go ahead and officially announce that the Provincial Bank of Truro is open for business, with you, of course, as the nominal head.' It went unspoken between them the reasons for that choice. A viscount or his son might sit on an executive oversight board of a bank, particularly if the bank was in his own area of the country, but he would never overtly sully himself with such work as the daily running of the bank.

Danforth rubbed his hands together in delight. 'I am glad to hear it.'

'As am I. The sooner we can begin loaning funds to the smelting companies and the mining corporations, the sooner we can have our cartel.'

'And the sooner we have our cartel, the sooner we control the market. Everyone will be in our pockets,' Danforth remarked shrewdly.

'Not just the market, but the world,' Lucien said meaningfully. He didn't expect Danforth to understand. The man's financial acumen was daunting on a domestic scale, but he had yet to grasp the implications of the new British mining colonies springing up in the Bolivian and Argentine territories. That was Lucien's gift to the venture—futuristic foresight.

His eyes strayed to the window. His foresight and exquisite planning would come to naught if he couldn't control the Cambourne interests. The strength of his cartel and its ability to regulate tin and copper prices would be minimal if the Cambourne mines and other associated industries remained outside the cartel's umbrella to compete against it with prices.

St Just was an unfortunate distraction, but not insurmountable. He would have to send to London for news about the returning viscount. With nine years in the diplomatic corps, there must be dirt on the man somewhere—real scandal beyond his rakish reputation with women.

Lucien had yet to meet a diplomat who couldn't be bribed to shape foreign policy. Not that there was anything wrong with greasing palms. Lucien was man enough of the world to know it took a bit of well-placed oil to keep that world running smoothly. But Philippa was another sort altogether. She believed in ideals, like the miners' school the late duke had let her open.

Lucien rather thought she'd take badly to the news that the dashing St Just was not only a womaniser—a fact openly known in certain London circles—but a man who'd been involved with darker dealings, selling 'opportunities', as it were, to become involved in the great British Empire for a price—things like rights to waterways or trade commodities. Those were things that quietly went to the highest bidders and not necessarily those who deserved them most. Such injustice would not sit well with Philippa.

However, until he could manage to tarnish St Just's sterling image a bit, he'd follow the old adage of keeping one's friends close and one's enemies closer. It was time to pay a visit to the garden.

Chapter Five

Philippa didn't see Lucien approach, but was instead alerted to his arrival by the sudden tenseness in Valerian's pose and the feral light that lit his green eyes. She tried to slide her gloved hand discreetly from Valerian's grasp, but the effort was nothing more than an afterthought. The stormy visage Lucien wore made it clear that he had already seen her hand in Valerian's.

She resented the intrusion. For a short while, she and St Just had been companionable, simply Philippa and Valerian again, like they had been on the dance floor. She'd liked the soft, intimate tones between them as they discussed her marriage to the duke. She'd liked the absence of witty repartee designed to spear the other, the social politics of claiming and possession. With Lucien's interruption, all that was back, and back in force. The moment Valerian had spied Lucien, he'd become all St Just again—the rakish diplomat who would not be cornered or made to feel guilty for his actions by any man.

'Philippa, it's freezing out here,' Lucien said, rubbing his hands together for good effect and trying to minimise Valerian's presence by ignoring him. 'What could possibly bring you outside?'

'We're reminiscing, catching up,' Philippa offered smoothly. It was true. They'd been talking of the past, nothing more.

'My dear, that is why we have a dozen sitting rooms, expressly for the purpose of talking.' Lucien forced a laugh.

'Is that true or is it merely an example of hyperbole?' Valerian put in, shielding his eyes against the wind and making a great show of surveying the manor as if he could count all the sitting rooms and doubted the manor was large enough to uphold Lucien's boast.

Philippa couldn't decide what she wanted to do first: laugh at Lucien's bluff being called—the manor was large by Truro standards, but there weren't twelve sitting rooms unless one counted the small salons attached to a few of the larger bedchambers—or strangle Valerian for poking at Lucien's pride so deliberately and with no greater purpose than to antagonise the man.

'St Just has an interest in gardens. I thought he'd enjoy seeing yours,' Philippa interjected quickly.

Valerian smiled beside her. 'Yes, the family seat has extensive gardens over on the Roseland Peninsula. I am eager to get back to them.'

Lucien smiled back. 'I hope you aren't in such a

large hurry to get back that you won't stay on with us for a while? Perhaps I could entice you with a visit to some excellent gardens nearby?' Lucien offered magnanimously. 'I've heard rumour that the new vicar in Veryan, just a few miles from here, has been rebuilding the vicarage and has plans to expand the gardens. I could arrange for you to ride over tomorrow and talk about plants and whatever else you gardening types enjoy talking about.'

Philippa turned to Valerian. 'Please say you'll stay. I know the vicarage. It's lovely and you would enjoy meeting Samuel Trist, the vicar. He's an avid landscaper. The two of you would have much in common.' The thought of Valerian leaving, after having only discovered he'd returned was suddenly unpalatable. But he wouldn't stay if he thought he was beholden to Lucien in any way.

'Who knows what other pleasant surprises might crop up if you stay long enough?' Lucien put in, playing the expansive host to the hilt. 'With luck, you could be one of the first to congratulate me on my good fortune. I have proposed to our dear Duchess this very morning. I thought it was best to start the year off on the right footing, beginning as I mean to go on and all that.'

Philippa felt the colour go out of her cheeks. How dare Lucien call his angry, jealous retort a proposal. She was keenly aware of Valerian's probing stare.

'Has our "dear Duchess" accepted?' Valerian asked of Lucien, although his eyes didn't leave her.

'She has—' Lucien began glibly.

'She has *not* accepted the proposal,' Philippa

broke in angrily. Who knew what kind of fiction Lucien would fabricate? If he was willing to risk portraying their quarrel as a proposal, he might be willing to go so far as to say her storming out of the library was akin to 'thinking it over'.

Philippa stared hard at each of them. 'I will not stand here and be talked about as if I am invisible. That goes for both of you. However, since my presence is not intrinsic to this conversation, please feel free to stay out here and continue. I'm going in.'

She must have been momentarily mad to think she wasn't ready for Valerian to leave. *Valerian.* That was another thing. Some time between his arrival two nights ago and this afternoon, she'd started thinking of him as Valerian again instead of St Just. Out in the garden, he'd been her friend, so reminiscent of the old days, and then he'd become St Just. On an instant's notice, the mask had slid into place as assuredly as the one he'd worn to the ball last night.

Was that what it was? A mask? Why she was so certain the mask of cold, sharp wit was the facade? It could just as well be that the friend was the front instead.

Up in her room, Philippa threw her cloak onto the bed and paced in front of the window, her thoughts in turmoil. For a woman who'd thought herself well armed against the dubious charms of Viscount St Just, her defences had proven to be woefully inadequate. Already, she was willing to cast off what she empirically knew to be the truth for the old fantasy he'd spun once before in her girlhood.

Why was it so easy to fall back into believing those old myths? Especially when she *knew* they were myths. Inspiration struck. She would prove to herself that Valerian Inglemoore was not to be trusted with her affections. Yes, if she could visually see the proof with her own eyes, it would be harder to stray from the truth the next time he held her hand or led her in a waltz.

Philippa drew out a sheet of her personal stationery from the escritoire and sat down. Purposefully, she drew a line down the centre of the paper, dividing it into two columns: one for myths, the other for realities.

When she was done filling in the columns, she had three myths and five truths. Myth number one: he had loved her in their youth. Myth number two: he'd meant to marry her. Myth number three: he'd returned and hoped to woo her, to atone for bad behaviour in the past. Yes, those were the things she wanted most to believe about Valerian.

Then there were the dismal truths. Truth number one: he'd blatantly acknowledged their little *affaire* was nothing but a young man's fleeting fancy.

Truth number two: he'd never meant to marry her. He'd known that very night he was leaving for his uncle's diplomatic residence. What else could explain such a rapid departure? He must have been planning it for months, perhaps for even longer than their short-lived infatuation.

Truth number three: he'd never asked her father for permission to court her and certainly not permission to ask for her hand. If he had, her father would have told her, she was sure of it.

Truth number four: he had made no effort to contact her or Beldon in his absence.

Truth number five: he'd come home with a reputation to match the behaviour he'd shown her that long ago night in the Rutherfords' garden.

The bottom line of her analysis convicted him. With the exception of a few fleeting moments, nothing corroborated the behaviour she wanted to see in him. Nothing supported the items listed in the myth column. Everything supported the facts both past and present. The stark truth was that Valerian Inglemoore was a seducer of women—a very good one at that. So why was it so hard to resist him, even with the truth staring her in the face? And why was it so hard to accept that truth?

Was it possible there was another side to Valerian that he deliberately kept hidden? Perhaps there was a side that he couldn't afford to expose. There might be reasons for his tightly tied mask, reasons that had to do with his work for his uncle. Philippa drew out another sheet of paper. She had friends in political circles who could find out. All wishful thinking aside, it suddenly seemed of paramount importance she knew the truth about Valerian Inglemoore.

Philippa sanded the letter and set it aside, nagged by a growing sense of guilt. She didn't feel right about the inquiry. It felt too much like spying, going behind Valerian's back. No, she wouldn't send it, at least not right away. Now that her initial anger was waning, she was beginning to recognize she had done little to get to know the man Valerian had become.

Before she sent off a letter of inquiry prying into the man's background, she should try to exhaust more direct routes available to her. After all, she sat at the same dinner table with him and there was the outing to Vicar Trist's in Veryan tomorrow if Lucien's request was accepted. Those were prime opportunities to reacquaint herself with Valerian and determine the truth on her own.

The evening was a relaxed contrast compared to the prior two nights. Many of the guests who had stayed over after the New Year's ball had departed late in the afternoon for short journeys home. In addition to Beldon and Valerian, only two couples remained, a Lord Trewithen and his wife, and the ageing Baron Pentlow and his wife from the Penwith area, who were friends of Lucien's father and had come to the ball en route from London on their way home.

With the exception of the queer Mr Danforth, Philippa knew the other guests as regular acquaintances from the Cornwall community during her marriage. It was a simple task to make conversation over dinner and have a congenial time with the two ladies after the meal in the music room while the men took their port.

Afterwards, the men joined them for a short night of cards. She and Beldon offered to play whist with the Trewithens. At the far end of the music room, Lucien already sat at the cluster of chairs and sofa, talking avidly with Danforth and Pentlow, to the exclusion of all else, leaving Philippa to consider what to do with the elderly Lady Pentlow.

Unlooked for, Valerian rescued her admirably. 'Duchess, would you mind if I played the pianoforte this evening? I haven't a desire for cards at the moment or for business.' Valerian gave a quick nod to Lucien's group deep in discussion, his tone indicating how inappropriate he felt such a topic of discussion was in this setting.

'It would be delightful to hear you play again, my lord,' Philippa said, inwardly laughing at the formality of their exchange, so bland and perfect compared to the heated, more imperfect exchanges they'd exchanged in private.

Valerian inclined his dark head in a gracious nod. 'Lady Pentlow, if I might impose on you to turn the pages for me? I recall at dinner you said you enjoyed the country pieces. Canton has a decent collection of music, perhaps you could sort through it and select a few.' Valerian offered Lady Pentlow his arm and escorted her to the pianoforte, bending his head low to catch the woman's excited chatter.

Philippa watched them go with gratitude. How deftly Valerian had managed the situation. Lady Pentlow was a dear, sweet lady and Philippa hadn't wanted her to feel left out or in the way. Valerian had sensed the need and adroitly stepped in. *Unlike Lucien.* For a man she'd considered eminently eligible marriage material, she'd certainly had a lot of uncharitable thoughts about him recently.

Philippa shot a glance at Lucien's coterie, wondering what they could be talking about that would raise such an interest that Lucien would forgo his guests? Typically, Lucien was an excellent host with an eye for details, showing every guest the utmost courtesy due them in polite society. Tonight, he'd left that task entirely to her. She didn't mind. She was there to play hostess, after all. Still, such behaviour wasn't like him and it seemed odd that he would commit such a *faux pas* in order to talk to Mr Danforth, a man whom Lucien had claimed not to know two days past.

'Are you coming? We're ready to play,' Beldon called from the card table.

Philippa smiled and took her seat. 'I hope my brother has warned you how competitive he is.'

Their game was lively and they rotated partners at the end of each rubber. The Trewithens proved to be capable players, demanding all of Philippa's attention. Usually she was quite good at cards, whist and piquet being two of her favourite games. But tonight, too many distractions competed for her attention, not the least being Valerian's quiet ballads coming from the pianoforte. On occasion, she caught snatches of Lady Pentlow's trebly voice singing a few lines.

At last the tea cart arrived, signalling the end of the evening. Philippa poured out and then went to stand with Beldon as the group congenially sipped their tea. 'What do you suppose has Lucien so interested?' she asked quietly.

Beldon gave a soft laugh, part-teasing, part-cynicism. 'I see the privileges of being a male prevails here. If you'd been allowed to stay at the table, you would have been treated to Mr Danforth's announcement that he was opening a bank here in Truro, the Provincial Bank of Truro or some such nonsense.'

'Nonsense?' Philippa queried. 'Why would you say that?'

'You know what these country banks are really like, Phil. They're investment firms.'

Philippa nodded in agreement. Cambourne had done business with Praed and Co., a bank in Truro that invested in high-risk ventures such as inventions and new technologies. If one was clever, these investments paid off. Cambourne had had good luck with them, but it was no surprise that these country banks went bankrupt far more often than the style of bank one would do with business with in London.

She better understood Lucien's potential interest now. Lucien was always interested in money. 'Does Lucien think he'll invest?'

'More than that. Mr Danforth has offered Lucien a place on the bank's board of directors.'

'For a sum, I'm sure.' Philippa offered thoughtfully.

'Definitely for a sum. But Lucien would be in charge of directing the investments. He seems quite taken with the idea.'

'He'd be good at it. Lucien is no fool when it comes to money.'

'But not women, at least not you.' Beldon eyed her over his teacup.

'Valerian told you?'

'Hmm. Rather cowhanded of Lucien to think you could be politely coerced, if not into an actual betrothal, then at least as far as a publicly announced engagement. Are you thinking of accepting?'

'I haven't given it much thought,' Philippa murmured vaguely. Marriage to Lucien Canton had been a foregone conclusion until the very unsuitable Valerian had arrived. Now, she believed she'd been rather naïve not to have thought about it more deeply, to look beyond the simplicity of an arrangement between two friends who enjoyed each other's company. What other reasons could there be for a man with Lucien's looks and prospects to choose to marry a childless widow when there were so many eligible débutantes available to him?

Beldon looked as if he would press her for more details. She stalled him with a shake of her head. 'This is not the place for such a discussion.' Lady Pentlow was starting to nod off in the middle of her conversation with Lady Trewithen. The evening was coming to a close. Her guests would want a good night's sleep before beginning their respective journeys in the morning. They would look to her for the sign to retire.

Beldon assented. 'Promise me we will have that discussion soon.'

Philippa smiled at her brother's protectiveness. Even with childhood long behind them, he had not forsaken his role as a doting brother. 'I promise. There is something I want to ask you, too, something about Valerian.'

Chapter Six

Beldon returned his empty cup to the tea trolley and said his goodnights to the group as they began to depart upstairs. He wasn't as ready for sleep as the rest of them. His agile mind was alert, pondering the little dramas of the holiday, and Canton had excellent brandy in the library.

In general, he found people to be an interesting area of study. Younger men of his acquaintance dreaded the routine of a house party unless hunting was involved, but he found them to be intriguing affairs. The gatherings were a constant source of amazement to him, full of the dramas of intersecting lives.

Even in a group as small as the one here tonight, the web was tightly woven—Lucien and that merchant-cum-banker Danforth establishing a business tie together; he and Lucien, friends established through their common tie in Philippa; Lucien and Philippa and the budding drama of Lucien's proposal; Lucien and Valerian, enemies on first sight. Why? The two men did not know each other. They had only Philippa in common between them.

Philippa was the only possibility. Did Valerian have a liking for Philippa? It was fantastical to think Valerian had fallen in love with his sister at first sight, and yet Val's animosity towards Lucien had seemed palpable the moment he'd walked into the manor. A hypothesis began to take embryonic shape, events of the past starting to form connections to one another instead of existing as isolated occurrences. But Beldon was interrupted before he could decipher what the link was that bound them all together.

'A farthing for your thoughts.' Valerian strode into the library as if conjured from Beldon's own mind. He'd removed his jacket and waistcoat, shirt sleeves rolled up.

Beldon shifted in the comfortable chair he'd taken up residence in. 'My thoughts are worth far more than a farthing, old chap. Pull up a chair. Canton has a superb brandy collection.'

Valerian gave a short chuckle at that. 'Is that his chief requirement in being your friend? Since I've met him, his cellar seems to be his primary recommendation.'

Beldon waved his snifter. 'Well, you have to admit the Veuve Cliquot was superior at New Year.' He paused, stopping to consider the play of firelight on the amber liquid swirling in the snifter's bowl. 'In truth, I'd thought Canton was quite an amicable fellow, a bit aloof at times, but otherwise acceptable, until you showed up. Why do you think that is, Val?'

Beldon studied his friend closely, watching him adopt a comfortable slouch in the opposite chair, his feet resting negligently on the fireplace fender as he pondered the question.

'Do you want me to answer that question or is it rhetorical? I seem to recall you made a habit of telling us what to think in school.' A teasing smile hovered at Valerian's lips before he sipped from his glass.

'*Touché*, I am wounded,' Beldon said. 'The accusation is true. However, in all fairness, you must admit most of our friends *didn't* think. I did them a grand favour by doing it for them.'

'Then carry on. Clearly, you have ideas.'

Beldon set his drink on a small side table next to his chair. He leaned forwards in earnest, elbows resting on thighs. 'Tell me the truth, Val. I don't have all the angles worked out yet, but I think you have a penchant for Philippa.'

It was telling that Valerian didn't meet his eyes, but chose to look straight ahead into the waning fire. 'Philippa is an attractive young woman who is intelligent and confident. I am certain many men desire her. She would be an asset to any peer's household—'

'More to the point,' Beldon broke in, not swayed by the general terms of Valerian's response, 'you desire her *and* you have for some time. This is no incident of love at first sight. You're both past the first blush of such fantasy. How long have you carried feelings for her, Val?' How had such a thing as his best friend's affections escaped his notice? Beldon felt a twinge of betrayal. He and Val had been closer than brothers and yet Val had not confided in him. Still, such an omission from Valerian was apparently not amiss. He'd not shared his plans to join his uncle until the night of his departure.

Valerian straightened and turned to face him, this time not avoiding his gaze. 'I've loved her since we were young together. I was head over heels for her by the time she made her début.'

'You didn't tell me,' Beldon said slowly, his mind whirring to adjust the pieces of this puzzle, how it fit against the backdrop of what had transpired. 'Did she return your affections?' There was a pit growing in his stomach. It was a horrible feeling to know that the two people he was closest to had fallen in love and he hadn't known or been told.

Valerian must have sensed the direction of his thoughts. His answer was simple. 'Yes.'

There it was. Valerian had not kept the secret alone. They had conspired together to keep the secret from him. 'Why didn't you tell me?'

Valerian shrugged. 'How could I? Cambourne had offered for her.'

'And you stepped aside?' Beldon asked sharply. 'That doesn't sound like your typical behaviour at all.' The Valerian he knew had championed the underdog at school, standing up for the principle of right, even when the odds were against him. He'd earned more than a few bloody noses for not knowing when to back down. In fact, the Valerian he knew didn't believe one ever backed down. What had changed that when it came to Philippa?

Valerian tossed him a warning glance. 'Beldon, I

must ask you to stop your inquisition right now. The hour is late. In my experience, late hours are good for confessions between friends, but not necessarily for understanding them. Be satisfied to know that I have loved Philippa for years from afar. Be satisfied also to know that I would still claim her if she would have me.' Valerian rose, putting an end to the conversation.

Beldon put out an arm in a restraining motion. 'You can't leave me on tenterhooks, Valerian.' He gave a snort. 'No wonder you were such a fine diplomat.'

'Go easy on me, Beldon,' Valerian said wistfully. 'I have the utmost confidence in your mind's ability to solve the rest of the riddle in short order and I will be waiting to confirm your conclusions. You know I value our friendship too much to ever cheat you out of the truth.'

Beldon nodded. 'I know. Sleep well, Val,' he said in all sincerity.

'Aren't you coming up?'

'No, I want to sit a while longer.' Beldon held up his half finished snifter. 'Wasting fine brandy is a sin of the highest order.'

'Enjoy,' Valerian said from the door. 'Remember, I did answer your question.'

'And gave me a hundred more to think about in return.' Beldon offered him a sardonic toast. He would sleep shortly. Valerian was right in one respect. Part of the riddle in terms of Valerian's dislike of Canton was appeased. They both wanted Philippa.

Beldon would wager it was for vastly different

reasons. Valerian loved her. And, well, love was not a commodity Lucien Canton was known to trade in. Canton wanted her for something else.

For a long while, Beldon had entertained the idea that Canton appreciated the intelligent companionship Philippa offered. She understood the man's talk of finances and business since she'd been well groomed by Cambourne for appreciating that aspect of the Cambourne holdings. The duke had believed a woman should understand her worth and seen to it that Philippa had.

After watching Canton and Danforth tonight talking over the new bank, Beldon had to wonder if Canton's interest in Philippa was and had been financial. He'd not thought of it before, since Canton was not without his own wealth or the ability to increase it on his own. Canton had no obvious need to find a wealthy bride.

Valerian's sudden reappearance had certainly acted much like a clarifying solution, throwing the muddied depths of their lives into sharp relief. If it was up to him, Beldon much preferred that Philippa married Valerian.

Valerian was a man of honour, a man who could be trusted to do right even in the most dire circumstances, which brought his thoughts for the evening full circle.

Why had Valerian stepped aside when Cambourne offered for Philippa? What would Valerian have seen as a more honourable pathway than the chivalry of fighting for his heart's desire? Who or what had Valerian been protecting that would have compelled him to set aside Philippa and leave his own country? They had not spoken of his abrupt departure, but Beldon felt certain the two were connected.

Beldon smiled to himself in the near-darkness. The fire had died down to mere embers. He loved a good mystery and this was proving to be an excellent one. He'd need his sleep in order to be fresh for the trip. He could hardly wait. Who would have thought such a seemingly innocuous jaunt to view plants at a vicarage could provide so much drama? Oh, yes, the morning promised to be very interesting indeed.

Cornwall could always be counted on for oddities when it came to weather. When the rest of Britain's estuaries froze, the streams near Truro and Falmouth were full of migrating eider and goldeneye ducks. When many parts of Britain thought the dark winter would go on endlessly, the sheltered south of Cornwall celebrated an early arrival of spring. So it was that the weather for the trip into Veryan was mild for January, even though the day before had been plagued with bitingly cold winds.

The last of the guests were gone by eleven o'clock after a late breakfast that would preclude the need for lunch, and the group of four was seated comfortably in Lucien's shiny black coach with large glass window panes by half-past the hour for the short trip. Philippa would have preferred to ride, since the distance between Veryan and Truro was negligible and the weather promised to remain true. But Lucien insisted on the coach.

'What's the point of having such a splendid vehicle at one's disposal if one does not make use of it?' Lucien said.

Philippa secretly thought it more likely Lucien preferred the attention the elegant equipage drew as the coachman tooled through Truro. 'Still, there aren't many days in the winter when the weather holds for a long ride. It seems a shame to waste one of them,' Philippa replied.

'Ah, but that's just it, my dear. I doubt this weather will hold.' There was a slightly condescending tone to his voice. 'Certainly, the skies appear safe at midday. But I predict clouds and rain before tea this afternoon.'

Valerian stirred in his seat across from them, a glint in his eye that made Philippa uneasy. 'You sound quite sure of your prediction, Canton.'

'I am, St Just. I've spent the better part of the year these last few years living here,' Lucien boasted.

Valerian nodded, gesturing to Beldon and Philippa, 'I've spent, as the rest of us present have, the better part of our lives living here, and I say the weather will hold.' Valerian glanced out of the window and tilted his head to catch a view of the sky. 'In fact, I would go so far as to say the sun will show itself by two o'clock.'

'Care to wager on that?' Lucien responded.

Philippa stifled a groan. The weather was supposed to be the one safe topic of English conversation. Wasn't that the rule one learned growing up? Somehow, Valerian and Lucien had turned the weather into a competition as if either of them could control it. Although, if she had to place her bets, she'd bet on Valerian. Lucien knew mining, but Valerian knew the climate. His estate on the Roseland Peninsula contained some of the rarest plants and flowers known to grown in Britain.

'Twenty pounds,' Valerian said. 'The sun shines by two o'clock with no rain until after five, I win. Canton here wins if the sun fails to shine *and* it rains by tea at four o'clock.'

Beldon broke in, drawing his attention away from the window where it had been riveted for most of the trip. 'Who wins if the sun doesn't shine and it doesn't rain? Or the sun shines, but the rain comes early?'

Oh, lord, not him too? Philippa sent her brother a beseeching stare. Worse, Lucien and Valerian looked as if they were seriously contemplating the developments. By the time they reached Veryan, the two of them would have concocted such an elaborate wager it would be impossible to determine a winner.

'A draw then,' Valerian declared resolutely. 'If there's any discrepancy, it becomes a draw.'

'Fair enough,' Lucien concurred.

Philippa shook her head and shot Valerian a scolding glare. He fought back a smile and discreetly turned his head to look out of the window at the passing landscape.

The vicarage was a place of organised chaos when their coach pulled in. Samuel Trist, the new vicar, broke away from a cluster of workmen and strode through the soft mud and dirt to greet them, smiling excitedly. 'You're here! This is a great pleasure. I was delighted to get your note yesterday.'

Philippa liked the man immediately. He was tall and lean, moving with a loose-limbed gait. Even though he'd known they were coming, he still wore the cotton flannel clothes of a workman and mud-spattered boots. He stripped off his gloves and ran a hand through the shock of flax-coloured hair that stood on end. She recognised his type immediately. He was the kind of man who forgot all else when set on a project dear to his heart.

'It was kind of you to let us come on such short notice,' Philippa said, giving him her hand as she stepped down, glad for her sturdy half-boots and short-skirted walking dress of simple merino wool. She'd guessed correctly that anything more formal would be out of place, although Lucien had quietly disapproved of her informal attire.

'Watch your step there. Some of the mud is a bit squishy yet,' Trist advised.

'Reverend Trist—Viscount St Just. He enjoys horticulture. I immediately thought of your place,' Lucien said, making the introductions. Lucien surveyed the scene. 'Quite the ambitious project you've got going.'

'Yes, this is just the beginning. The vicarage had become seriously run-down during my father's last years. I took over as vicar and decided the place had to be brought up to standard. I want something more fashionable, more up to date.' Samuel gestured for a man to join them. 'This is my foreman on the project. He can show you the plans while I show the viscount around. There's not much out here yet in terms of a formal garden, but I have my hopes.'

Reverend Trist turned to Philippa, seeing that Beldon and Lucien were already poring over the new plans for the house. 'Your Grace, will you join us?'

Trist walked them through the garden, talking of plants and herbs. He stopped to check the tight, close-budded rhododendrons. 'Will only be a month and these beauties will pop open.' He stopped at the edge of the garden. 'Now here is where I've planned a lane of trees.' He gestured to lines of seedlings strategically placed. 'There's copper beeches and evergreen oaks.' Something twinkled in his eye. 'Look over there.' Samuel Trist pointed. 'That is my pride, a Chilean Pine.'

Valerian was immediately taken with the tree. 'What a curious species. May I?' He strode towards the tree, studying it intently with gentle hands. 'Philippa, come see this!' All formality was forgotten in the wake of his excitement over the exotic tree.

The tree was indeed a curiosity. Dark green in colour and covered with stiff needles, the tree had arm-like branches that stuck out haphazardly, becoming a complex tangle of maze-like arms that took up vast amounts of space. 'Why, I think it would puzzle even a monkey to climb it!' Philippa exclaimed, laughing at the intriguing shape of the tree.

'Perhaps that's what I'll call it,' Samuel Trist said, joining in her merriment. 'A monkey-puzzle tree.

That certainly sounds more exotic than "Chilean Pine.'"

'I've not seen anything like it,' Valerian said, his tone nearly reverent.

'I might boast enough to say that if I can get it to grow, it'll be one of the first planted in Britain,' Trist said.

'I'd like to get a cutting of this and have a go at it myself,' Valerian said. Philippa didn't miss the excited sparkle in his eye as he contemplated a new plant.

Trist nodded, glad to have found a fellow enthusiast. 'I need to get back to the vicarage, but feel free to walk farther. There's a grotto I am currently filling in to make a folly and I've got stakes laid out where there will eventually be a man-made lake. The walk is a bit rough this time of year, your Grace. You're welcome to come back with me,' he added.

Philippa flashed a look at Valerian. She should go back. Returning to Beldon and Lucien was the safest path to travel. There was no temptation there, just polite conversation. Valerian had proved to be the opposite. In the short time since his return, he'd managed to tempt her passions and her temper, two irreconcilable forces.

It was something of a mystery to her how she could resent the passion he awoke so easily and yet she had continually courted opportunities for him to stoke those same flames.

Valerian's sharp gaze seemed to sense her hesitation as she weighed her choices. 'Come with me, Lady Duchess. The weather promises to remain fine and you remarked in the carriage how much you wished to be out of doors. If the path proves too hard, we can turn back.' He held out his arm in a gesture that brooked no refusal. How could she gracefully decline a gentleman's arm without turning it into an outright rejection?

Reverend Trist was staring at her, confirming her suspicions that she'd contemplated her situation too long.

She smiled and said with forced brightness, 'Thank you, St Just. I think a walk is the perfect idea.'

She took Valerian's arm, telling herself that the bachelor vicar couldn't see her inner turmoil over the decision or even that he suspected anything amiss. Women took a man's arm all the time. But it did not escape her notice that the vicar glanced from one to the other before he set off towards the house, trying to understand what had really transpired. Philippa wished him luck with the conundrum, although she doubted he'd succeed where she had failed.

'Shall we?' St Just turned them towards the stone-strewn path leading to the folly site, which Philippa thought was aptly named in light of the fact that she'd had very little luck with Valerian when it came to gardens. The last time she'd been alone in one with him, he'd left her with a broken heart that had taken years to patch. She wondered what he'd leave her with today. She could already feel the seams of that patch starting to unravel against all logic and her better judgement.

Chapter Seven

'**Y**ou hesitated, Philippa,' Valerian said matter of
factly, guiding her around a large stone in the centre
of the path. 'Did you fear being alone with me?'

'Don't overestimate yourself.' Philippa fought the
urge to give an unladylike laugh. 'I recall the last
time we were alone, you ended up with my hand
across your face. If either of us should fear being
alone with the other, it should be you.'

Valerian tossed her a sideways glance. 'I must
correct you. *That* wasn't the last time we were alone.
Yesterday, I thought we did very well together. I
thought our conversation was quite civil. As for the
other time you are referring to, I am still not sure if
the slap was meant for me or if I was merely an
available target for your own personal frustration.'

The man's arrogance was phenomenal. But she
was thankful for it. Fighting with him was better than
wallowing in silence with her fantasies about the
man she wished he was. 'Enlighten me. What would

I be frustrated about, if not your outlandish assumption that I was inviting your attentions out there on the balcony?'

They called an implicit truce while Valerian helped her over a small pile of scrim. The path smoothed out and argument resumed. In a detached part of her mind, Philippa thought the scene would be quite funny if played out on stage—their courteous behaviours being interspersed with the contradiction of the verbal spears they hurled.

'Outlandish?' Valerian repeated with calculated incredulity. 'I believe "outlandish" refers to being odd or strange. My dear, I regret to inform you my "assumptions" were anything but "outlandish". You did not find my "assumptions" strange or odd in the least. Perhaps you're looking for a different word?'

'I don't know what that would be,' Philippa snapped.

Valerian gave a shrug and a sigh. 'I don't know either. Perhaps a word denoting "liking" or "appreciation"? After all, you did like my kisses. Point of fact, you liked them so much, you managed to kiss me back quite thoroughly *before* you managed to slap me. By the way, I find that deuced unfair— slapping *me* for *your* kissing.'

'No gentleman would ever speak to a lady in such a manner!' Philippa fumed. The man was more than arrogant. He was a positive boor. 'How dare you make such assumptions!'

'Oh, that word again, "assumptions",' Valerian parried with feigned blitheness. 'I think before we go any further we should define precisely what you mean when you say "assumptions". I'm starting to believe you and I use the word differently.'

Philippa's temper flared again. 'If this is your idea of diplomacy, Britain is lucky not to be engaged in a conflict of major proportions.' She regretted her words instantly. Valerian's face went strangely blank for a moment, his eyes giving the impression that his thoughts were suddenly far away. The impression was so fleeting that the next moment Philippa wondered if she hadn't imagined it.

'But this is not a diplomatic mission, my dear, it is a walk to a folly with an old friend who, frankly, seems a bit confused about her feelings.'

'You dare too much.' Philippa stopped and withdrew her hand from his arm, her voice as stiff as her spine. The cad had gone too far. She would argue with him about stolen kisses or 'assumptions' or whatever he wanted to call them, but she would not countenance this effort to make their past history her fault. Neither would she let him portray her as a wanton widow eager to bed down with any handsome house guest.

'You cannot come back into my life after what you did and expect to be forgiven on two days' notice. Neither can you expect me to engage in whatever kind of *affaire de coeur* you are used to carrying on with women of your acquaintance.' She knew very well the kind of women who peopled Valerian's diplomatic circles.

To her satisfaction, Valerian did have the decency to look penitent. 'Are you finished?' he said quietly, the toe of his boot digging out a muddy hole in the ground.

For a moment Philippa felt awful. She'd been too harsh. She'd let him get the better of her. But she found her resolve. She would not be won so easily. He had to be accountable for his actions. It was best for both of them to know how she felt. 'Yes, I believe I am finished.'

Valerian's voice was subdued. 'Suffice it to say, I didn't want things between us to end that way.' He shook his head as if to dispel unpleasant memories. 'I didn't want to make you cry. I don't expect you to forget what passed between us. However, I would welcome any forgiveness you'd be willing to offer. Over the years, have you ever thought once that maybe I had my reasons and those reasons had to remain secret? After all, you knew me to be a man of honour, Philippa.'

Philippa shook her head in denial, her voice matching him in despairing softness. 'No, Valerian, I know no such thing.'

'So be it,' he said quietly in tones that passed for the barest of whispers. He offered her his arm again and they trudged forth in silence, but Philippa was not immured from the hurt that had flitted across his face at her words. She was not a cruel person inherently or by design and she regretted her words, although she did not regret thinking them. They represented the empirical truth as she knew it. Still, a part of her did not welcome hurting Valerian, and that part worried her very much.

They did not speak again until they reached their destination. 'Ah, there it is, Trist's folly, or what there is of it,' Valerian said with a modicum of gallantry to cover the silence that had sprung up between them.

'Yes, there it is.' Philippa offered half-heartedly. She wasn't thinking of the stone grotto slowly being renovated, but of a different folly; this one being a handsome man with broad shoulders who was busy stripping out of his expensive coat and rolling up his sleeves a few feet away from her to better explore the rocks that lay haphazardly about the grotto.

Philippa found a flat slab of granite and sat down, to wait and to watch. *Handsome is as handsome does.* The nursery-room warning clanged in Philippa's head. Valerian had certainly proved the adage true. He'd stolen her débutante's heart with hard, full-mouthed kisses and soft promises that roused her budding sense of passion. Then he'd disappeared from England without a backwards glance or even a letter. Still, the old memories, memories that predated heartbreak and harked back to a better time, persisted, a time when she'd believed differently.

She'd enjoyed watching Valerian in gardens before. He would wander around in silence and then suddenly remark, 'wouldn't this be a lovely place for a fountain?' or 'a maze would be a splendid addition here'. In their youth they'd often used the pretence of looking at landscapes to steal a private moment. Only, it hadn't been so much a pretence since Valerian made a regular habit of mentally rearranging everyone's garden.

The recollection made her smile now while she watched him stroll about the grotto. Watching him, so absorbed in his study, she could almost believe time had stood still. Errant strands of his hair were being blown in his face by the light breeze. He bent occasionally to study the stones that seemed to intrigue him. The expensively cut shirt moulded his strong physique to perfection across the expanse of his shoulders and the exquisite muscles of his back.

Valerian turned towards her, a hand pushing his hair back from his face. 'Come and see this prospect. The view from the north-west corner is outstanding. I think I'll tell Trist he should build rockeries, too. The quartz-veined rock from Carne Quarry at Nare Head would be handsome here.'

At his words, a stab of yearning speared through Philippa, causing a near-physical pain. Hot words and devastating past aside, in that moment he was the old Valerian, the one she'd thought she'd loved, and she wanted him. This was no lustful coveting of his body. No, she wanted more than sex from him, although she wanted that, too. She wanted Valerian Inglemoore body and soul, the way she thought she'd had him when they were younger. She wanted to know what he was thinking the moment he thought it. She wanted to anticipate his every desire. It had been years since she'd felt a longing so complete, so intense, and never with anyone but him.

Time stood still, then fractured into a kaleidoscope of half-forgotten memories. She was in his arms, although she hadn't the faintest idea how she'd got there or when he'd moved. His lips were on hers, full and demanding. His mouth possessed her and she returned it with a possession of her own.

Someone was crying, and she had the vague impression it was her own sobs. Valerian's hands were rough on her body and his breath was ragged as he ravaged her mouth. She did not care. They were both frantic.

He was a master at this, kissing her with insistency, his tongue probing her mouth, his teeth nipping her bottom lip and sucking hard. His hands moved from her waist to expertly cup and caress her breasts, kneading them through the fine wool of her gown until they were erect with need.

Philippa caught fire. All she could do was wrap her arms about his neck and press into him until she couldn't tell where she ended and he began. But it wasn't enough. She wanted to throw off her clothes and let his hands range free on her body no longer hampered by the fabric of her gown and the undergarments beneath.

She could feel his body rise, burning hot and hard. His erection was full and insistent against the folds of her skirt. His hands had moved to gather up the material of her dress and she could feel his body, taut with desire and anticipation. No wonder he'd had half of Europe on its knees.

All reason fled. She cared not a whit for the hardness of the granite slab beneath her back or for the painful ghosts of the past. She cared for nothing save the heat of Valerian's body as it covered hers in an attempt to assuage the need that coursed through them both.

Valerian, green eyes forest-dark with desire, hesitated for a moment. 'Philippa, are you sure?'

'Val, I want…' She met his eyes, searching for what it was that she so desperately sought—that her Valerian existed, that this moment was the moment she'd thought to claim so many years ago. But it wasn't there, not really. This was wrong, no matter how right it felt. And she remembered why. She had loved him. He had shared her passion, but not her depth. He'd scorned her and sent her off to marry another man.

'Yes, what do you want?' Valerian panted.

'I want to believe,' she said softly, her arms twining around his neck, pulling him down to her in mute apology. 'But I can't. Not yet.'

'I can make you believe again, Philippa,' Valerian vowed. 'Let me try,' he pleaded, every ounce of his muscle straining in desire as he held himself in check.

She held him there, full against her. She couldn't deny that she wanted him, but she didn't want him, not as a fiction. 'Don't do this. I won't have it. You had your dalliance with me years ago. I won't be played for the fool again.'

'You were never my fool, Philippa.' He raised himself up on his arms, drawing back from his seduction only slightly. His eyes shut as if in an attempt to hold back the memories. 'We had a great passion between us once. We can have it again,' he coaxed. 'I want you, Philippa.'

Philippa felt the old animosity flare against her passion. 'I was the one left crying in the Rutherfords' garden. I thought you were going to propose and you *knew* I thought that.' When she had him, *if* she had him, it would be with an understanding of the truth of who he was. It was the only way she could protect herself from being hurt a second time. If she learned nothing else today, she'd learned that being hurt again was a distinct possibility.

A distant 'Halloooo!' reached her ears and the reality of their situation hit her. She'd done the most foolish thing of all—she'd almost let Valerian make love to her in the open, where they were no doubt visible to all sundry passers-by.

Valerian groaned a miserable 'Oh, God,' as he moved to stand, fumbling with his clothes. 'We have company.'

Philippa struggled up to see Beldon and Lucien tramping towards them. Good lord, how much had they seen? She and Valerian had been kissing in plain view of anyone coming in that direction. That was the problem with follies and prospects. They thrived in wide open spaces.

'I don't think they saw anything,' Valerian whispered reassuringly in her ear as if he could read her mind. Out loud, he called to them, 'What brings you out here?'

'Lucien's come to concede!' Beldon called back good naturedly.

Philippa's cheeks went scarlet. She didn't need a mirror to know her face was burning with mortification. *They had seen*. Beldon's reference made it perfectly clear.

'Steady, love.' Valerian chuckled. 'I don't think Lucien's coming to concede on that point.'

He made a show of pulling out his pocket watch

and flipping it open. 'Concession accepted, Canton. It's two o'clock and the sun's been out for ten minutes.'

If her cheeks could have reddened further, they would have, this time from anger. While Valerian had been seducing her with sweet words and kisses, half his mind had been on the ridiculous wager and she'd lost half of hers for falling temporarily to his seductive efforts—further proof that Valerian Inglemoore was no more than the sum of rumours and her past experience made him out to be.

'How's the prospect from here?' Beldon asked, striding to the area marked off with string where the folly was slated to be.

'It's lovely. You can see all the way to Truro,' Valerian said vaguely. 'Philippa hasn't seen it yet. Now, we can all see it together.' He led the way to the outcropping, very much aware that Philippa lagged behind, shooting not-so-subtle daggers at his back.

He could imagine with a fair degree of accuracy what she was thinking: how like a man to turn the situation so adroitly. One would never guess he'd been lying on top of her, proclaiming to be in the throes of passion and making impossible promises literally moments ago. Here he was, playing tour guide and looking for all the world like a man whose sole interest in coming up here had been to see the sights.

Well, she was wrong about that. He'd seen the opportunity to get her alone when the vicar indicated he had to go back. That had been the end of his inspiration. He'd taken the opportunity, but done nothing with it except compound Philippa's distrust. He'd meant to tell her Beldon knew about their past romance. He'd meant to confess the reasons for leaving her. But events had taken a different direction and they had ended up on the granite slab, apparently against Philippa's better judgement.

Her 'better judgement' rankled. It was one thing to know, to suspect, what she thought of him. It was another thing entirely to hear her articulate those ideas out loud. She thought he wasn't a man of honour. She thought she couldn't believe in him again.

And maybe she was right.

Valerian fought back a wave of self-doubt. He'd failed to help those people in Negush too, failed to find a way to peace before all revolutionary hell broke out. People who believed in him notoriously came to bad ends. It was not an accomplishment he was proud of.

Valerian cautioned himself to control his dark thoughts. He could not give in to the megrims that accompanied his guilty moods. This was not the place for it, on top of an overhang on a house-party outing. It would be the height of bad form to come down with one of his devastating headaches—compliments of the Phanariot revolutionaries.

Gathering his concentration, Valerian had to admit that the prospect did not disappoint. Once the actual folly was built, it would have a breathtaking command of the Truro area. The vicar would be pleased with the results. Beside him, Beldon took a deep breath and exhaled expansively. 'Ah, there's nothing like clean Cornish air. I swear there's no place on earth as grand as this.'

Valerian smiled at his friend's Cornish pride. It helped to lighten his mood. He too had loved growing up and living here. But Lucien seemed inclined to argue, suddenly much less 'Cornish' since he'd lost the weather bet.

'I think I prefer the Lake lands with their mountains. Much more rugged, more challenging. Makes the mountains here look like rolling hills.'

Valerian raised an eyebrow, indicating that he disagreed wholeheartedly. 'While I was away, I saw many different terrains—mountains, seaboards. Some places were blistering hot and others were cold enough to freeze a man's thoughts. When I couldn't tolerate the climates, I would think of Cornwall.' His eyes strayed to Philippa as he spoke the last. He had meant more than 'Cornwall' in the comment. The startled look on her face suggested she guessed as much.

Encouraged, he went on, blurring out those around them. 'I would think of the gardens, especially the gardens at Pendennys Hall and Roseland and all my plans for it. I'd imagine walking in the gardens in those places, sometimes making plans, other times finding peace.' Did she remember their walks? Their talks? They'd shared many secrets in their time.

Philippa broke away from his gaze and turned to stare out over the land. He hoped she'd heard the hidden message: *I thought of you; I treasured memories of our time together.* Most importantly, *you and you alone sustained me when I kept no hope for myself.* Although he doubted she'd fully comprehend how dark his life had been, how far from the light he'd wandered.

Beldon coughed discreetly, drawing his attention with an over-loud voice. He must have drifted off in his thoughts. 'Contemplating the weather again, Val? Lucien and I were wondering how you knew it wasn't going to rain.'

Valerian gave a negligent shrug of his shoulders, all glib aristocrat once more. 'Well, for one, I didn't say it wouldn't rain, only that it wouldn't rain before tea time. As for that, I do believe it will rain after six tonight and before nine o'clock. Double or nothing on that, Canton?'

Canton eyed him suspiciously and Valerian knew he'd be packing his bags tonight. It was a sure sign it was time to leave when one was reduced to the subterfuge of wagering on the weather in order to distract the host from the reality that his guest was bold enough to seduce his hostess right under his nose. Oh, yes, it was definitely time to go home.

Chapter Eight

Philippa was going home. Danforth's stultifying conversation at dinner decided it by the time the duck was served. She would leave in the morning. From the looks of things at the table, she wouldn't be the only one.

Immune to such uncharitable thoughts, Mr Danforth held forth ceaselessly about his bank throughout dinner, although it was exceedingly obvious no one was paying him serious attention except Lucien. But even Lucien appeared to have his mind on other things. Philippa didn't want to dwell too long on what those things might be for fear of discovering she was at the heart of them.

She was certainly at the heart of Beldon's absorption. Beldon, who was normally very adept at dinner conversation, seemed lost in his own thoughts, letting his gaze drift between her and Valerian.

Valerian had apparently used up his quotient of good behaviour the night he'd squired Lady Pentlow.

It was clearly not in evidence tonight. Valerian was in one of his blacker moods, not even making an effort to follow the conversation beyond sprinkling it with an occasional pointed comment regarding the risky nature of country banks. 'Venture capital is all well and good, but let's call it that instead of calling it "banking",' Valerian drawled over the last course.

Lucien took offence, which was probably what Valerian had been planning, Philippa thought. 'Exactly how is it *not* banking, St Just? We do what any other bank does. We loan money to those who wish it. We hold money for those who wish to deposit sums with us.'

Valerian sipped his wine thoughtfully. 'With the exception that you invest deposited sums in high-risk ventures without the benefit of safe investments to act as ballast should the risk fail. Frankly, you and I both know there is a significant chance people could not get their money back. It's why folk of our status bank in London at Childs or Coutts. Don't you find it telling that certain classes of people are rather limited in the banks they have access to?'

Philippa didn't like the gleam in Valerian's eye, but could find no way to intervene without giving the impression she was championing Lucien. For starters, Lucien didn't need a champion. He could handle himself well enough in a financial conversation. For the rest, she didn't want to give any impression to Mr Danforth that she'd be willing to invest in his provincial bank.

'St Just, are you implying that I would deliberately swindle investors by making promises I could not uphold?' Lucien was all cold ice, piercing Valerian with a stare that said he was merely a comment away from pistols at dawn. Philippa stifled a groan. The Provincial Bank of Truro was about to erupt into scandal and the doors weren't even open. She shot her brother a quick plea for help, but Beldon was enjoying himself too much.

'I am suggesting that there is something of a history of short-lived provincial banks, that's all,' Valerian said easily, his long fingers caressing the stem of his wine goblet. 'Their limited livelihood comes from the tendency to invest in risky enterprises. Odds are usually against them. It wouldn't be the first time something went amiss.'

'It would be for me, Viscount,' Lucien said evenly. 'I have yet to invest foolishly. Those who follow my lead reap the profits of their trust. Don't they, Pendennys?' He looked down the table to Beldon for confirmation, putting Beldon in a tight spot.

'That is certainly true, in my experience,' Beldon acquiesced. But Philippa noticed he didn't bother to elucidate further on the point. She could tell Lucien was disappointed. She knew Lucien had hoped Beldon would expound on the British-Bolivian mining colony in the Americas that the two of them had invested in. Beldon had sold his shares a few months back, reaping an enormous profit. It was left to Lucien to blow his own horn.

'Pendennys and I had a lucrative opportunity in Bolivian silver. We took a large sum in the proceeds when we sold. I'd be glad to guide any investments you might consider making as well, St Just. Your man of affairs is welcome to contact my secretary any time,' Lucien said with cold magnaminity.

He turned to the rest of the table. 'Since it is just the four of us, I'd like to suggest dispensing with cigars and brandy. It's been a long day with departing guests and the trip to Veryan. Perhaps, gentlemen, you would enjoy a game of billiards. St Just, if you'd like to play the pianoforte, feel welcome. Make free with my home. I find I have business to discuss with my gracious hostess. If you will excuse us?'

It was all skilfully done and moments later everyone was dispersed, leaving Philippa and Lucien to talk alone in his library.

The meeting was not at all what she was expecting. The last time they'd spoken, Lucien had been angry. Since then, they'd only spoken in the company of others. She'd anticipated a continuation of their former conversation. She'd anticipated an angry, self-righteous Lucien Canton. What she encountered was a very different face.

'Sherry, my dear?' Lucien solicited from the sideboard, pouring himself one of his special after-dinner wines.

'No, thank you. I have packing to oversee, so if you don't mind, I'd like to keep this short,' Philippa insisted, taking a seat in a deep-wing backed chair near the fire.

'I am sorry to hear that. My valet reported you were preparing to leave. I'd hoped you would stay on after everyone had left. We haven't had much time together this week,' Lucien said in sincere tones, taking the seat opposite her.

He drew a deep breath and exhaled, relaxing. 'This is nice, sitting with you by the fire. Two chums, taking their ease together, eh, Philippa?' He gave a charming smile, looking and acting more like the Lucien she'd known over the past three years than the arrogant man of the last few days. 'We are still friends, aren't we?'

'Of course, Lucien,' Philippa said quietly. In truth, as upset as she was about Lucien's behaviour, she could not logically throw out years of steadfast friendship with him over the matter of a few days and events; events she was responsible for. She imagined she might behave quite the same as Lucien had if she'd been in his place. No one liked being usurped in one's own house and there was no denying that Valerian hadn't hidden his dislike of Lucien Canton.

Lucien cocked his head to one side, studying her intently. 'My God, you're a beautiful woman, Philippa. The shot-blue silk becomes you.'

Philippa blushed. 'Thank you. But I am sure that isn't what you called me in here for,' she prompted gently. She wanted to be in her room, watching the maid pack her things. When she'd returned from Veryan, she thought some of her things had been moved, that her escritoire had been looked through, gently, of course, but still it felt like a violation. The letter she'd written, but never sent to London regarding Valerian was in a different spot than she'd recollected. For an unexplainable reason, the incident felt like more than just negligence on the part of an unobservant maid cleaning the room.

'Yes, our business.' Lucien nodded. 'I need to thank you for acting as hostess. Everything went splendidly, as I knew it would. I had time to talk business with my guests and you took care of the rest.

'I also need to apologise. I have not looked after our relationship as I should. I was reckless and self-centered. Such behaviour caused me to jump to poor conclusions.' Lucien reached for her hand and closed his fingers around hers.

His hand was warm and she thought the gesture was meant to convey reassurance. But she wasn't re-assured at all. She had the distinct feeling they were being watched, and coupled with the fact that Lucien was not a man who would admit to such shortcomings, something was afoot, although she couldn't put a finger on it.

'You have nothing to apologise for,' Philippa offered, hoping quick absolution would end the conversation. But Lucien wasn't finished.

'I have everything to apologise for. I didn't understand how close you and St Just were, that he was your friend as well as your brother's. I misunderstood your desire to simply spend time with an old friend. He had your time, Philippa, and I didn't. It made me a bit jealous and jealousy can cloud a man's judgement, make him see things that aren't there or put incorrect constructions on what is there. I am guilty of doing that. I spoke harshly to you on New Year's Day. You were right. Jealousy does not become me and, indeed, there is no place for jealousy between us.'

Lucien ended his pretty speech and reached inside his evening coat. 'I have something for you, Philippa.' He took out a square, blue velvet box and opened the lid to reveal a sapphire pendant on a thin gold chain, tasteful and expensive. It had not come from a local jewellers. 'I made a shambles out of things New Year's Day. No woman wants to be asked to wed in a haze of anger.'

'You don't have to do this. You don't need to atone for anything,' Philippa began to stall. Right now would be the perfect time for Mr Danforth to burst in and start babbling about his bank. The odd man hadn't bothered to follow any protocols of polite conversation at the dinner table, why not put all that lack of couth to good use and barge in now, when it would be useful?

Lucien was prosing on about his growing senti-ments for her and she supposed she'd better pay at-tention. 'Although I regret my behaviour during St Just's visit, I do not regret what his visit has caused me to see. That is, I want to spend my life with you. We are well matched in status and intellect. In you, I see more than a wife and mother to my heir. I see a partner. Would you consider doing me the honour of marriage?'

He was even down on one knee. Philippa was struck by how different her response to this scene might have been had it occurred a month earlier. She might have said yes immediately, as a logical con-clusion of their long-standing friendship. Companionship was worth marrying for, even in the absence of passion. Her first marriage had been based on mutual companionship and it had not been a poor experience. But now, everything was somehow different.

Still, she was not foolish enough to toss away a modicum of happiness and security on a whim. Neither was she so much of a sapskull that she would ignore the assets of marriage to Lucien Canton. As her friend, he deserved more from her than an out-of-hand dismissal.

'Lucien, you pay me a great honour. It deserves thinking about. Rest assured that your proposal will be in the forefront of my thoughts as I return home to Cambourne.'

'Then take this pendant as a token of my esteem and my affection, Philippa. It will serve as proof that I am in your thoughts.' Lucien was too gallant to refuse as he fastened the sapphire pendant around her neck. 'Now, off to your packing, my dear. Rest well. I will be up to see you off in the morning.'

The wall panel to the left of the fireplace slid open and Mandeville Danforth came out of hiding. 'That's quite a room you've got back there,' he chortled. 'Right out of Bonnie Prince Charlie's time.'

'That went well, I think,' Lucien said, uninterested in Danforth's thoughts on the priesthole.

'Yes, indeed. Although, she could have said "yes",' Danforth was quick to point out.

'At least she didn't say no. St Just has turned her

head, but how far is hard to say. We're not the only ones making inquiries in London. She's thought about it. My valet found a letter in her room. Still, her doubts about St Just are enough for us to exploit if we must.'

'We must. It is a foregone conclusion,' Danforth corrected. 'She must marry you or sell you all her mining rights and ancillary companies. You have to control the Cambourne interests. I don't see her selling.' Danforth's eyes narrowed in thought.

'We could stage another accident, perhaps several of them, that would convince her to sell.' He began to plot.

'No.' Lucien cut him off sharply. 'Properties with accidents don't inspire investors to cough up their pounds. It would do us more harm than good in the long run. Besides, she's stubborn and sabotage would take too long. We need those properties by late summer.'

'Then it looks as if the Duchess should reconcile herself to being a June bride,' Danforth said in a tone that suggested Philippa Lytton would find herself at the altar, whether she wished it or not.

Lucien raised his glass. 'Here's to the end of my bachelor days.'

Chapter Nine

She was glad to be home! Philippa put down her pen and looked up from her ledgers, taking a moment to stretch her back and survey the glorious view spread before her through the long windows of the library. Not even the fine mist that blurred the landscape could dim her appreciation. The vast lawns spread before her, green even in winter. The pond floated on the horizon, filled with ducks. In good weather, she would have been tempted to throw open the windows in order to hear their squawking.

In all, she'd been gone two months; first up to London for the Little Season and the Michaelmas session of Parliament, wanting to support some early discussions on mining reform; then to Richmond for Christmas and Lucien's for New Year. Now she was home for three months before she'd need to return to London after Easter.

Home. Her kingdom where she reigned supreme. She did the ledgers, she oversaw the transactions of daily business, she visited the tenants, the fields, the home farm, the mining interests. Here, she was not ruled by any man.

Philippa knew how rare her situation was. It had not come easily, but at the price of sacrificing a youthful dream. She'd wanted to marry for love, the passionate romantic kind of love found in fairy tales and Minerva Press novels. Instead, she'd married the man of her family's choice and found a quiet companionship with him.

Perhaps that was better. Her experience with Valerian had been quite illuminating about the quality and strength of romantic love. It had its limitations. But companionship had its limitations, too. Cambourne had been kind and generous with a giving that extended far beyond his purse. He'd educated her in business and finance, delighting in her interest in his estates.

In the beginning she'd become interested to keep her mind off Valerian's desertion. She had to do something to fill her life. Later, she'd seen the genuine need to take an active part in the life of Cambourne's holdings. She'd built the school for miners' children and it had become one of her favourite projects.

Then Cambourne had died so suddenly, firing her involvement in legislation concerning mine safety. Oh, yes, there was no disputing that her life was full these days. She'd remade herself admirably as the young Duchess of Cambourne and then again a few short years later as the Dowager Duchess. But refashioning oneself was hard work and she had no desire to do it again.

Philippa fingered the sapphire at her neck. She'd worn Lucien's gift today out of a need to honour her word. There was no one to see her, no one to hold her to her commitment. But *she* knew. She'd told Lucien she'd consider the offer. Wearing the pendant was a reminder of what she'd promised. She owed at least some consideration of his offer. Although, if he could read her thoughts, he'd probably wish she hadn't felt so obliged. Marriage to Lucien would definitely require some re-fashioning.

Most likely, she could get her solicitors to design a betrothal contract that would protect her property, but it would be difficult. Not even a dowager's possessions were safe from a new husband's rights. She would have to give him something. It wasn't that she didn't trust him precisely. It was more the issue of having to give up the control she was so used to having.

Control would be given up in other areas, too. Lucien would expect her to stay with him wherever he went. The year would be divided up between Truro, London, his father's estate, and then Cambourne. There wouldn't be time to live as she liked. Her interests would give way to his and when his father eventually died, Lucien's responsibilities would increase. Becoming the future viscountess to Lucien Canton would require quite a lot of re-fashioning, leaving very little room to be the Dowager Duchess of Cambourne—obliterating it, in fact.

And for what?

Security? She didn't need security. She had it aplenty with her own holdings.

Finances? She was far wealthier now than the Pendennys family had been during her growing-up years. Marriage to Lucien didn't enhance her wealth in any meaningful way.

Companionship? Certainly they rubbed along well together, but that was already something she enjoyed with him, not something she needed marriage to gain.

Love? Definitely not. In spite of his protestations the night before she left, Philippa knew without question that Lucien didn't love her any more than she loved him. She appreciated him, but one didn't marry for appreciation. She wasn't sure Lucien was capable of a great love, the kind of love you married for, because you knew with a pure certainty that this was the one person in the entire world whom you could find fulfilment with.

There were none of the usual reasons that women typically married for. She couldn't think of a single reason why she would want to marry Lucien and give up all she had. It all provoked the question—why Lucien had asked in the first place? Surely he knew?

But Lucien needed the one thing she didn't. He needed an heir and he was approaching thirty-five in a couple of years, the magical age when heirs finally decided it was time to start their nurseries and look to their futures. Perhaps he'd looked about for a wife and decided she would be better suited for him than one of the débutantes peopling London's marriage mart.

That was a conclusion she could understand. Lucien would not tolerate an insipid wife. He would want someone with intelligence and social skills. It was the only conclusion that made sense. Like her, Lucien didn't need additional wealth. Being a man and his father's heir gave him inherent security. He didn't need to marry for companionship.

Philippa sighed and took off the necklace, carefully laying it in a desk drawer for the time being. She'd take it upstairs later. Lucien would be disappointed in her answer and it could very well scotch their friendship. He would want to know why. He would try to resolve her misgivings with promises he'd mean to keep, but that social pressure wouldn't allow him to—like the right to live her own life. He would say, laying out his assets like a balance sheet, 'Why not me? Do you think someone better will come along?'

In fact, she did. At least she hoped. She'd married once for the sake of her family. If she married a second time, it would be for her. For someone who considered herself to be fairly conversant in the realities of the world, she was hard pressed to let go of her romantic notions.

It didn't mean she had someone specific in mind and it absolutely didn't mean she was holding out to see if Valerian could be brought to heel. He'd already proved he couldn't be. But his kisses were hard to forget and served as potent reminders that one did not have to settle for the convenience of lukewarm companionship.

Philippa rose from the desk. The drizzle had stopped. She would change into a habit and take a ride between showers. When she came back she would write to Lucien and tell him of her decision. There was no sense in waiting. Bad news didn't get better over time and the longer she waited to dispel him of his matrimonial notions, the more likely it was that he'd build up his expectation of being accepted.

Expectations being what they were, Lucien was not all that troubled by the arrival of Lady Cambourne's letter at the manor in Truro the first week of February. In fact, he was precipitously jubilant. The New Year had got off to a perfect start.

Danforth's bank had been well received by local men with money to invest. Cornwall was rich in many resources and not all of them came out of the ground. Industry bred invention. Plenty of men like Dabuz, Bolithio and Williams had seen the need for other industries like tin-smelting and gunpowder. Dabuz and Fox swore that smelters and gunpowder works were more profitable than the actual act of mining. From the amount of funds at their disposal, Lucien was inclined to agree with them.

It had been the simple work of a few dinner parties to corral the financial resources needed to start investing and buying. These men were as avaricious as he was. They immediately saw the merit in banding together to form a cartel that controlled the outside world's access to tin and regulated the prices at which that outside world would have to pay for the commodity.

They'd also seen how important it was to control the mining interests in Britain's new South

American colonies. If those resources were allowed to compete against the cartel, it would diminish the profit. But if those colonies were controlled by the cartel, then the prices would be controlled as well.

Lucien had hand-picked the men who would serve on the new bank's board of trustees and all had agreed buying up shares in the largest British mine in South America would be the first place they'd start with the building of their overseas control. Monopolies and cartels were tricky things. It wouldn't do for there to be a large broadcast of their intended plans until they had some leverage.

So with his finances firmly in hand, Lucien had complete confidence that all else would fall into place, too. The letter from Philippa had arrived as if on cue. Just that morning at a bank meeting someone had asked about the Cambourne mines. He'd given the man an enigmatic smile and said vaguely something to the intent that he hoped to have more concrete news to share shortly. Then, like magic, the letter had arrived.

Lucien ripped open the envelope and scanned the contents, reading it twice and then again a third time to make sure he understood its contents correctly, his blood turning to ice.

Damn Valerian Inglemoore.

Lucien crumpled the note in one angry fist. The man's name hadn't been mentioned once in the missive, but he could read between every line. Although Philippa would deny it, St Just had turned her head. Whatever the man had once been to her, whatever claims, spoken or unspoken, had lain dormant between them during her marriage and his long absence, they had been awoken once more.

The man had kissed her at least once since his ill-timed return, making Lucien highly suspicious that St Just's tenure away from fair Albion's shore could be directly linked to Philippa's marriage. Lucien didn't like surprises. It galled him there was something of that nature he didn't know about Philippa.

Lucien's secretary knocked and asked for the day's correspondence. Lucien sent him away. 'No letters to write today. Take time to work on cataloguing the library.' The door shut on the office. Alone again, Lucien took out a sheet of crisp paper. There was one letter to write, but it was too private to entrust to another pair of eyes.

Lucien dipped his pen into the inkwell and began to write. St Just stood in the way of his bid to build a mining empire; for that, the man must be ruined.

Something had ruined the relationship between Valerian and Philippa, Beldon mused, and not for the first time since he'd parted ways with Valerian at Roseland three weeks ago.

After seeing Philippa off in her coach bound for Cambourne, he had ridden with Valerian to Roseland, stayed a few days to see his friend settled and then turned for the Pendennys lands outside St. Mawes.

Today, as he rode home from his weekly visits with the tenants and his meeting with the vicar, the subject dominated his mind, perhaps because he had little else to think of. He was a social creature and this was a lonely time of year for him. There was small need for him to be in London and Philippa was busy with her own interests before she had to be back in town.

It wasn't that he didn't have options. He could go up to London anyway and Philippa would always welcome him at Cambourne. Roseland was close by and now that Valerian was home, he'd probably ride over to Roseland on occasion to ease the isolation he felt rambling around alone in the big Pendennys country house.

Certainly, he had options, but, in truth, his own estate needed his attention too. He'd worked too hard to save it from genteel poverty in the years since his father's passing. Of course, he couldn't take all the credit. Without the generous loan from the Duke of Cambourne, all the effort in the world could very well have been useless. When he'd first starting going over the ledgers, that fact had become glaringly apparent. Cambourne's wealth had kept the Pendennys family afloat. He'd silently thanked the fates Philippa had married well, if precipitously, and at such a fortuitous time.

Beldon drew sharply on the reins, bringing his horse to a rather sudden and jarring halt. The answer to his riddle hit with full force. Cambourne's money had been the 'something' that had come between Philippa and Valerian.

He kicked his horse into a hard gallop, covering the remaining distance home as fast as he dared. Once home, he raced into the estate office, pulling down old ledgers from the shelves. Beldon didn't even wait to take off his coat, only taking time to strip off his gloves so as to turn the ledger pages better.

Hours later, when he'd finally removed his outer wear and his jacket, rolled up his shirt sleeves and eaten sporadically from the tray the housekeeper had sent up after she realised the young baron would not be swayed from his task long enough to eat in the dining room, Beldon had his answer.

The office was a mess, with books open to various pages strewn across any available surface. Ledgers from nine years ago had simply been a starting place. He'd had to go back further to determine why the Pendennys barony had needed the funds so badly in the first place.

What he found had been devastating. The office had paid the price of his sleuthing and so had his memories. It was almost like learning the life he thought he'd had was only an illusion. His father had not confided in him, not really.

He'd known about the loan from Cambourne, naturally. But he'd thought very little of it beyond the exorbitant expenses of a few years. Philippa's Season and début were costly affairs coming on the heels of supporting his time away at Cambridge with Valerian. At the time, his father had only said that the wars with Napoleon had placed the economy under undue stress.

Beldon had believed him. When he'd taken over the reins of the barony, he'd not looked back far enough in the ledgers to see that while there was truth in what his father had offered as an explanation for Cambourne's loan, there was also much else. The Pendennys finances had been in a slow decline for years. He could trace a string of investment losses and a decline in the production rates of the mines. Too much money had gone out and too little had come in to cover the losses.

The loan had been used to shore up the failing coffers and Beldon had used part of the funds later to diversify the family holdings. In anticipation of a future where the copper and tin mines wouldn't produce as much ore, never dreaming that future was already coming to pass, Beldon had bought a tin smelter. Later, he'd invested wisely with the Perran Industries gunpowder works. Both had paid off handsomely. A tin smelter was to the mines what a miller was to farmers. Grain needed to be ground into flour and tin—well, tin needed to be smelted. The smelter would continue to pay out long after his own mines had exhausted their resources.

Beldon pushed a hand through his hair, leaning back in his chair. It was all embarrassingly clear now. They had been in dun territory and Philippa had been married to Cambourne in order to save the family—in order to save him, really. He was the heir. Without her marriage, there would have been little to inherit but trouble. All his life, he'd thought he was protecting his younger sister, watching over her at balls to see that she didn't dance with the wrong sort of gentleman, making sure she went nowhere unescorted, and all the while she had been protecting him. There was a certain amount of guilt that went with that realisation.

Had she known? He remembered vividly the night he'd found her in the Rutherfords' garden. She'd been crying although she wouldn't admit it. At the time, he thought it had been the shock of the sudden engagement to Cambourne. Had she known why their father had favoured the match?

Beldon remembered too his brief encounter with Valerian that night. Valerian had been brusque and out of sorts. His friend had paused only long enough to tell him that Philippa was in the garden. The next weeks had been chaos. Valerian had gone and Philippa's wedding had to be planned. He'd had little time or reason to ponder the turn of events or even to see his friend's disappearance in connection with the wedding.

In retrospect, Beldon began to think it was highly plausible that Valerian and Philippa had met secretly in the garden and that she was crying for a different reason. He couldn't quite puzzle out that bit yet. Still, on one hand he had more answers. Cambourne's money had likely come between them. Cambourne's money had not been a serendipitous godsend as he'd always believed, but rather a calculated move on his father's part to save the barony.

Beldon took stock of what he had: some answers, more questions, and one damning hypothesis beginning to form—if the move to woo Cambourne had been planned, then Valerian had to have known, otherwise he would not have willingly stood down from his claims on Philippa's hand.

The mantel clock struck midnight, late hours for

the country. It was time for bed. He had a long day ahead of him, beginning with a ride over to Roseland.

Chapter Ten

Valerian was in the greenhouse, working with his new rose hybrids, when Beldon arrived the next day. He looked up from his pots and cuttings in glad surprise. He had been alone too much with his thoughts lately in lieu of any available company. 'I'm hoping to get a yellow rose with pink highlights,' Valerian said, brushing off his hands on a towel.

'It's good to see you. What brings you over so suddenly? I hope everyone is well.' For a moment his stomach tightened. He hoped the news wasn't about Philippa. A hundred images of all the things that could go wrong raced through his mind. She could fall from her horse on uncertain terrain, she could take ill with a winter cold, she could have accepted Lucien's ridiculous marriage proposal.

Apparently, his concern was obvious. 'At ease, old friend,' Beldon chuckled. 'Everyone is well. Philippa's well, if that's what you're worried about.'

'Would you like to go inside?' Valerian offered.

'No, don't let me stop your work.' Beldon waved the offer away, pulling up a tall stool next to the long work table. 'I came to talk. Some things about our riddle were niggling at me,' he confessed.

Valerian nodded, pushing a wooden crate across the table. 'You can sort seeds while we talk.' He knew precisely what Beldon meant by the riddle and he could guess with approximate accuracy what Beldon had unravelled and what he hadn't.

Beldon grabbed a packet of seeds and starting sorting the menagerie by flower type. 'Good lord, what are all these for? There must be a hundred packets in here, Val.'

'They're all wildflowers. I want them for the south garden. Sort them by type, not colour,' Valerian instructed.

'You're making plans. That must mean it feels good to be home again,' Beldon said.

Valerian looked up from his clipping and smiled gently at his friend. 'First, yes, it does feel wonderful to be home. I am finally starting on the plans I once had for this place. Second, you don't have to ease into it, Beldon. We've been friends a long time. I'd like to think you could ask me anything and our friendship would not suffer for it.'

Beldon snorted at that and Valerian knew he was thinking of the irony of that statement, thinking that Valerian had not felt he could tell Beldon his own great secret years ago. 'Perhaps you'll think differently about why I didn't tell you, when you're done with your questions,' Valerian said softly, apologetically. There was so much he had to account for. Today would be a start.

Beldon drew a deep breath. 'All right—what do you plan to do about Philippa now that you're home to stay?'

Valerian chuckled, intent on the plant before him. 'It's not so easy as what I intend to do, Beldon. Philippa's a stubborn woman. She'll do what she pleases and I am afraid she's not convinced I am in her best interest.'

Valerian looked up in time to see Beldon's brows furrow as he tried to work through his statement.

'I don't really understand the difficulty,' Beldon began. 'The two of you were in love once, she's free to pursue her own interests now and you're still in love with her. Beyond a little wooing, I don't see the problem.'

Poor Beldon, Valerian mused. He knew so much and yet so little of the details. Valerian took mercy on his friend. He set down his garden shears and leaned across the rough-hewn work table. 'Listen, Beldon. The night you found her crying in the garden, she wasn't crying because she had to forgo me and marry Cambourne. She was crying because I purposely broke her heart. She thought I was going to propose that evening.

'Instead, I told her I wanted her to marry Cambourne, that what we shared together was nothing more than a young man's dalliance.' Valerian winced at the last. Surely, Beldon would forsake his seed sorting and send him a rounder across the jaw. He deserved no less.

Beldon stopped his sorting, his fists hardening into tight balls, white at the knuckles. 'Why would you do that?' His voice was that of an angry older brother. 'Philippa was never anything but good to you. She adored you and apparently in a way far deeper than I guessed. You were her hero.'

Valerian nodded his assent, countless images of Philippa as a young girl, hair still in braids and skirts still short, tromping beside them during the long summers; Philippa slightly older, still coltish with her long legs, begging him to partner her during dance lessons.

Oh, yes, Beldon could not be more right. He'd been her hero. Once upon a time, he'd revelled in her adoration. There had been a type of strength in knowing that someone believed in him so thoroughly. The power of her young girl's adulation had got him through the darkest year of his life—the year his parents had suddenly died in a tragic hunting accident up in Scotland and he'd become the young Viscount St Just at the age of fifteen.

Philippa had been a rock, listening to him grieve when he gave in to his blacker moods. Beldon had been the consummate friend, just as Beldon's parents had been loyal to their son's young friend. Valerian owed the family fiercely for what they'd done. They'd sheltered him, protected his inheritance when there had been concern over his young age, and, most of all, they had loved him. He'd no choice but to return that offering in kind when the time came, even if it meant hurting Philippa for the larger good.

Valerian sighed, moving to a tomato plant he was growing indoors. He began checking the leaves for any fungus. 'I've felt guilty enough over the years for what happened. I've wondered if I should have handled it differently. Mostly, I blame myself for starting it in the first place.' It was easier to talk if he kept busy.

'I am not so interested in how it started, Val, as to why it ended with a broken heart,' Beldon encouraged.

Valerian heard the unspoken message. Beldon understood how deuced awkward it was to talk about romancing one's best friend's sister. Those memories were too intimate, too private, memories that rightly should be only for him and Philippa.

'Philippa was not wrong. I had meant to propose that evening. She'd only been out a little over a month, but I'd known long before her début how I felt about her. That afternoon, I went to speak to your father.' Valerian hazarded a quick glance at Beldon.

'My father refused you?' Beldon's reaction was incredulous. 'He loved you.' But something else was working in Beldon's mind. 'The money,' Beldon said quietly. 'I came today because I spent most of last night going over the Pendennys's accounts. We would not have survived without the generous loan from Cambourne.'

Valerian gave a slight nod. 'Your father asked me to step aside. He said he was entertaining an offer from the duke.' He didn't need to say any more of the difficult words. Beldon was quickly piecing the rest of that interview together.

Beldon's voice was full of disbelief when he spoke. 'What my father did was dishonourable. He sold his daughter in marriage when she loved another and that other was willing to marry her and give her a respectable life—'

'Don't be angry with your father,' Valerian broke in. 'I didn't tell you this to drive a wedge between you and his memory. He was a good father to all of us. I do not think it is a sign of dishonour to try to protect your family from ruin.'

Beldon protested. 'It's not as if you were disreputable or poor or untitled. You were Philippa's equal in all ways.'

'He did what he thought was best,' Valerian said with finality. 'I must take some of the blame. I knew Cambourne was interested. The betting book at White's attested to the fact. But I went ahead and put your father in the position of having to refuse me. It might have been better for all if I had just let the romance dwindle, or I hadn't started it at all.'

Beldon shook his head. 'It is so typical of you to bear the burden of another's choices. At school, you were so quick to champion the underdog and to protect others, even when they should have shouldered their own responsibilities.'

'Still, it had to be done. You know I couldn't access my full inheritance until I was twenty-seven,' Valerian reminded him. 'If the family could have lasted five years, I would have thrown every pound I owned into seeing the family redeemed, but your father could not wait.'

Beldon went back to sorting the packets. 'I understand.' But his tone suggested otherwise. Valerian knew it would take Beldon a while to come to grips with the realities of the past. He appreciated that, for Beldon, the past was being rewritten.

'Your father asked me to break it off with Philippa in a way that didn't place him as the villain or jeopardise her willingness to marry Cambourne. You know Philippa. If she thought there was any chance of coercing her father into changing his mind, she would have tried. She could not know about my offer.'

'So you played the cad and told her this "*affaire*" meant nothing to you.'

'Essentially,' Valerian admitted, then added, feeling the need to clarify that there were limits to how much of cad he'd been willing to be, 'It wasn't an "*affaire*" in the truest sense of the word, Beldon. I left her untouched. You needn't assume the worst about me, whatever the rumours have asserted about me since then.'

'Rumours aside, I've always found you to be a man of honour,' Beldon said, meeting Valerian's gaze evenly.

'Yes, well, you might, but consequently Philippa does not. The past and the present—the way she understands them—fit together all too well. My performance that night in the garden was quite convincing. Perhaps you can see for yourself the implications that now impede any courtship I might conduct with her at present.'

Beldon tossed the last packet into a pile of violet wildflower seeds. 'I absolutely see what a mess you've got yourself into. She thinks you really are a cad for using her so poorly in the past and now doubts that your affections are sincere.'

Valerian gave him a wry smile. 'It's worthy of a Drury Lane farce.'

'I don't know if "farce" is the right word,' Beldon replied. 'Do you think your efforts will be in vain?'

'If they are, we'll call it a drama. If I am successful, we'll call it a comedy. It can't be a comedy unless the ending is happy.' Valerian was glad for a bit of levity. The conversation had been far too serious, but necessary. If his time abroad in diplomatic circles had taught him anything, it was that the past always came back to roost. He'd known the choice to come home would mean facing his old demons. But he'd chosen to do it anyway. There was only so far a man could run and only so long.

Valerian set aside his work. 'Let's go up to the house and see if Mrs Wilcox can set out tea for us.'

'I agree with the going up to the house part, but tea, Valerian?' Beldon raised his eyebrows. 'I suspect we'll need something stronger before we're through.'

Valerian gave Beldon a chary stare. What else did his friend want to winkle out of him today? Certainly there were more secrets to impart, but he'd shared all he was capable of sharing in one day. Professing one's soul took a lot out of a man.

Beldon came around the table and slapped him on the back, laughing. 'From the look on your face, you'd think I was the Spanish Inquisition, Val. I mean, we have plans to make. The way I see it, we have to convince Philippa that you were play-acting that night and all for a good cause, paint you as the noble fellow you are, and convince her to put her trust in you again.'

'You make it sound so easy,' Valerian groused, shutting the greenhouse door behind them. The weather seemed exceptionally cold after the humid warmth of the orangery.

'Well, it would be easy if she was here to be convinced,' Beldon drawled, stopping to stare at the back side of Roseland, looming impressively in all its sandstone majesty. They began the short trek to the back terrace. Beldon stopped shy of the granite steps. 'Aha! I have an idea.'

'Oh, no, your ideas—' Valerian began.

'Are good ideas,' Beldon finished for him, fixing him with a stern stare. 'Listen, here's your "situation" as it were: you've just returned from years away and have never really lived here since you came of age. You find there is much to be done to make Roseland liveable, modernised.' Beldon pitched his voice dramatically. 'But, alas, you are a feeble man with no brain for interior design. If left to your own devices, you'd have striped chintz curtains with polka-dot-satin bed comforters.'

'I see where you're going with this.' Valerian glared. 'You want me to ask Philippa to redecorate Roseland.'

Beldon shrugged. 'She'll do it anyway if you marry her. Might as well get a jump on it.'

Valerian laughed at his friend's practicality. 'You're an optimist.'

Beldon sobered from his earlier jocularity. 'I

mean to see you both happy. She doesn't have to choose you unless she wants to. It's a bitter pill to swallow, to know all that happened, happened for me. I was the heir. You can't sugarcoat the bottom line, Val. I was the one who benefited most from Father's choices. It's been a hard discovery, finding out that your sister and best friend gave up their personal happiness for your benefit.'

'She doesn't know,' Valerian put in, foolishly thinking for a minute that might ease Beldon's guilt.

'Ah, but she will. To win her, you'll have to tell her everything,' Beldon said. 'Making a clean breast of it will probably make your road with her easier to travel.'

Valerian scuffed his foot in the dirt in mild protest. 'Since when did the shortest distance between two points become confession?'

'Since confession was good for the soul,' Beldon laughed, stomping the mud from his boots as they mounted the terraced steps of Roseland.

Beldon was right. He did have to tell Philippa. He'd seen how painful the story had been for Beldon and he did not relish going through it again with Philippa. But it would go a long way in explaining things to her.

However, Valerian was acutely aware that it might not go far enough. He acknowledged what Beldon had not yet realised. He'd led a very different life the nine years he'd been gone and he had a reputation to contend with from that life. Mr Danforth had made that blatantly clear at the dinner table. But there were other 'pigeons' too from his time abroad that would come home to roost, pigeons far more damaging than his wenching. It would only be a matter of time before they migrated north.

Reputations could be damnable things, Lucien Canton reflected, rereading with ill-concealed glee the extensive missive that had arrived in the mails from London. He splayed his hands wide on the smooth surface of the cherrywood desk that denoted his power at the Provincial Bank of Truro.

He came in daily to read the post and the week-old Times financial section and to conduct private business for the bank. The local squires and gentry found it comforting to apply directly to him for a loan. It lent an air of status to know that they were able to do business with a viscount's son. Lucien traded on that cachet liberally and often.

Danforth knocked and stuck his head in Lucien's elegant, private office. 'Good news, I hope?' he asked solicitously.

Lucien smiled and said only, 'Yes, very good. Thank you for asking.' He'd learned the power of information was a highly prized commodity. He had no intention of letting anyone, especially not that status-sucking, tailcoat-riding, self-fashioned banker, Danforth, in on his latest *on dit*. Technically, it wasn't an '*on dit*' yet, but it would be when he chose to let it out. And really, the gossip would be the aftermath. All the action would have occurred already.

It was all Lucien could do to refrain from rubbing his hands together in unabashed joy. He re-read it a third time. It seemed the Viscount St Just had participated in an ill-fated rebellion in a town called Negush. There'd been a massacre, the town had burned. Women and children had died brutally. St Just had failed to quell the rebellion before such atrocities occurred.

Lucien had no idea where Negush was and since he had no mining interests there, he cared very little what part of the map it was on. But St Just would care a great deal if such information got out. If the tale was told in just the right way, St Just could be made out to be a murderer of innocents, which he likely was, even indirectly. If Lucien spun the tale skillfuly enough, he could have the *ton* thinking St Just capable of treason for his part in the uprising. At the very best, St Just would hang. Not even peers were immune from treason, especially not if his father and cronies at Whitehall decided to make an example of them. At the least, the man would hang in a different way. The *ton* would not countenance a man capable of such actions either from his own negligence in quelling the rebellion before it got out of hand or from actual participation in such meaningless bloodshed.

St Just would pay and Philippa would come running to him. Really, Lucien thought, he couldn't lose. Philippa would shun Valerian and congratulate herself on avoiding being taken in by such a monster, or, if she had fallen for the man, she'd come running, willing to bargain all she had for his clearance. Lucien would be in a prime position to offer that protection, to call off his father's watchdogs.

Maybe he would look up Negush on the map after all, since apparently he owed the success of his future to the little speck. Lucien walked to the small sideboard and poured himself a brandy and toasted his imminent success.

Chapter Eleven

*T*he conflagration was spreading rapidly. Soon the flames and smoke would reach the unprotected villagers caught between the oncoming Ottoman army and the burning remains of their homes. Surprised and unsuspecting, women and children had run into the night, giving no thought to where they ran, thinking only of immediate escape from the scorching inferno that consumed their village.

A child fell. A woman screamed. The carnage of Turkish retribution had begun. Under the cover of darkness, Valerian did what he could to protect a few of them. In the heat of battle, who could say with any certainty that it was he who had killed an Ottoman soldier or a Phanariot revolutionary fighting desperately with whatever weapons were at hand?

Through stealth and a warrior's skill, Valerian made his way toward the burning huts, yelling her name. After all, he'd promised Dimitri he'd do what he could. The smoke sucked the very breath from his *lungs, rendering his voice hoarse, the flames licking dry the cold sweat from his body. Someone cried out his name, barely audible above the roar of fire and the screams of panic.*

Valerian turned towards the sound. There she was, as foolish, as selfless as ever, a sword in one hand, her eyes wild, holding off two soldiers, using her body as a shield to protect the three children with her.

She did not stand a chance. If she was lucky, the soldiers would cut her down before realising what a prized prisoner she'd make, sister to one of the Phanariot leaders. She deserved better. She'd not asked for any of this. She'd pleaded with her brother to take the peaceful surrender the Ottomans had offered.

Valerian hefted his knife and drew his other dagger. He would need them both along with speed and surprise. He began to run, issuing a hoarse roar with the remnants of his voice. It was enough. The soldier closest to him looked in his direction. Valerian threw his knife, taking the man in the throat. He covered the distance, leaping over the fallen man's body, and made quick work of his comrade.

His hands were soaked in blood, but he took no time to wipe them off. Fire was his biggest enemy now. 'Help the children. Give me the baby,' he yelled hoarsely over the flames to Natasha, who had already grabbed the oldest child's hand so as not to lose him in the tumult. The girl gave him the baby she'd so diligently cradled and took Natasha's other hand. Valerian put the baby in his left arm, leaving his knife hand free. He needed it twice before they gained the dark sanctuary of the forest.

The horrors of the night were not over. Ottomans burst into their safe harbour, skewering Natasha in the side with a wicked curved blade. The beautiful young woman fell. Valerian charged like a bull, taking one man down by sheer force, his blade ripping into him in retribution. He fought like the devil himself, stabbing, slicing, killing, aware only briefly that the boy had picked up Natasha's blade to help him. When he was done, the ground ran red from his efforts, the last Ottoman fighter slain from his beserk rage. But some time in the fight, the boy had fallen too and lay deathly still not far from Natasha. He had failed Dimitri. One of the children was already dead.

He pushed down his grief and crawled to Natasha's side. She lived yet, but it would be only a momentary condition.

He took her hand, feeling her clutch at it with a last mad strength. 'Save the children.' She gasped. 'Find Dimitri.' Then her eyes widened with terror. 'Val, behind you.'

He had the disturbing sensation this had all happened before. He was losing her again. She deserved better than a bloody hand holding her own as she slipped away. He wouldn't lose her. He called her name. No, not the darkness. He didn't want the darkness, not yet. He hadn't saved the others. He wasn't ready.

Valerian woke in a sweat, his head throbbing, his body trembling. Breath choked in his throat. Bile rose. He groped blindly for the bowl next to his bed, set there in anticipation of just such a purpose, and retched until the trembling subsided.

The dream again; the night in Negush that he never wanted to relive, but seemed doomed to do so. Valerian steadied himself, drawing deep breaths. It was the first time he'd had the nightmare since returning home.

Valerian threw back the covers and got out of bed, slipping into a robe. He lit the lamp, knowing he wouldn't sleep again that night. The fear of the dream coming back was too real. He couldn't do anything about the dream, but he could minimise the headache.

Valerian poured himself a glass of water from the carafe on the bedside table and rummaged in the drawer, looking for a small vial. He pulled the stopper and put a few drops into the glass. He drank it down and sighed with relief. In twenty minutes, his headache would numb to a dull throb thanks to his special herbal potion. He went nowhere without it. Until then, he'd have to sit and tolerate it.

Valerian sank into a chair near the cold hearth in his private sitting room. He hated the dream. More, he hated what the dream represented: his failure to protect people he cared about.

It had been his job to help the Turks negotiate a peaceable surrender after the Negush district had rebelled against Ottoman rule. The district had actually succeeded in temporarily liberating themselves. It had spread to neighbouring villages, but eventually the revolutionaries were no match for the

Turkish army. He'd been sent to advise the revolutionaries to lay down their arms. But they'd not relented. They'd been shown no mercy by the Turks, who'd slaughtered the soldiers, rounded up prisoners, sold them into slavery and relocated any who had escaped those two fates deep into Macedonia. The district of Negush had been effectively erased from the face of the earth.

But he'd known the Phanariot rebels. He'd feasted at their tables, stayed in their homes. They were regional aristocrats. Natasha had been like a countess, her brother an earl of sorts. They'd reminded him intensely of Beldon and Philippa.

Originally, Britain had charged him with the mission of befriending the Phanariots, but then switched sides when it became apparent that a weak Turkey needed British support if Britain wanted to stand against Russia in that part of the world.

Even now, eight years since the disastrous 1822 uprising, the whole event filled Valerian with self-loathing. Britain had changed sides, seen innocents slaughtered all for the sake of maintaining British-friendly waterways to India.

There were no ideals behind what they'd ordered him to do, simply pure capitalist greed. Britain liked having a weak Turkey in its pocket. It did not like the idea of people throwing off the Ottoman yoke to form a new, powerful Christian nation that might compete against England.

Natasha, Dimitri and Dimitri's gallant young son had died for their ideals of freedom all because Britain couldn't countenance the emergence of a new, large Christian nation that might unite eastern Europe into a competitive force.

Valerian fought against the grief that rose up at the thought of the loss: Natasha bleeding to death in the copse; the boy fighting futilely against men twice his size; Dimitri executed with the other leaders two days later in a gruesome display of Turkish revenge.

He supposed he'd technically committed treason that night, stabbing the ally Turks as he fought to save Natasha, but he could hardly care when the reasons for supporting the Turks had been so mercenary on England's behalf to start with. He'd done his duty by attempting to negotiate peace. Then he'd done his duty by Dimitri and got the two other children to relative safety. He hoped it had been enough.

That had been the beginning of a stalemate in the region between the Great Powers, each checkmating the other in their bids for dominance. It had also been the beginning of Valerian's own disillusionment with diplomacy. Diplomacy was not, as he'd originally believed, a chance to participate in history, to leave one's mark on the world.

The remainder of his time in Europe had been marked by a constant shifting of allegiances as Britain attempted to pre-empt Russian control and pull Ottoman strings. Towards the end, the balance of power was shifting again. Britain had gained control of Cyprus and no longer needed to control Turkey in order to control waterways. Further proof that Dimitri had died for nothing, not even for the posterity of the waterways. The cause for which

Dimitri's dream had been pushed aside had been fleeting. The Turkish alliance had only held for a few years until Britain had achieved its objective.

Valerian had come to the conclusion that if he wanted to leave a legacy, it would best be done in the beauty of his gardens, where the focus was on living and peace, and in his nursery where he could raise a child. But he needed a wife for that. He needed Philippa.

She would be here at Roseland by tomorrow afternoon. She'd responded to his request affirmatively, no doubt because of his promise to have Beldon on hand. He'd promised many things in that letter, anything that would get her here and give him a chance to prove his worth to her.

He was a man of action, but in his desperation to claim her, his actions had all been wrong. He'd rushed his fences. He knew the whole of his story, but she didn't. She needed time to know him again, believe in him again as she once had.

Philippa sighed and carefully refolded Valerian's letter, placing it back in her reticule. She was twenty times a fool for coming. She was inviting all kinds of madness. She and Valerian had proved they could not behave rationally in one another's presence. The few times they'd been alone had led to all sorts of mischief. Yet here she was. There had been something plaintive about the note, a personal plea of one friend to another, that she found she could not refuse.

Philippa looked out of the window of the coach.

She was nearly there, if memory served. The tall, square tower of St Justus Church was coming into view and Roseland was a mile down the road after that. She'd only been here once, right after Valerian's parents had died. Her family had come over to help settle the estate. She had been twelve at the time, but she remembered the journey with remarkable clarity. The road veered south past the church's lych gate, past the tidal creek that ran alongside the building and up one last hill to the vast park and gardens of Roseland.

At first glance, Roseland looked no better than it ought for a place that had been masterless for nearly a decade—even longer if one counted the years after Valerian's parents' deaths. The magnificent gardens that had once been Roseland's fame were overgrown, rhododendron bushes crowding out old woody hydrangeas, and bluebells growing wild where they willed.

But at second glance, Philippa could already see Valerian's expert hand at work as the coach tooled up the long drive toward the house. Gardeners swarmed the lawn with long scissors, trimming and shaping the ragged edges and uneven patches of lawn. The gardens closest to the house teemed with workers digging restraining walls and clearing flower beds.

The coach pulled into the circular drive in front of the house and Philippa marvelled at the elegance that greeted her. The cobblestoned circle was free of any intrusive weeds that might grow between the stones. The stones looked freshly paved, smooth and evenly laid one against the other without any uneven ground between them that might trip an unsuspecting guest.

Philippa dismounted, staring in wonder at the centre of the driving circle and its *pièce de résistance*, a magnificent stone fountain spilling water into a pool at its base. To add colour to the centre, the fountain base was surrounded by a bed of flowers in bright blues, whites and reds.

The fountain was done in the classical style to complement the architecture of Roseland and reminded Philippa of something one might see in an Italian piazza.

She could not resist the lure of splashing water. Thinking she was alone, Philippa gave into the temptation to put her hand beneath the spilling water, laughing as she did so.

A man's chuckle answered her laughter. She swiftly pulled back her hand and gathered her dignity, looking around.

'Your Grace, welcome to Roseland.' A dignified man walked down the stairs leading up and to the front door. 'I am Steves, the Viscount St Just's butler. He instructed me to watch for you.'

Philippa stifled a groan. What an image she must paint. Steves would think her quite gauche for engaging in such childish behaviour.

'The viscount will be pleased to know you liked the fountain. It is new. Milord put it in just this past month. He laid the cobblestones himself.'

Philippa could very well imagine Valerian doing such a thing. If Steves thought the news would surprise her, he would be disappointed. 'His crafts-manship is excellent as always,' she said.

Steves nodded and said meaningfully, 'Indeed it is. He hoped you'd like it.'

She blushed and fought the urge to ask Steves to clarify. It would show too much eagarness to probe. Instead, she asked. 'Where is the viscount, Steves?'

'He's out on the back terrace, my lady. If you would follow me? A footman can see to your trunks.'

'Out on the back terrace' was something of an understatement, Philippa realised shortly. *She* was on the freshly swept terrace with its sturdy wicker furniture. Valerian was engaged with four other men in the process of moving an enormous planter containing a type of tree Philippa had never seen.

Apparently, the gigantic container was to go on the edge of the terrace, situated so that it could shade the cluster of wicker furniture grouped on that side. Valerian caught sight of her and waved, motioning that she should take a seat and wait.

He looked glorious. His hair shone in the sunlight and he wore only his shirt, the sweat of his efforts plastering the thin material to his back so that Philippa could plainly see the play of his muscles as they strained to set the planter into place.

The men gave the planter a last push and Valerian stepped back, satisfied with its placement. 'Perfect. It's exactly what I was hoping for,' Valerian explained, stripping off his thick workman's gloves and coming to take a chair next to Philippa.

'It's a marvellous tree, Val.' The old nickname slipped off her tongue before she could catch herself.

She bit her lip. To his credit, Valerian did not comment on it.

'It's a Chusan Palm. I sent a seedling back from Italy several years ago. My head gardener saw to it and here it is today.' Valerian rose and walked over to study the mop of green fronds that topped the palm, estimating its height. 'I don't imagine it will get much taller than this. The gardener I talked to in Italy said the plant stays shorter in colder climates because of the winds bothering its top leaves. Of course, in the Mediterranean regions it grows much taller.'

'I didn't know you were in Italy,' Philippa said in surprise. She was just starting to realise it was only one of many things she didn't know about him.

'Just briefly. It was a trip only, nothing permanent.' Valerian shrugged. 'I took full advantage, though. I visited every garden I could. I even went up to Florence when my work in Rome was concluded so I could see the Boboli Gardens.' Valerian laughed suddenly, looking very young and very happy, if one ignored the tell-tale dark circles under his eyes. 'I've been in the dirt so long, I've lost my manners. Here you are, newly arrived, and I am rambling on about plants. My apologies, Philippa. I am glad you're here. Do you think you're up to the task?'

'You don't need to stand on ceremony with me.' She smiled back, lost in the wondrous moment of being with her friend. This was the Valerian she missed. 'The place looks good. I like the fountain.'

'It will look better once you and I are through with it,' Valerian said. 'I want the gardens to shine again, on equal with Trewithen and Trebah,' He cited two large, nearby estates famed for their botany. Valerian sobered a bit. 'I was gone a long time and this place shows it.'

Philippa sensed he was scolding himself. She wanted to say something to ease the guilt she heard in his voice, but what could she say? She had no idea why he'd stayed away so long. She'd always thought he'd liked being away, that it had been a choice. Now, something in his tone indicated it might have been otherwise.

Valerian shook himself and his smile returned. 'Would you like to see inside? See what you're up against? Beldon won't be back until supper.'

Valerian had been right—the house did need a lot of work. Philippa made mental notes as they strolled through the large, airy rooms of Roseland. Beeswax and lemon could only do so much. Wallpapers were faded and needed replacing. Curtains were dusty. She wouldn't know how deteriorated they would be until they'd had the dust beaten out of them. Carpets were thin with wear over time. But she was up to the challenge. She'd cut her teeth on Cambourne's townhouse in London and had turned it into a showcase for his works of art by the time she was finished.

Valerian threw open the double doors leading to the ballroom. Philippa was not ready for the rush of memories the empty room evoked. The room itself was not special. The floors were scarred from years of hard dancing, the polish having worn away. The paint was faded, chipped in places. Curtains hung limply at the long Georgian-style windows that lined the far side. The niches where enormous crystal vases could stand, filled with flowers from Roseland's hothouses, were empty. The room's only piece of furniture, a long pianoforte, was covered with a dust cloth in the far corner.

No, the room was nothing spectacular. In fact, it was just short of shabby. But to her eye, she was twelve again, seeing the ballroom for the first time. 'I remember you bringing me here,' Philippa said softly, drifting into the centre of the room.

Valerian followed her in. She was acutely conscious of his presence behind her. He gave a warm laugh. 'You declared this your favourite room in the house. You told me that yellow was the best colour for a ballroom.'

'And I was right,' Philippa teasingly protested. 'Look how well it has weathered the years.'

'You tried very hard that day to cheer me up,' Valerian said quietly.

'I don't remember.' Philippa replied awkwardly. She didn't want him to do this—to be so nice, so kind, to make her believe she hadn't imagined the man she'd once known. Of course, she did remember, quite vividly, what she'd done to cheer him up.

'I remember.' Valerian swung her around to face him and swept her into his arms. 'You danced with me, you talked the whole time about all the parties we'd hold here later, how Roseland would be a happy place again.'

'I must have been very annoying,' Philippa said,

startled to find herself in his arms, his body moving them into the opening turns of a silent waltz. Good lord, he was irresistible. How was she to stop her heart from loving him in spite of her better judgement?

'Val, is this wise?' Philippa asked, letting him whirl them down the length of the ballroom floor at an exhilarating pace.

'We won't run into anyone. We're quite alone.'

'Don't be glib, Val. I am well aware that we're alone. That's what has me worried. We can't fall in love again, or whatever you want to call it.'

Valerian brought them to a hard stop. 'What are you saying?'

Better to eat her pride now rather than later, Philippa thought. 'If you invited me here to help with decoration efforts, that's all right. However, if you invited me here with other intentions, perhaps those of a—a—a—romantic sort...' Philippa paused, groping for the right phrasing. But there wasn't any. 'If you invited me here to seduce me or romance me, or to relive an *affaire* of your youth, I'll have no part of it.' She shook her head. 'I understand what constitutes a relationship with you and I can't do it. I loved you all those years ago and I fear that I could love you again. I would be devastated when you left. I wouldn't survive such heartache again.' She gathered the courage to meet his eyes after her foolish speech, feeling much more like an eighteen-year-old girl than a full-grown woman of twenty-seven.

'Shh.' Valerian put a finger to her lips, his voice

a mere whisper. 'What if I told you I loved you, that I never stopped loving you? That the night I played the jilt, it was all a lie? That is what all your worries are based on, isn't it?'

A wild hope surged in her, raising all kinds of confusion. Did she dare to believe these fantastical claims? Then she remembered and her hope fell. 'And the women, Val? Was all your wenching on the Continent a lie too?' she asked in a sad, teasing tone, trying for a brave smile.

'They were a fool's stratagem to try to forget what I had left behind,' Valerian whispered, his eyes pleading for a chance.

Philippa tried to pull away, but he held her tight. 'Let me tell you my story, Philippa. Let me give you permission to love me again.'

Chapter Twelve

'I don't know what to say,' Philippa said after Valerian's account of their fateful evening came to an end. His revelations left her at sea, awash in uncertainty. She'd built her mental fortress on the foundations of that evening, that he'd spoken the truth when he'd jilted her, cast her off as no more than a dalliance. The reasons for her distrust and harsh words stemmed from that night.

In the single telling of the tale, Valerian managed to make those foundations unstable. If she believed him entirely, her foundations were reduced to nothing more than rubble. Her world had shifted. Everything had changed. She could love Valerian again. Her one reason for attempting to withhold her affections had been swept away.

'Say you believe me, that you find me to be a man of honour.' Valerian answered quietly.

His hands held hers tightly. They had long since given up standing and had seated themselves on the floor of the ballroom. The shadows had lengthened into early evening, the bright room growing darker. The floor was a hard seat, but Philippa would not have moved from the dusty wood floor for anything. Valerian's tale had riveted her from the beginning. It had made sense, why she'd found such incongruity in his statements that evening. All that nonsense about needing society's approval had not sounded like the Valerian she'd known.

A voice from the doorway caused her to turn her head. 'I'll vouch for him, Phil. The Pendennys's ledgers support all he says. We needed Cambourne and Father arranged for it to happen.' Beldon pushed off from the door jamb and strode towards them.

'Beldon, you know?' Philippa stood up awkwardly, shaking out her wrinkled skirts.

'I suspected as much.' Beldon gave a short laugh. 'I started thinking how serendipitous it was that Cambourne's money came along just when we needed it. The pieces started to fall into place. I searched the family ledgers and I discovered there was nothing lucky about the appearance of Cambourne in our lives. He was Father's last great campaign to save us.'

'I wish you had told me.' Philippa turned to Valerian, quiet censure in her voice.

'How could I tell you? You were desperate enough that night. If you'd thought there was any chance of undoing your father's plans, or if you thought I could be won over, you would never have agreed to marry Cambourne.'

'So you decided for me?' Philippa's temper began

to simmer. 'You decided it would be better to let me believe the worst about you, about my own judgement, for nine years?' She saw Beldon slip out the door, trying hard not to be noticed. Very well, this was between her and Valerian.

'Your father asked it of me,' Valerian answered with a rising anger of his own. 'If you knew, we'd have ended up running off to who-knows-where with nothing but the clothes on our backs.'

'It was my life.' Philippa stomped her foot in irritation. She was tired of having men decide what was best for her. First her father, then Lucien and now Valerian's disclosure. Did all men think women were such sapskulls? 'I expected better from you, Valerian.'

Righteous indignation fired Valerian. 'Better? In what sense?' He should have known this would be Philippa's response. For once, why couldn't she be like other women? Other women would be won over by the romance of his sacrifice and the long constancy of his affections. But Philippa challenged the realities of the situation.

Her sharp eyes studied his face, testing his reactions for truth. 'You should have trusted me instead of trying to bear that burden alone.'

Valerian pushed a hand through his hair in frustration. He'd bared his conscience, confessed the greatest sin Philippa knew him capable of. And, yes, he'd expected to be believed. More than that, he'd expected to be accepted. He'd rather thought—and foolishly so—that her heart would welcome him back on the spot. It seemed quite unfair to be treated to her scolding instead and he'd had enough of it.

'Regardless, it was done with your best interest at heart. I regretted hurting you. I regretted denying myself happiness. But I won't stand here and be tongue-lashed for upholding your father's wishes and doing what was best for the family. There were no easy answers or choices, Philippa.' He was aware he'd raised his a voice in his agitation. He controlled it, bringing it down a notch. 'I feared if I told you, you would hate me and then your father would know that I had failed him.'

'I ended up hating you anyway,' Philippa said sharply. Her hands were knotted into fists at her sides, her voice full of impotent frustration. 'Nine years is a long time to hate, Val.'

'It's also a long time to love,' he said softly, walking towards her and taking her hands in his, un-curling them from their tight fists. But he knew what she meant. She could not be expected to change course suddenly. The news was too raw, too unfiltered. She had the permission she needed to trust in him again, to see him as the friend she'd once known, but it would take time. She had her permission. The rest was up to her.

Valerian relished the thought of that challenge. He would woo her gently. While she was at Roseland, he would court her as sincerely as he had once dreamed of doing. The idea of Philippa thrilled him enormously. This time there would be no sneaking off under the facade of excuses to steal hasty kisses, there would be no fear of being caught. He would court her openly, starting with this kiss.

Gently, he tipped her chin up and captured her

face between his hands, taking a chance to drink of
her countenance, the creamy skin, the brilliant blue
of her eyes, the tremulous smile that played uncer-
tainly at her lips while she waited, her own gaze
searching his. Then he brushed her lips with his,
softly, tenderly. This kiss lacked the roughness of
their heated engagement at the folly, but was no less
intense for that absence.

Slowly, he could feel her body soften, the rigid
posture with which she'd held herself in her anger
relaxing against him, arms finding their way around
his neck as he took her weight. He'd waited his entire
life for this. He'd come back for this. The darkness
of his world receded in the wake of the peace that
flooded through him from the simple act of holding
her tight against him.

'I will not be so foolish as to let you go again,' he
vowed, pressing a kiss to the top of her head.

'You may have to for dinner,' Philippa joked, her
voice muffled against his shoulder.

'Well, just for dinner, then.'

The next days were heady ones for Valerian. True
to his word, he hardly let Philippa out of his sight.
They rode in the early morning along the coastal
bridle path between St Just-in-Roseland and St
Mawes. They picnicked with Beldon in the hilly
meadows above the St Justus churchyard, watching
the small wildlife run through the fields. They took
long walks beside the tidal creeks that bordered
Valerian's property. It seemed that he talked endlessly of his plans for the future in those days: plans

for his gardens, his landscapes, his stables. He couldn't help it. Life, full and pure, coursed through his veins again. There was purpose everywhere he looked. He was young and fit with the wealth he needed to bring his plans to fruition…and the woman.

Philippa was intoxicating. Her very presence in the same room could steal his attention for minutes at a time. The curve of her neck when she bent over a book during their quiet times after dinner drove him to distraction, making his hand itch to gently massage her exposed nape. The lilac scent of her light perfume lingered in the air long after she'd passed through a corridor. Her soft music at the pianoforte lent a cultivated feel to the house, filtering through the halls from the music room.

There were signs of her presence everywhere, from the cut-crystal bowls filled with colourful flowers placed on tables throughout the house to the very obvious redecorating efforts. Painters had come to paint and others had come to hang the drawing-room walls with a damask silk of deep crimson. It was more than simply noticing the difference a woman's touch made in transforming a house into a home. Valerian was struck afresh daily that it was his home, his woman.

She smiled easily these days, she laughed, she stared at him with a dreamy look in her eyes when she thought she had him unawares. Most of all, she'd found her ease with him again. They roamed the hills, comfortable in their conversation and in their touch. She'd take his hand or reach out to brush a strand of hair back from his face without thinking.

If he were naïve, he'd say it was like the old days of their youth. But those days were gone. Only a fool would think they could be reclaimed in their entirety. These were new days, new times for them, and Valerian was not careless with that reality. He treasured each knowing look, each shared laugh as spring came to his beloved Cornwall. He'd lived too long in places where life changed at a moment's notice to discard the simple pleasures he found in Philippa's company. As the days passed, he had reason to believe she felt that way also. Her own life had not been without the pain of loss that had come too early.

On St Piran's Day, they rode down to St Justus to put flowers on the graves of miners and to join in the village celebrations. The weather was fair for March and everyone for miles around had turned out for the festivities honouring the legendary hero-saint who, legend held, had imparted the wisdom of tinning to early Cornish miners a thousand years earlier.

Valerian found himself to be something of a celebrity. Although several tradesmen and day workers had been tramping up the hill to Roseland since his return, he'd not spent much time in the village re-establishing ties yet. He was proud to make his entrance with Philippa at his side, looking splendid in a rich brown riding habit trimmed in black with a small hat to match, her russet hair twisted into an exquisite knot at the back of her neck. He wanted people to get used to seeing her with him. She would be his countess soon. Valerian thought of his quietly sworn New Year's resolution and smiled. All he'd ever truly wanted was within his reach.

Philippa did not disappoint. At the village, she dismounted from her horse, immediately engulfed by a group of children with daisies in their hands. She took the little bouquets, some already wilting, exclaiming over each one in delight until she'd compiled one big one. The children were charmed. Two little girls seized her hands and led her to the village green where preparations for celebrations were just finishing. She tossed a smile back at him as the children merrily towed her away.

Valerian lifted his arm in a brief wave and followed at a slower pace behind the excited children, stopping to talk with a few men as he progressed. Booths were set up around the perimeter of the green and he caught up with Philippa and children at a booth selling Cornish pasties.

'We were deciding if we were hungry or not,' Philippa called out.

A little girl with dark curls piped up. 'We've decided that we are.' Excited cheers went up from the little coterie and Valerian found himself handing over coins for nine pasties filled with savoury beef. He was starting to think the children might be with them all day, when a handful of mothers bustled up to claim them.

'We're so sorry, your lordship, milady. I hope they didn't bother you too much,' one woman said in apology, casting a stern look at her three youngsters.

Valerian assured her it had been no trouble. But

the children's eyes began to fill with tears regardless of his reassurances. Philippa knelt down swiftly, taking their hands. 'Come and see us this afternoon. I think I heard there are to be games.' Her offer dried their tears and Valerian thought he could literally feel his chest swell with pride at her kind efforts.

'That was very generous of you,' he remarked as they began a slow stroll past the booths.

Philippa shrugged. 'Children make the world brighter. It's a shame the world doesn't do more for them in return other than to force them to grow up too fast and assume adult responsibilities.'

'Perhaps that will change. I hear there is legislation in Parliament regarding child labour.'

'I hope it goes through. I have thrown whatever political clout I have behind promoting such laws. Perhaps you will too?' Philippa cast him a cautious sideways glance.

Valerian raised her hand to his lips and kissed it, his eyes returning her gaze. 'Absolutely.' For a fleeting moment he thought of Dimitri's young son forced to be a warrior, forced to flee from a village that had become a war zone. He wished Dimitri's children could have had a village like this one, a day like this one, and the security of knowing there would be other days.

'What is it, Val? You're miles from here,' Philippa asked with concern.

He pushed his sad thoughts aside. Today was about the future. 'An old memory, that's all. There's a vendor with some good lengths of ribbon over here.' He tugged on her hand and the moment passed.

* * *

They shopped the rest of the morning. Philippa bought several lengths of ribbon and cakes of soap. At the last booth she bought a bag of peppermints.

'Sweet tooth, my dear?' Valerian inquired teasingly.

'They're for the children,' Philippa protested and Valerian smiled. She hadn't forgotten her promise.

Valerian spread out a blanket on the green near where the games would take place that afternoon and went to assemble a luncheon of sorts from the different stalls. By the time he returned, Philippa was surrounded by her court of children again. She sat placidly in their midst, weaving daisy necklaces for the girls and crowns for the boys.

The scene made his heart lurch, not this time for the boy who had died fighting beside him, but for the children that might be—his children with Philippa. Yes, six or seven little ones seemed just about right.

After lunch, he let the children talk them into playing some of the children's games. Philippa was quickly snatched up to partner one of the girls in a three-legged race. One small boy shyly asked him to play too. The little boy's name was Geoffrey and he barely came up to Valerian's waist. It would be a terribly difficult race with the difference in their heights, but Philippa was already at the starting line, smiling her approval. In the end, he and Geoffrey took third and the vicar's wife awarded them a shiny white ribbon that made Geoffrey's eyes light up in delight.

'He'll remember that for ever,' Philippa commented as they left the children to admire their prizes. 'The day he raced with the local viscount in the three legged race and took third on St Piran's Day.' She looked at him with a wealth of meaning in her eyes. 'Old wives say there's a lot of good in a man who has such joy in children, Val.'

That did it. He'd been wanting her all day and not just because of how lovely she looked in her habit or the graceful way she'd moved, but because of her easy way with the children, the way everything at the simple fair had pleased her, the way she made people feel good about themselves when they were with her, even him. That had always been her gift and he loved her for it.

Valerian drew her round the back of a wide tree. What he intended was meant to be private, out of sight of children and families.

'What are you doing?' Philippa whispered, picking up on his need for secrecy.

'I want to kiss you,' Valerian confessed, his eyes falling on her lips. 'I've wanted to kiss you all day.' His tone was playful. He felt like a young boy with his first miss. He bent to kiss her and all boyishness faded. There was no mistaking that he was all man with a grown man's urges. At the brush of her lips, he felt himself go hard, passion and want surging through him in an irrevocable tide of longing. He'd held himself in check since that day in the ballroom, giving her time to accept him again. But his grip on those reins was starting to slip.

Philippa gave a little moan of pleasure and pressed against him, a hand going to his hard length where it jutted against his buckskin trousers. Her palm found the sensitive head of his manhood through the fabric and she gently rubbed her hand over it.

Valerian groaned, deepening his kiss, desperation to have her flooding him. He wanted to rip off all his clothes and lie naked in the grass with her. 'We must have more than this, Philippa. I don't think I can survive on kisses alone much longer.'

'Nor me,' she breathed, her eyes full of a pure desire that shook him to his core. This was not the calculated gaze of a woman who wanted him solely for his looks and bedroom skills. He'd seen that assessing gaze far too often in his years abroad. Philippa wanted him body and soul, heart and mind, perfection with imperfection, and he'd never felt more complete in his life.

'Tonight,' he whispered, kissing the column of her neck.

'Tonight,' she affirmed.

The rest of the day held a heady tension for him, the activities of the fair acting as a form of exquisite foreplay, knowing that each hour moved him closer to the moment he craved.

Reluctantly, he gave into Philippa's cajoling and joined in the knife-throwing competition. He won easily, to which Philippa remarked, 'I had no idea you could throw a knife like that.' He shrugged and said nothing.

The paper lanterns were lit, surrounding a squared-off space for dancing. Shadows lengthened. Night was coming. Valerian felt his anticipation ratchet up another notch. They'd be expected to dance, of course. It would be wrong to leave before the dancing was underway and he found he wanted to dance. Tonight it would be all country dances and polkas, furries and scoots in the Cornish fashion. It would be thirsty work. The taverner had already set up barrels of ale on the perimeter.

He and Philippa led off the first dance, a rowdy, hand-clapping country dance. Philippa danced the next polka with the greengrocer's son and Valerian took to the sidelines to watch. Her hair had come loose and she'd given up any attempt of putting it back in place. Now, it hung in a heavy chestnut sheet down her back, flying behind her as she and her partner took a turn. She threw him a joyous smile as they passed and he smiled back.

'She's a wonderful woman, milord,' the vicar's wife said at his side, following his gaze. 'Should I be so bold as to set aside a date at St Justus for you?'

Valerian chuckled, his confidence high. 'I have hopes in that direction.' If he had his way, he'd marry her tomorrow. That being an impossibility, he'd like to marry her at the summer's end, after the hubbub of the London Season.

The dance ended and he went to claim Philippa for his turn. She was light in his arms. If he hadn't known what awaited him at the end of his evening, he might have been convinced to dance with her all night. But he did know. They'd both pledged it and, from the look in her eyes, she knew it too. There was no reason to wait any longer.

The dance ended and he leaned towards her to whisper one simple word. 'Home.'

Chapter Thirteen

Philippa shivered on the threshold of Roseland. Her anticipation had grown to a fever pitch on the short ride home in the dark. Valerian was beside her, lighting a candelabrum left on the entry table, taking her hand, leading her up the stairs to the master's chambers.

Inside, he set the brace of candles on a small table and turned to her. He held up his hand. It trembled in the candlelight. 'See how you affect me?' His voice was husky. 'I want to please you so badly. I've thought of nothing but this for longer than you can know. Most of my adult life, really.'

Philippa smiled at his confession. She went to him, slowly removing the cravat wound about his neck. 'I know.' They'd come close to this on a few occasions, reckless with hot youth. Her hands moved down to his shirt. She unbuttoned the shirt and pushed it back, his shoulders flexing to push it off. She ran her hands down the length of his chest, exploring the sculpted torso and the sensation of smooth, male skin. Her fingernails lightly raked his nipples, causing Valerian to gasp in sensual delight.

Empowerment swept through Philippa. She reached for the waist of his trousers and the rigid length of his manhood. At her touch, everything transformed. They came alive as lovers, no longer tender friends but something much more demanding, more animate.

Heat engulfed them. She felt Valerian's hands on her body, caressing as they made short work of her clothing until she was entirely naked to his hot gaze. His green eyes burned with an incinerating desire. In a fluid motion, he bent and grabbed her up in his arms and carried her to the bed. He followed her down on to the mattress, surrounding her with his taut body, aroused and ready for love.

She offered up her body and he took it, suckling at one breast, then the other, worshipping with every kiss and caress. Philippa arched against him, caressing his hair, his shoulders, anywhere she could reach. The man who rose over her was magnificent and wild, treating her to pleasures she had not imagined existed. She parted her legs for him, feeling herself growing unabashedly damp from his efforts. He sank between her thighs, taking himself in hand and manoeuvring smoothly to her entrance. He tested her readiness. She felt herself stretch at the fullness of his member, accommodating, taking, begging for more until she felt his sex pressing against her very womb, so deep was he inside.

He moved and began the ancient rhythm, his breathing coming in ragged pants. She closed her eyes and gave herself over to the sensations surging through her. She felt as if she was standing on the edge of a cliff, each step taking her closer to an edge where something wonderful awaited if she would only jump.

She wrapped her legs about Valerian's waist, urging him on, to help her jump. Her hands clung to his muscled shoulders. She could feel the unbridled strength of his arms as he kept his full weight from pressing down on her. She started to shudder.

'Open your eyes, Philippa.'

Her eyes flew open at the last moment. She heard herself gasp in pleasure as she plunged over the cliff, soaring and falling at the same time. And Valerian was with her, shuddering his own release, his eyes dark with his passion, his body slick with his exertions. He collapsed against her, spent. She could feel the fast thump of his heart and knew her own pulse was racing in the glorious aftermath of what they'd done.

Valerian shifted to his side and she snuggled into the nest of his body, revelling in the safety and warmth of his strong arms. Nothing could hurt her here, nothing could reach her. 'Val?' she whispered.

'Hmm?' His hand tightened around her waist.

'I never hated you. I couldn't bring myself to do so, not really.' In her drowsy state, she recognised it for the truth it was. She'd wanted to hate him, she'd forced herself to it. But it had been a hard battle and tonight she was glad it was one battle she had lost.

Philippa awoke late the next morning, giddy with her realisations. She was free to love Valerian. For the first time in years, she could follow the dictates of her heart and never mind the doubts her mind tossed up as facts. Valerian's arm was still around her waist. When had she ever slept so soundly that she hadn't moved an inch? But when had she ever felt so secure that she could lay down her burdens long enough to sleep undisturbed?

Behind her, Valerian began to stir. She squirmed experimentally and felt the jut of his straining morning erection against her buttocks. Wanton desire rocketed through her, along with a healthy measure of curiosity. Could last night be repeated or was the intensity of her feelings unique? Would she feel that way each time she made love with Valerian? She was out of her depth here. It had never been like this with Cambourne. She'd not known how powerful a coupling could be until last night.

Valerian nipped at her earlobe, whispering love words as he positioned himself. Dear lord, he was going to take her from behind. Such a strange position caused her a moment's panic. She tensed. 'Val? What are you doing?' She knew, technically, but she wasn't sure it worked in practice. 'Does this actually work?'

Valerian gave a low, sensual chuckle and hugged her close. 'Yes. Relax and let me show you. I won't hurt you. This is new to you?' His free hand gently rubbed her shoulders, massaging away the tension. 'This position is a woman's gift to a man. She is at her most vulnerable here,' he explained softly. 'But it allows a man to penetrate her more deeply than other positions.'

He gave a gentle thrust. Philippa gasped. There was something exceedingly decadent and yet wondrous about the position. There was no doubt that she had all of him and she revelled in the feel of him so completely entrenched inside her. It didn't take long for either of them to reach their pleasure, Valerian holding her tight as he poured his warm seed deep inside her.

He held her close, letting his release shudder over him in waves. She was silent, a sure sign her mind was rampant with questions, thoughts.

She dared her question once the initial wave of ecstasy had subsided. 'Is it supposed to be like this all the time?' She turned in his arms to face him, pushing hair back from his face.

'No, not always.' Valerian answered carefully. It was inevitable she'd ask, wonder about the rumours that had floated back to England, most of them clear exaggerations of a truth only he knew. He rather wished she hadn't asked at such an inopportune time, though, when he'd rather lie with her in peace instead of fencing with her dragon of a temper.

She seemed to contemplate his answer. 'Has it been like this for you before?'

An even worse question than her first one. 'Not really.' How could he explain to her that a man could enjoy such a release on a purely physical level without the emotions that had accompanied what passed between them? How could he make her understand that there was a different sort of satisfaction to be had, but that it didn't compare in the least with what he'd done with her? Nothing ever would.

She was poised to ask another question. Valerian raised himself up on one arm. 'This is neither the time nor the place for such an inquisition, Philippa. There is not room enough in this bed for anyone else you'd care to drag in here.

'However, since you have raised the topic, I will tell you this—I was not a monk those nine years, but most likely the reports of my licentious behaviour were greatly overestimated. Those women meant nothing. They were a poor excuse to forget what had happened in England. They wanted my body and they understood that was all they'd ever get from me. My heart was engaged elsewhere—with you—and it always has been. I'd prefer to put paid to that part of my life.'

Philippa smiled her assent. 'I didn't mean to pry. I was curious. That was all.' She blushed and looked away. 'I never knew…' she stammered, shy in her embarrassment.

'Not with Lucien?' Valerian knew he was pressing her, but he had to know. She'd had her inquisition and he had things he needed to know too.

She shook her head. 'No, Lucien and I have never been together and Cambourne…well, that is to say, Cambourne and I didn't achieve…'

Valerian pressed a forefinger to her lips. 'Shh. You needn't say any more.' He understood perfectly what she meant and it thrilled him, deep down in some primal core of his being, that while he hadn't been the first, he'd been the one to bring her true pleasure. And he'd be the last. If he'd had any doubts on that score, he would have used a sheath to prevent a child.

* * *

The Jezebel! Lucien Canton was furious. The man standing in his office at the Provincial Bank of Truro looked away anxiously and Lucien tried to remember it was bad form to kill the messenger.

It was not the messenger's fault that Philippa had not been at Cambourne Hall when he'd arrived to deliver the note. It was not the messenger's fault that he'd followed her to St Just-in-Roseland and caught her in what seemed an obvious case of *in flagrante delicto* with her hand on the viscount's bloody cock. The messenger had assured him the little moment had been done in privacy and good taste. He'd been the only one to see them. Such assurances didn't change the fact that Lucien wanted to hit someone and since Valerian Inglemoore wasn't available at present, the messenger just might do after all.

Everything had been going well. He should have known that was when the bottom usually dropped out from beneath you. Philippa had rejected his marriage proposal out of hand so that she could go traipsing around Cornwall with the viscount. Good lord, she'd been seen at a peasants' fair fondling the man's private parts. It didn't matter that the messenger had been full of assurances that no one else had seen them. They'd been discreet. She'd refused his proposal because she'd felt he'd had nothing to offer her. That was about to change. She would discover shortly he had something she wanted quite desperately.

He would not be played as the cuckolded suitor.

Everyone in London knew he'd been her strong right
arm these past years. Everyone expected something
to come of it. His reputation would suffer if he turned
out to be nothing more than Lady Cambourne's jilt,
to say nothing of his finances when the bank's board
of trustees understood that he did not control the
Cambourne mining interests.

He would confront St Just with his treason, force
Philippa to barter for the man's freedom and then
make sure there would be no happy ever after for
them. St Just would not forgive Philippa if he
believed it was by her hand that such treasonous
issues had been brought up. Fortunately, Lucien had
the letter to infer such a thing. He would have his
bank, his revenge and a wife too. Not a day would
go by that Philippa wouldn't be reminded of the
favours he'd done for her and how much she owed
him. He would start by going to her as a wolf in
sheep's clothing.

Philippa sat in the small sitting room she'd com-
mandeered as a lady's parlour at the back of the
house. The windows gave her a view of the back
terrace where she could watch the men working on
the new flower beds Valerian had designed. She
could look up from her writing at the elegant escritoire Valerian had moved in there for her and see him
at his labours on the lawn. All in all, it was a very
domestic arrangement.

She was seldom disturbed in this room. She used
it primarily when Valerian was out, as he was today,
working in the ravine garden on the edge of the

estate. And Beldon had taken himself off on long visits and explorations these last few days to give her and Valerian some privacy. Knowing this was her preferred time of day for correspondence, the maids left her alone as well. No one bothered her here unless something was wrong. Which was why she was surprised to see Steves at the door.

'Is something wrong with the dinner menus?' she asked with a pleasant smile.

'No, milady. This letter has arrived for you. It came by special messenger. I thought it might be urgent.'

Philippa looked at the envelope. It was from Truro. Her initial worry that something drastic was wrong at Cambourne eased. She didn't know anyone in Truro well enough to warrant a letter by special messenger. In fact, the only person she knew in Truro of any real significance was Lucien. But Lucien had no reason to send such a letter. The regular post would do for any business they might have.

Philippa opened the letter, reading the back first to see who it was from. Lucien.

Philippa flipped the paper over and began to read.

My dearest Philippa,

Thank you for your kind words and polite refusal of my proposal. I appreciate your considerate words as much as I regretted your need to decline. As for me, I shall remain your obedient friend and servant in the hopes that my offer might meet with your fondest reconsideration.

It is my sincerest hope that any impetuosity on my part might be forgiven. It is also my sincerest hope that you keep yourself safe. To demonstrate that sincerity, I feel compelled to bring you news of great concern regarding your family friend, the Viscount St Just. Lately, it has come to my attention that he is suspected of having dealt in some behaviour of a treasonous nature while serving Britain in the Balkans—something to do with a little town called Negush.

I do not know all the details or even how true such claims are. But I thought you should know. You know him better than I and are perhaps best placed to help exonerate him should these charges become more than speculation and rumours at Whitehall.

I would encourage you to be vigilant on your friend's behalf. Look for anything that might prove him innocent if need be.

I was surprised to discover you had gone to Roseland. Do have a care with your reputation. I would not wish to see you suffer simply by association should St Just be branded a traitor.

As always, I stand your true friend,
Lucien

Philippa clenched the paper, wrinkling the fine linen bond with the strength of her hand. Treason? What nonsense was this? But it wasn't exactly 'nonsense'. There was no reason for Lucien to make any of this up and, really, one couldn't fashion charges of treason out of whole cloth and expect to get away with it. If Lucien didn't think it was the truth, he'd hardly have bothered writing about it and sending the news by special courier.

That worried her. The letter had been sent with all haste possible. The letter had been written with the express intention of sharing that news with her. He'd made no mention of the bank or of any local news. In the past, the letters they'd exchanged had been full of such events. It was unlike Lucien to write an entire letter without making a single financial reference. She'd not known he was capable of it, in fact.

Worry twisted in her gut. Philippa looked at the little clock on the wall. Eleven. Valerian wouldn't be back until tea time, four hours away. Four hours to search the house, looking for some proof that it was all balderdash, whatever those charges might be. But she had no idea what she'd be looking for.

She was suddenly struck with the thought that she didn't know anything about what he'd actually done during his time abroad. In order to look for clues, one usually had to have something to start with. Philippa had nothing but the name of a place she'd never heard of.

She would start with that. There had to be an atlas in the library. Then she could practise how she'd ask the man she loved if he'd committed treason.

Chapter Fourteen

In the end, Philippa elected to say nothing. Valerian had returned late, barely in time for supper, out of sorts over a retaining wall in the ravine garden that had collapsed. A day of hard labour had hardly made a dent in the damage done to the eroding hillside.

Valerian's bad mood aside, Philippa reasoned she'd be better off waiting until she had proof of something before she brought the subject up. Otherwise, she'd have to confess her interest in the topic stemmed directly from the potentially spurious letter Lucien had sent. Knowing how Valerian felt about Lucien, she felt it best to leave Lucien's letter out of the situation. If she wanted to investigate Lucien's concerns, she needed to do it under her own power.

Philippa let Beldon carry the dinner conversation. He was animated about a meeting with an inventor by the name of William Bickford. 'He's created a method for inserting a strand of yarn into rope fuses that makes the fuse more predictable.'

Beldon paused long enough to take a sip of wine. 'The funny thing is, Phil, he's from your area. He lives in Tuckingmill, outside Cambourne. He's just here on a visit with friends. You should meet him, help him get established. Can you imagine what this might mean for promoting mining safety?'

Of course she could imagine it. The tubes of reeds currently used as fuses for blasting were erratic. On several occasions they were known to go off too early, and on other occasions they went off after a long delay. Either way, men were hurt or killed by the faulty fuses. 'I should like to meet him,' Philippa said noncommittally.

Tonight, her mind had difficulty concentrating on business, her thoughts already occupied by Lucien's disturbing letter. Every time she looked down the table at Valerian, the thoughts kept creeping in. Had he committed treason? She knew very little of what he'd done in the diplomatic service of his country. This was difficult territory to navigate. He was a man of honour. His sacrifice for her family's greater good proved her initial instincts about him had not been wrong. However, she also understood that he valued honour above all things, including her opinion and her desires and his own.

From what she knew of her own experiences in political London, loyalty to one's country or party often conflicted with one's sense of honour. It was entirely possible that what Valerian viewed as the honourable path had, at some point, become a treasonous path. That particular juxtaposition concerned her gravely.

Before now, she'd always imagined traitors to be deceitful spies out to make a quick pound for selling out one's country. She was starting to see where that interpretation might be a bit limited in its scope. If the charges proved to be founded, how would the public see it? Would they share the same latitude she was willing to give or would they paint Valerian with a traditional traitor's brush? More than his reputation would be tarred. She knew very well the price for treason. Being a peer would not protect him.

She shuddered at the last, drawing a strange glance from Beldon. 'It's just a chill from the sorbet,' she said lightly, forcing her mind to push away such dire thoughts.

She was putting a very big cart before the horse with her suppositions and conclusions. She had taken the afternoon and discreetly searched the house, looking for any information that might help her understand Valerian's post and service. But she'd found nothing. She couldn't even find the place called Negush on any of the four maps of Europe Valerian possessed.

'Are you sure you're all right?' Valerian asked, too.

'Yes, both of you are old mother hens,' she teased and dipped her spoon into the sorbet to prove it.

Convinced, Valerian and Beldon returned to their conversation about Bickford's fuse. 'Invention is one thing,' Valerian was saying, 'production is another. It won't matter how incredible an invention is if it can't be produced in quantities.'

Beldon waved his hand in a dismissive gesture.

'That's what has impressed me so much about Bickford. He's thought of everything. He's in the process of finishing his design on a machine that performs the task of winding rope around a central core of gunpowder, then winding a second strand of rope in the opposite direction to keep the fuse from untwisting. He's already talking about ways to waterproof the rope by using a special varnish. He's got the plans with him. He'll be in St Mawes for the rest of the week. We could ride over and see him, Val.'

'I'm free tomorrow. The materials for repairing the retaining wall won't arrive until the day after so there's nothing more I can do. Philippa, would you like to come?' Valerian inquired.

'I would, but the men are coming to hang the silk in the music room tomorrow. I should be here for that.' It would also give her a chance to look around the house to further assuage her fears. Perhaps it was a good sign that she couldn't find anything. Perhaps his diplomatic work had been as bland as all the reports indicated. Maybe he had spent all his time hosting parties and squiring around delegates' wives. That might not be all bad.

She was suddenly less jealous of his parade of women if they'd kept him from harm. After all, how busy could he have been? He'd had time to visit Italy and study gardens. He'd mentioned at Lucien's that he'd been actively studying the piano. Those didn't sound like the hobbies of someone who had time to hatch a treasonous plot against the crown.

'You can advise me as to the wisdom of helping this Bickford with his invention, whatever he is calling it.'

'Safety rods,' Beldon put in.

'Safety rods,' Philippa repeated. 'If you like, you can write to Lucien and tell him about it. It might be the type of investment Danforth's new bank is looking for.' She made the offer to be helpful. It did indeed seem to do both sides a favour. Bickford would need funds to build a factory and Lucien needed Bickford's type of business to make the bank thrive.

But Valerian clearly disagreed. He pushed back his silver-stemmed sorbet dish and all but glared at her down the length of the table. 'I'd be very careful what I sent Canton's way.'

'He has money and good business sense. What could be the problem with that?' Philippa protested, not so much out of a need to stand up for Lucien, but out of dislike of having her judgement questioned.

'Too good, if you ask me,' Valerian said pointedly. 'Have you ever wondered why the financially savvy Mr Canton has his fingers in so many pies?'

Philippa leaned back in her chair and folded her arms, entrenching. 'No, I have not thought about it beyond the simple fact that he understands wealth is based on diversified holdings. Apparently, you think otherwise?'

'I do think otherwise. I suspect he wishes to corner the market, as it were. From there, he could regulate the prices to his whim and squelch any budding competition.'

Philippa laughed. 'Hah, that is theoretically how such a manoeuvre works, but, realistically, it would be almost impossible to perform such a feat with mining. It wouldn't be enough to control the mines, you'd need the other industries too, the smelting and the gunpowder. And I don't see how it would be possible to regulate the new mines in South America. They'll always provide some level of domestic competition to keep the price of ore fair. Valerian, not even Lucien could pull something like that off.'

Valerian quirked an eyebrow. 'Really? Why do you think he was so interested in Danforth's bank? I rather suspect Danforth's arrival was less spontaneous than you might have been led to believe.'

'You're spinning out of whole cloth now, Val,' Philippa said. 'He'd have to control Cambourne to at least make a start and I am not sure I am interested in the merits of a cartel at this point.'

Valerian pushed back his chair with a rough shove, his eyes glittering like sharp, cutting emeralds. 'Why do you think he wanted to marry you?'

Philippa rose out of her chair, horrified. 'Why are you attacking him in this manner?'

'Why are you defending him so vigorously?' Valerian shot back.

Beldon rose, eyeing each of them charily. 'Let's take some time and think this through,' he said slowly. 'Somewhere along the line we stopped talking about Bickford's safety rods and started talking about something else. I am not convinced we're really talking about Lucien Canton's bid to establish a tin cartel.'

'My apologies,' Valerian said stiffly. 'I'll be in the music room.'

Philippa watched him go with a sigh and sat back

down, suddenly weary now that the fight was over. Beldon was right. The fight had been about something else. 'He's upset about the garden wall,' Philippa said by way of a facile explanation for his outburst.

Beldon relaxed into his chair. 'Don't play me for a fool, Phil. Has something happened between the two of you? I thought things were going rather well.'

Philippa toyed with her spoon, drawing it through the melted remnants of her sorbet. 'Things were going well, but it is to be expected we'll have some rough times. Nine years is a lot of time to account for. We have to learn about each other again.'

Beldon would not be put off. 'Something has happened to make you question him again.' He shook his head. 'Certainly there are events in his life that you do not know about. But you know him and you know how Valerian would handle those events. You know that he can be trusted to act with honour at all times.'

'That does not reassure me,' Philippa said quietly. 'It is what concerns me the most. I had a letter from Lucien today.'

'Does Valerian know? That would explain his pique.'

'He might.' Philippa could see how that would be possible. Valerian may have asked Steves if there was any correspondence and Steves could have reasonably answered that there had been none but a letter from Truro for the Duchess. 'I never thought of Valerian as the jealous sort.'

'Of course not. Valerian is the least covetous man I know. But he's also the most protective. He doesn't trust Canton. Protection is honourable. Coveting is not. That's the difference between him and Lucien— one of them, at least.' Beldon shrugged.

Philippa stared at her brother. His insights, as usual, made perfect sense. When it came to people, Beldon was a genius. 'I think you could have been a splendid fortune teller, Beldon. You see people so much more clearly than the rest of us do.' She rose, laying her napkin on the table. 'Excuse me, brother. I have to go mend fences with Val.'

The music drew her down the hallway. Valerian was an exquisite musician, his playing both technically perfect and emotive. Tonight, he played a quiet nocturne.

She listened for a while at the doorway, unwilling to interrupt. 'The piece is very soothing,' she said softly.

'That's why I chose it. I hoped it would help clear my head and my heart,' Valerian said, his fingers still on the keys, his back to her.

'Has it?' Philippa moved to stand behind him, her hands on his shoulders, gently kneading away the tension there.

'To a certain extent.' Valerian sighed. 'That feels good. I think I will feel better once I apologise for my boorish behaviour.'

'I came to apologise for mine. I didn't mean to defend Lucien. He assures me that he remains my friend, but I think my refusal of marriage has fractured that friendship regardless. I have not sought him out, even in correspondence, since I declined his second proposal.'

'His second? I hadn't known.' Valerian stiffened, leery of such news.

'He asked again the last night in Truro. But I have refused him. He has no reason to hope that my feelings will change. However, he wrote today, citing his prolific friendship for me.'

Valerian nodded, confirming what she had suspected. 'Steves mentioned it in passing.' He put off her hands and stood. 'I am sorry for the way I behaved at supper, but I am not sorry about my motives for doing so. May we speak reasonably for a moment? Do you think our anger has subsided enough for that?'

Philippa took his arm and they began to stroll the halls, coming to the long portrait gallery that ran the length of the second floor. Their anger had indeed passed and the peace between them was a balm to her earlier agitation.

'What shall we talk about?' Philippa said after a while, sensing Valerian's reluctance to break the quiet.

'In all honesty, have you considered why Lucien felt compelled to offer for you?'

'I did think about it, but I could not come up with a reason beyond his need for an heir.'

'I did not say it well at dinner, but have you considered that the reason is that he would gain control of Cambourne when you married? Marriage to you would solidify the cartel's success. Without the Cambourne mining interests, the cartel is nothing but businessmen with venture capital. Without Cambourne, they can't regulate prices or control the supply and demand in the marketplace for ore.'

Philippa took a deep breath. 'No, I had not thought of that. I overlooked the issue of holdings simply because he had no obvious need for my wealth. He has plenty of his own.'

Valerian gave a deprecating snort. 'A man like Canton always wants more. He's greedy and ambitious. He can never have enough. I fear that that avarice puts you in danger, my dear.'

'I can handle Lucien,' Philippa said. 'You forget I've been on my own for some time now. I know how to take man's measure.'

Valerian stopped their strolling and turned to face her directly, placing his hands on her shoulders. 'If you will not be guided by your lover, be guided in this by your friend and listen to my advice as that friend. Canton will not brook your refusal lightly, not because his feelings are hurt—I doubt the man has any—but because it now puts his purse at risk. He *must* have Cambourne or give up his dreams of a cartel entirely. Your refusal has put him in an untenable position. Short of trying to coerce you into selling out or breaking up the unentailed holdings, he has no options left.'

'Coerce?' Philippa said. 'I am far too intimidating to be forced.'

'Coercion doesn't have to be obvious, Philippa. It could be sabotage.'

Sabotage. Philippa blanched at the word. Surely Lucien would not betray her in such a way? He'd been a steady friend, someone she'd counted on in numerous ways. Friends didn't sabotage each other, they respected each other's decisions.

'You mean like causing accidents to happen at the mines?'

'Possibly.'

'Well, I wouldn't worry on that account. Accidents now hurt his profit, if he later acquired the mines.' No, she felt confident that Lucien would not resort to such ridiculously extreme tactics.

'What did Lucien write to say?' Valerian said, veering on to another topic of conversation.

'Only to reassure me of his friendship,' Philippa said, glossing over the letter's contents. She was more than glad she'd waited to discuss Lucien's concerns. Tonight was definitely not the time to mention them.

She had too much to think about. Valerian's comments had placed Lucien's letter in an entirely different light. She *had* thought that the letter seemed odd, not Lucien's usual style. Now she wondered if the letter hadn't been a strategy of some sort. Lucien would see Valerian as an obstacle. If Valerian were out of the way, perhaps Lucien believed she might reconsider his offer. But the consequences were too terrible to think of. She couldn't believe even Lucien would see a man dead or ruined simply to achieve a goal.

A shiver ran down her spine.

'Are you sure you're not catching a cold? That's the second time tonight,' Valerian inquired.

Philippa smiled up at him, playing the flirt. 'Perhaps I am a little chilled, after all. Why don't you take me to your chambers and warm me?'

Valerian flirted back readily. 'I do know a clever trick they use in the Danubian provinces during the cold winters for warming up people.'

Philippa gasped in mock modesty. 'Do tell!'

'Well, they take off all of their clothes and crawl beneath a blanket and hold each other.'

'It sounds scandalous.'

'Not scandalous, *scientific*. The belief is that the body of the warm individual is passed to the colder recipient. With clothes, so much heat is lost in the transfer.' Valerian made a great display of shaking his head. 'A shame for so much heat to go to waste.'

Philippa laughed for the first time since Lucien's awful letter had arrived. She put her arms about Valerian's waist. 'What are we waiting for? Do you by chance know a cure for lightheadedness?' she asked, teasing heavily.

'Why?' Valerian looked wary.

'Because I think I might swoon.' Philippa passed a dramatic hand over her brow and let Valerian take her full weight.

'Minx, you just want me to carry you to our room,' Valerian laughed at her theatrics.

With a quick sweep of his arm beneath her legs, he hefted her up, making it seem so easy. Philippa rewarded him with a kiss. 'I hear kisses heal almost anything.'

Valerian held her gaze, his eyes merry, but his voice soft. 'I've heard that about love, too.'

Philippa was glad he was holding her or she might have really swooned, so powerful was the effect of his simple words. He loved her. And the very knowledge of that held her fears at bay, like a night fire against the wolves.

Chapter Fifteen

Philippa was in the music room overseeing the hanging of the wallpaper and new curtains when the summons came. The usually unflappable Steves appeared to be slightly winded as he delivered his message. Philippa thought it highly likely he had run all the way from the front door.

'My lady, there is a woman here to see the viscount,' he puffed, trying to hide his rapid breathing.

Philippa began untying the apron she wore, her mind working quickly. The caller was unexpected. If Valerian had had an appointment, he would not have agreed to ride out with Beldon to talk with the fuse inventor. The caller was also a stranger. If she'd been from the area, Steves would have recognised her and have been less flustered.

'I shall see her, Steves. Did she have a card?' Philippa said calmly. In spite of the spontaneous nature of the call, it was not beyond the realm of acceptability. There could be any number of reasons that a chance visitor had stopped at Roseland: a broken carriage part, a desire to see the gardens, or an old acquaintance passing through the area. Those things had happened often enough at Cambourne. The Duke had had an enormous number of acquaintances and they had on several occasions dropped by.

But Valerian hadn't been home long enough for that, nor had he publicly announced his return. She'd sensed he was waiting to make his return official once the Season was under way in London.

'Where did you put her? Does she have a name?' Philippa asked, smoothing her skirts and catching a glimpse of herself in a mirror to make sure she didn't have a bit of plaster in her hair. It wouldn't do to meet the caller, whoever she was, looking like the housekeeper.

'I put her in the small receiving room downstairs. She said her name was Lilya Stefanov.'

Worry came to Philippa for the first time. She started to understand the source of Steves's unease. The woman's name indicated she was foreign. Was she someone, then, from Valerian's past? She fought a sudden wave of nausea at the implications. Was this woman one of his reported lovers? Perhaps more than a reported lover? Surely they had shared some substantial connection if she felt she could call on him.

'Did she say what she wanted?'

Steves shook his head and said quietly, 'No, your Grace. However, she does have a young son with her.'

Philippa's stomach roiled again and she was doubly glad only toast and tea had appealed to her at breakfast. She chided herself. She was not acting like the Dowager Duchess of Cambourne. The Duchess would regally sweep down the stairs and take charge of the situation. She would not be standing in the music room letting nerves get the better of her.

The problem was, she hadn't thought of herself as the Dowager Duchess for more than a month. In the six weeks she'd been at Roseland, she'd been Philippa Stratten again, a woman in love and resident lady of the manor. She'd not thought of herself as anyone's duchess, widow or viscountess; she'd rather liked defining herself as a person instead of a title.

Now it was time to put the cloak of official authority back on. Philippa straightened her shoulders, reminding herself that it wasn't appropriate to show emotions or weakness in front of the servants. Loving Valerian had made her more careless than she'd realised over the past weeks. 'Have Cook send a tea tray to the parlour, Steves. We'll show our guest the best of Roseland's hospitality, whatever her mission may be. Tell Cook to put some of her special sugar biscuits on the tray and a cup of milk for the boy.'

Steves smiled his approval. 'Yes, your Grace,' he said crisply, his relief evident that someone other than he was about to handle the delicate situation that had arrived on Roseland's doorstep.

Philippa drew a deep breath and headed downstairs. The parlour had been one of the first she'd re-done. She just hadn't planned on using it so soon to receive callers. Soft voices in a language she didn't recognise drifted out into the hall. Philippa was struck with a fresh thought. She hoped the woman hadn't come to tempt Valerian with any more treasonous activity. Philippa checked her thoughts and amended them. Assuming he'd already been tempted before.

'Good morning, Miss Stefanov.' Philippa swept into the room. 'Viscount St Just is not at home right now, but perhaps I can assist you.' She was the consummate polite hostess.

The woman on the new yellow striped sofa rose, smiling her relief. 'You are too kind to receive us.' The boy beside her stood stiffly at her urging. 'This is Constantine.'

'How do you do, Constantine?' Philippa greeted him. The poor boy was terribly uncomfortable, trying hard not to fidget in his suit of clothes. He was a handsome boy with thick, dark hair and dark eyes. She judged him to be seven or eight years of age. He was old enough to be Valerian's son, a child fathered a few years into his tour abroad. But the girl didn't seem old enough to be the boy's mother.

'Please, be seated. A tea tray will be here shortly and you can refresh yourselves. Have you been in England long?'

The girl, for that was what she was now that Philippa had a moment to study her, shook her head. 'We arrived two days ago. We came straight here. We know no one else in this country.'

The tray arrived and Philippa used the time to assess the girl while the servants laid out the tea things. She looked to be in her mid-teens and uncommonly beautiful. Like the boy, she had ink-black hair. She wore it twisted up in a tasteful hairstyle with a pretty jewelled comb to fasten it. Her skin had a slight olive cast and was flawlessly smooth. And her clothes were well made. These two were not country peasants. Wherever they hailed from, they were people of means.

The boy was delighted with the milk and sugar biscuits. The girl smiled her thanks at the thoughtful gesture. 'Our journey has been long and we have not eaten as well as we should.'

She was brave and proud, Philippa thought, watching her over the rim of the tea cup. 'Where are you from? Your English is very good, but I detect an accent.'

The girl blushed. 'Please call me Lilya.'

'Is that a Russian name?'

'No.' There was a hint of defiance in her 'no'. Philippa wondered where that came from. 'It's a Balkan name, a Macedonian name.'

Philippa maintained her smile, but a slow coldness began to spread through her. She could guess where this girl was from. 'I don't know terribly much about the Balkan region.'

A shadow of sadness passed over the girl's face. 'I am from a village that doesn't exist any more. It was called Negush, but it was destroyed. Since then, I've lived wherever there was peace.'

Philippa started at the mention of the village. She

recognised it from Lucien's letter. Her stomach lurched. Was Valerian in true danger from something that had happened there? Was Lucien serious about what he'd uncovered? A thousand questions rioted through her mind. It took a large amount of self-control to keep from quizzing the girl. The truth about Lucien's claims likely sat across from her. Her curiosity raged. Philippa tamped it down, opting instead to be selfless. The girl had undergone a difficult journey and was now in foreign surroundings. She needed empathy, not an inquest.

'I'm sorry.' Philippa offered quietly. In spite of her concerns for Valerian, she felt her heart go out to the girl. Her phrase, 'I've lived wherever there was peace', spoke volumes about her struggles. Philippa could hardly begin to comprehend what that must have been like. She'd grown up during the wars with Napoleon, but that was different. The war hadn't been fought, thank God, on English soil. She'd been able to remain insulated from a first-hand encounter with the terrors of war.

Philippa set down her tea cup. 'I confess, I have a thousand questions for you.'

'Please, you may ask us anything,' Lilya said. 'But first, would you tell me your name?'

Philippa had the good grace to laugh at her oversight. She'd been so worried—still was worried—about what these newcomers would mean to Valerian. 'I'm the Dowager Duchess of Cambourne, but you may call me Philippa.'

Lilya's eyes widened with something akin to excitement. 'You're the one who has the brother, Beldon.'

Philippa was caught entirely off guard. That was the last thing she'd expected the girl to say. 'Yes. How do you know about my brother?'

The girl seemed to relax for the first time. 'Valerian used to tell us stories about the three of you.'

'Valerian.' She was quite free with his name. She did not call him by a title or his surname.

'I hope the stories were all good,' Philippa said wryly. 'Perhaps we should start with how you came to know the viscount?'

The girl's reserve was back and she sat straight as she told her tale. 'The viscount was a regular visitor at my father's house. We lived in the Negush district. We were Phanariots. Do you know the word?'

Philippa shook her head.

'The Phanariots were high-ranking Christians in the Ottoman system. Our family held an important position in the government. I suppose you could say we were a type of ruling elite. We had wealth and power and we controlled huge portions of business, especially in the area of shipping.'

Philippa nodded her understanding, noting how the girl spoke of these Phanariots in the past tense.

'Valerian came to our home to talk about British shipping and trade. He was a diplomat. He'd been charged to discover whether or not it would be profitable to establish a business relationship between us and the British government.'

The pieces were starting to come together. Philippa knew how valuable shipping routes were to the British government. But this charge seemed rather straightforward to carry out. It sounded as if the Phanariots had British sympathies.

'Valerian visited us often. I've known him since I was a little girl. I would practice my English with him. Languages were important in our house.' A wistful look passed over the girl's face and Philippa could well imagine she was recalling a happier time.

'Valerian befriended my father, Dimitri, and my Aunt Natasha. He stayed with us even after the negotiations proved to be unsatisfactory.'

'Unsatisfactory? In what way?' Philippa seized on the words.

'I was only eight, as young as Constantine is now. I hardly know exactly. But my father was furious. I do remember him shouting, "By God, we have six hundred ships between the Black Sea and Venice!"'

'But Valerian remained your family's friend?' Philippa pushed, wondering what would have caused him to pursue a personal tie.

'Right until the end. He risked everything for us. We would have died without him that last night.' Her face grew cloudy.

Philippa felt guilty for bringing it up. Perhaps she'd pushed too far on such short acquaintance. She wanted to ask more, but refrained. 'You're tired. Valerian won't be back until later in the day. He's gone to see an inventor with my brother. Perhaps you'd like to rest?' She did a quick mental inventory of the bedchambers upstairs. One of them had just been completed a few days earlier with fresh linens and paint. She would have the day maids Valerian had hired open up the nursery wing for the boy. He might enjoy the chance to be the master of his domain.

Lilya looked relieved at the suggestion. 'It has been an exhausting set of weeks.'

'Do you have trunks or any baggage?' Philippa inquired. No matter what this girl or boy were to Valerian, she could not send them away knowing they had nowhere else to go.

Lilya nodded. 'I left them at the posting inn in the village.'

'I'll send a cart for them. You will have them by dinner. Until then, ask for anything you need,' Philippa offered graciously, leading them up the stairs.

The newly finished pale green room at the end of the hall was perfect for Lilya. A small sitting room opened on to a large, airy bedchamber that overlooked Valerian's prized herb garden. Philippa threw the long windows open to let the scent of lavender waft up from below. Lilya was enchanted.

'I'll have the nursery wing ready for you, Master Constantine, in a few hours, if you'd like,' Philippa said to the boy. Her curiosity was killing her. Was this solemn young boy with his dark hair and the beginnings of a broad-shouldered build Val's son? If so, there were a hundred other questions burning in her mind, not the least being who and where was his mother?

He nodded his thanks and Lilya quickly explained that his English was not that good. She gave an elegant shrug. 'I've taught him what I could, but…' Her voice trailed off and Philippa suspected that life spent running away from war zones allowed little time for formal schooling. It also struck her that times had changed for this apparently ex-class of ruling elite. Speaking any language other than the local tongues might call unwanted attention to two people who had their own reasons perhaps for remaining inconspicuous.

Philippa left them in the chamber. She glanced at the clock. She couldn't expect Beldon and Valerian for another two hours at the earliest. She felt a bit fatigued, too, after the interview with Lilya. She'd have liked to have lain down as well, but there was too much to do before Valerian returned.

She knew herself well enough to know that if she laid down she wouldn't sleep at all. All the thoughts rolling through her mind would keep her awake. She would be better off keeping busy. Philippa concocted a mental list in her head.

She would check on the workmen in the music room and tell them to be done by four o'clock. She wanted all the peace she could find for Valerian's return home. On that note, she stopped to report briefly to Steves and suggest he send a groom out to find Valerian. She penned a quick note to send with him. Valerian might appreciate being forewarned.

With that done, Philippa went to the kitchens to let Cook know there would be two more people for dinner. She left instructions for the table to be set with the best china and the good wine to be decanted for the occasion.

Finally, she went upstairs to see how the maids were progressing with the nursery. In hindsight, she'd wished she'd put the nursery wing higher up on the priority list for redecorating. But it had ended up one of the last, there being no hurry with it at the time.

Fortunately, it was not in bad shape. The paint was faded, but a good dusting and beeswax had made a lot of difference in a short time. Like most nurseries, this one contained a large centre room used for playing and for school work. Off the big room were a series of smaller bedrooms.

Philippa helped the maids remove the holland covers shrouding the chairs and tables in the playroom and then wandered on to take stock of the bedrooms. Some were empty, some were partially furnished. They'd probably never been completed. Valerian had been an only child. There'd been no need.

Philippa selected the largest of the four bedrooms for Constantine and called for a maid to help her move some furniture from the other rooms. When they finished, the room looked presentable, with a small chest of drawers and a bookcase to hold personal items.

The housekeeper brought fresh linens for the bed, and clucked appreciatively over the change in the quarters. 'This used to be young Master Valerian's room. You've done well in a short time. It looks very respectable.'

'I didn't know it was his room,' Philippa said thoughtfully. By the time she'd known Valerian he'd moved out of the nursery and she was too old to be in the habit of visiting boys' bedchambers. Thinking of Valerian playing here brought a smile to Philippa's lips. It would have been a cheery but lonely nursery.

'A sad thing it was too that there weren't brothers and sisters to fill the other rooms,' the housekeeper said briskly to cover the little catch in her voice. 'But he found you and the young baron. You've done well for him.'

Philippa coloured a bit at the housekeeper's praise. 'Thank you.'

'The viscount will be proud of what you've done today. It can't have been easy to be so kind to those people. But you've done it anyways. It's what the master would have wanted if he'd been home, I think.'

Philippa nodded. The staff was probably abuzz with speculation. Perhaps the housekeeper thought Philippa might share some information with her that she could take back to the staff. But Philippa knew no more than they did. Her own curiosity remained as unsatisfied as theirs.

Philippa went back out to the main room and turned about, studying their efforts. They had done well. Improvements could be made later, but, for now, the room was inhabitable. Still, she felt as if something was missing. Her eyes fell on the long window seat and the empty cupboards below. She knew what it was.

'Mrs Wilcox, are there any of the viscount's toys left somewhere?'

The housekeeper's face brightened. 'Yes. They're packed away in the attic. I'll send some footmen for them right away.'

Philippa was delighted with the crates brought to

the nursery. She spent the remainder of the afternoon unpacking boxes, dusting off toy soldiers, a wooden chess set, and other myriad treasures for a boy Constantine's age. Soon, the cupboard beneath the window seat was filled and a few books lined the small bookcase in the bedroom.

She'd left strict instructions that she was to be notified the moment Valerian and Beldon were sighted, but the nursery windows overlooked the front drive and she saw them coming long before a footman could race up the three flights of stairs to tell her.

Careless of her appearance, Philippa sprinted down the stairs. Her note had been short, saying only that two unannounced guests had arrived from far away.

Valerian came through the door in a rush with Beldon close behind, his face anxious and his hair wind-tossed, evidence that the groom had found them. 'Is everything all right, Phil?' He gripped her hands hard, searching her face.

'I think so. It's hard to say,' Philippa said slowly. 'I've put her up in the green room and opened the nursery for the boy.' Now that he was here, she wasn't sure precisely what to say.

Valerian looked perplexed. 'A girl? A boy? Do they have names?'

'She says they're from Negush, that you knew their father.' Philippa cast about for the name. The girl had mentioned the man's name. 'Their name's Stefanov. Dimitri, that was the man's name. Yes, Dimitri Stefanov.'

'My God, they're here?' Valerian looked unsteady. Philippa couldn't tell if it was from genuine surprise or fear.

A young voice called out from the top of the stairs in blatant delight. 'Valerian, we've come. Oh, thank heavens we've found you!'

Valerian looked beyond her shoulder, his eyes blazing with emotion, his grip quite shattering on her hand. 'Lilya! Constantine! You're safe. Thank God.' He moved past Philippa, his throat working hard and his arms wide open. The pair flew down the stairs to meet him and he enfolded them in his embrace.

Philippa watched the teary reunion. She'd seldom seen Valerian so deeply moved and the sight of it caused her own eyes to blur. He held them tightly, then Lilya stepped back slightly and Valerian knelt down eye level with the boy, his hands on the boy's shoulders. He was speaking the language Philippa had heard them speak in the receiving room earlier.

There was no mistaking the tears on Valerian's cheeks for anything other than joy as he spoke to the boy. Seeing them together, Philippa was overcome by the sensation that she was watching a father being reunited with his son.

Chapter Sixteen

Valerian rose from his crouch to face Beldon and Philippa, an arm around each of the visitors. 'I am pleased to introduce Beldon Stratten, Baron Pendennys, and Philippa Lytton, the Dowager Duchess of Cambourne.'

He was glad to see Lilya make a nice curtsy and that Constantine had manners enough to sketch a light bow. He gave Lilya credit for that. It was unbelievable that they were here. Even with Lilya's resourcefulness, the journey was an arduous one. For a young girl and a boy alone, the journey was almost beyond comprehension. They would not have had the means to travel easily in private coaches or the funds to stay at quality inns. He started to note how thin Lilya was, although it did not detract from her delicate beauty. It didn't matter. They were here now and he would take care of everything for them from now on.

Valerian had to slow his mind down before plans

ran away with him. He'd do well to finish his introductions. 'Philippa, Beldon, this is Miss Lilya
Stefanov and her brother, Constantine. They are my
wards. Their father was one of my closest friends
during my time in the Balkans.' He knew he was
beaming with ridiculous joy but it was completely
overwhelming to know they were here after years of
separation.

He watched Beldon and Philippa's reactions.
Beldon was normally a dab hand with manners, but
he seemed quite tongue-tied as he greeted Lilya.
Philippa's response was harder to gauge. She
seemed relieved? Shocked? Then her eyes met his
above the exchange of pleasantries and a warm smile
lit her face especially for him. Whatever worries
she'd had would have to wait until they were alone.
For now, there were questions to answer and stories
to tell.

Beldon had already begun. 'How did Valerian
come to be your guardian?' he was asking Lilya.

Lilya looked at him for direction and Valerian felt
guilty for not having mentioned if before. 'I am their
guardian in the absence of any of their countless
aunts and uncles,' Valerian offered, glossing over the
fear that had prompted Dimitri to place the children
in his care. Dimitri had been afraid the Turks would
wipe out the entire family, leaving the children
orphans if they lived at all. And Valerian had known
in that part of the world, orphans were as good as
dead.

Lilya inserted herself into the conversation. 'My
aunts and uncles have generously taken us into their

homes these last years, but now there is a new war between the Turks and the Russians. Nowhere is safe. This war won't be the last and it won't change anything. Not for people like us.' She turned dark, pleading eyes on Valerian. 'I know there is talk of peace, but upheaval takes many different forms. I had to try to make a better life for us.' She gestured to the silent Constantine.

'You are welcome here,' Valerian assured her. He knew all too well what the aftermath of so-called peace brought. Peace in the Balkans would net the Western powers a chance to insert their own economic revolutions into the area, which was exactly why the West had been meddling there in the first place. There would be 'upheaval'—as Lilya called it—of the social and economic type for years. But perhaps the bloodshed would be less and, after a while, perhaps even the quality of life would be better. A man could make himself a fortune in postwar economies, but such places were not safe for a woman or a child.

Philippa gently ushered them upstairs and suggested everyone change for dinner. Valerian was grateful for her thoughtful intervention. In the midst of all the excitement, he'd forgotten they were still standing in the middle of the wall.

Valerian washed and changed as quickly as his valet would allow it. He wanted a chance to speak to Philippa before dinner. It could not wait until tonight, when he would share her bed.

Philippa was sitting before her dressing table,

letting the maid do her hair when he came in. She wore a pale sage-coloured dressing gown of silk that fell softly over the full swells of her breasts, reminding Valerian of how delectable her body was. He felt his own body stir in longing. He wanted to dismiss the maid and take his ease. Was that a trick of the mirror or did her breasts look fuller? He had an irresistible urge to palm them and test them himself.

'Val.' Philippa turned from the mirror and murmured a few words to the maid.

'You saved me the effort of doing that myself,' Valerian joked, taking a seat on the bed as the maid shut the door behind her.

'I assumed you needed to talk.'

Valerian nodded. 'I need to thank you for all you did today. My valet insisted on regaling me with all your efforts. According to him, as he heard it from Mrs Wilcox, you left no detail overlooked, from the dinner menus to getting chambers opened up, even the nursery.' Valerian paused here and reached for her hand. 'My valet says that you behaved honourably and denied the guests nothing, not even when there was speculation the boy was my bastard son.' He said it in kindly tones. But Philippa tensed.

He'd had to drag that confession out of his valet. His valet had suddenly fallen silent at some point in their very one-sided conversation, aware that he'd said too much. But Valerian had not let him stop. It explained the odd look on Philippa's face downstairs. She'd thought it was possible.

'His dark hair and age made it a distinct possibility,' Philippa answered. 'But, Val, I did not condemn you for it. If Constantine had been your son, I could not blame you for that. I had no claims on you during those years. It is not realistic to expect you would form no attachments.'

'You are too kind, Philippa. I hardly deserve it.' Especially, Valerian thought, knowing that she understood him to have been a very different man during that time, thinking that he'd truly shunned her.

'Do you have any more secrets, Val?' Philippa queried.

'None I can think of at the moment.' Valerian drew her to him, settling her on his lap. 'But thinking is deuced difficult when I am so distracted.' He kissed her neck, his hand working at the belt of her robe. His need for her had intensified to the point he knew he couldn't control himself for the duration of the evening. If he didn't have her now, he'd be sneaking off with her for a quick tumble on the billiards table.

Philippa laughed between kisses. 'Do you think there's time?'

'Steves won't serve dinner without us.' Valerian grinned and rolled her on to her back.

If they were twenty minutes late coming down to the drawing room where the others patiently waited, or if anyone noticed that Valerian's cravat was tied in a less than complicated knot, no one said anything.

Conversation hovered around Lilya's journey and

news of acquaintances Valerian knew. Occasionally, he'd lean over to Constantine, who sat on his left and say something in Koine, the language spoken by the Phanariots. He would have to see to tutors for the boy immediately so that Constantine could start learning English. He wondered where he'd find an English tutor who spoke one of the Balkan languages. Constantine spoke some Turkish and Russian. Surely there was someone in London or at one of the universities who would be able to converse with him?

'You still remember!' Lilya was delighted to hear Koine. She directed the rest of her comment to the table at large. 'Valerian has the most wonderful command of languages. He learned Koine while he was with us, but he also speaks French and German and some Russian and Turkish too.'

Valerian felt uncomfortable under the aegis of her praise. Philippa was smiling at him. 'I had no idea, aside from the French,' she said.

'It seemed the best way to accomplish my work,' Valerian said shortly. 'One can hardly be assured of fair negotiations, even with a translator present, if one doesn't know the language.' Beside him, a tired Constantine yawned. Valerian was thankful for the well-timed interruption.

Philippa and Lilya rose. 'Let's get Constantine settled for the evening while the men have their port,' Philippa suggested. 'Don't take too long,' she instructed as she led a sleepy Constantine from the room.

For a moment Valerian let his mind fantasise that it was his son and his wife heading upstairs. Those

kind of domestic fantasies had taken up a consid-
erable amount of his time lately. Whenever he saw
Philippa in her little office or talking to the housekeeper about menus or arranging flowers for the
many vases sprinkled about the house, he could not
imagine Roseland without her.

'German? You learned German?' Beldon was
saying.

'Yes. It wasn't that hard. English came from
German, you know.' Valerian dragged his thoughts
back to the present.

Beldon was thoughtful for a moment, studying his
friend. 'Is that why you were in London at Christmas?'

'Whatever can you mean?' Valerian schooled his
features into a look of utter confusion, as if he could
not grasp the connection between his fluency in
German and being in the capital in December.

Beldon wasn't fooled for a moment. 'It was.
There had been a rumour that the Russians and the
Turks were willing to negotiate peace. Britain and
France were to broker the treaty. Those talks are in
process right now. The papers are calling them the
"London Protocols".'

'One would hardly need to speak German for
that,' Valerian said, pushing the remark aside as he
reached for the decanter of brandy. Talk about his
diplomatic skills always made him self-conscious.
He didn't want people making the mistake of
thinking he'd been a modern-day knight, dashing
around broken kingdoms and restoring peace with
his diplomacy.

Beldon toyed with the stem on his brandy snifter. 'Unless, of course, one was talking with Prince Otto about overseeing an independent Greek kingdom. Then German might come in handy.'

'Yes, well, perhaps I had a small hand in that. The German delegates needed an escort and it seemed as good a time as any to return home.'

Beldon chuckled. 'You're positively astounding, Val. Why so shy about your accomplishments? Why did you let the gossip paint you in another light?'

'It suited my cover at the time. It's not all untrue, at any rate. In the beginning, my uncle needed me to act as a host and I needed to learn quite a lot about the business of international politics. I spent a vast amount of time at parties, listening and learning, becoming self-educated about alliances and the people behind them. I'm sure from the outside, it appeared that I was doing little but enjoying myself.'

'Well, I am proud of you and Father would have been too,' Beldon said charitably.

'I think its time to join the ladies.' Valerian swiftly redirected the conversation. He didn't want praise. Beldon couldn't realistically give it to him anyway. Beldon only knew a tiny portion of what he'd been involved in. Beldon only knew that he spoke several languages and had participated in a few high-profile negotiations. Beldon didn't know about the diplomacy conducted at knifepoint, gunpoint, or sword point. Beldon didn't know about the men he'd killed.

He wondered what Beldon's reaction would be if he knew about the night in Negush when Valerian had turned his blade on British allies to save rebels. For that matter, what would Philippa think?

In the music room, Philippa was chatting easily with Lilya and it did Valerian's heart good to know that Philippa and Lilya had taken to each other so well. He hoped Philippa would be able to guide Lilya through a Season next spring. Lilya would be eighteen and it would be high time to help her find a husband and settle her life in England.

Valerian played the piano for a while, letting the ladies talk. Beldon read quietly, casting a furtive look at Lilya every few moments. Valerian had never seen his friend quite so taken with a woman before and he found it amusing. Beldon spent so much time studying others and watching the drama of their lives unfold; he seldom gave his own life the same consideration. It would serve him right to finally have some drama of his own. Perhaps while Philippa was matchmaking for Lilya, she might do a little matchmaking for Beldon.

This time next year was promising to be very interesting. Valerian stumbled over a stanza, recognising certain assumptions about that claim. He was assuming Philippa would be married to him. This time next year, she'd be the Viscountess St Just and in a position to help his young ward come out. It was time to ask her. There was no more reason to put off proposing. Her actions today proved that she had no further reservations about him.

But he should wait a few days, let the excitement of Lilya and Constantine's arrival wear down. She needed to see the proposal as something between them, born of their love. He didn't want her to think for a moment he wanted to marry her because he needed help with his wards. Lilya would shortly move on to be mistress of her husband's home. But Constantine was young. He'd be a long-term responsibility. Valerian knew such a responsibility would be asking a lot of Philippa, but she'd been generous with the boy today and she'd genuinely enjoyed the children at the St Piran's Day fair.

The situation with his wards wasn't the only reason for delay. There was one last secret to share with Philippa before the path was clear to claiming her. And he had to share that secret soon.

He smelled lavender and knew Philippa was behind him before she laid her hands on his shoulders. 'Your playing is lovely, but it's been a long day. Lilya and I are going to bed.'

Valerian stood to wish them goodnight, noting that Philippa did look fatigued tonight. She was usually so energetic, but the day's exertions had left signs of weariness about her eyes and she seemed paler than normal. It was all understandable given the demands of the day.

'May I come to your room?' Valerian asked, *sotto voce*.

Philippa gave him a wan smile. 'I think it would be best if you didn't.' She gave a slight nod, indicating Lilya. 'I'll want to be available if she or Constantine need anything during the night. Sleeping in new places can sometimes take getting used to.'

'I will miss you.' Valerian covered her hand with his where it rested on his sleeve.

In part, he was relieved by her decision. He feared the nightmare. He'd not dreamed it since Philippa's arrival. But all the talk of the past at dinner and seeing the Stefanov children again had brought those concerns to the fore. Before he could propose to Philippa, he had to tell her about the night in Negush. It would only be a matter of time before Lilya confided in Philippa. He wanted no secrets between himself and Philippa when they wed. Tomorrow, he told himself. He would find a way to tell Philippa tomorrow.

Philippa's maid woke her at nine o'clock the next morning, under Philippa's strict instructions. She'd been in the habit of oversleeping lately and was determined not to laze the morning away. In Philippa's opinion, nine o'clock was late enough. She'd prefer getting up at seven or eight. A note, and a yellow rosebud tinted with pink at the edges, waited for her on the small table near the window.

'What's this?' Philippa asked, crossing the room to look at the envelope.

The maid giggled. 'It's from his lordship. He had me bring it in so you'd have it when you woke up.'

Philippa smiled and opened the envelope. 'He wants me to join him for breakfast on the back terrace.'

'It's a beautiful morning for it,' the maid said, throwing back the curtains to reveal the sun. 'Shall I lay out the jonquil muslin?'

'Perfect. A sunny dress for a sunny day.' Philippa's pulse raced at the prospect of a breakfast with Valerian. Something was afoot, she could sense it.

She arrived on the back terrace thirty minutes later almost breathless from her flight down the stairs. She stopped to gather herself at the French doors. The sight that met her gaze almost undid her, so moved was she by it.

A white-clothed table set with breakfast china and crystal glass sat under the Chusan palm, looking like something out of an Italian painting. But what held her abject attention was the man standing beside it, his back to her as he surveyed the lawns.

She'd thought Valerian handsome as a youth, but none of that compared to the manly beauty he exuded now. This morning, his hair was brushed forward on to his forehead in raven-black waves, the way she liked it best. He'd been for a ride and was still dressed in his tall boots and riding jacket, looking like a prince of the world.

Philippa went to him, wrapping her arms about his lean waist and laying her head against the broad strength of his back. 'Good morning, Val. This is lovely.'

Valerian turned and kissed her gently. 'Good morning—did you sleep well?'

'Yes. I feel much recovered.' Philippa smiled easily and sat in the chair he held out for her. 'And you, did you sleep well?'

'As well as a man can when he has so many things on his mind,' Valerian confessed.

Indeed, he looked slightly ragged about the edges, Philippa thought after a good look at his face. His jaw was smooth, evidence that his valet had been up early this morning, but there were the beginnings of tired circles beneath his eyes. 'You should have come to me.'

'I needed time alone to think.' Valerian shook his head. 'I needed time to think about us.' He passed her a basket of warm toast covered with a cloth napkin.

'You've been at Roseland for nearly two months. I can't imagine this place without you. You've been generous with your time. I know Cambourne is a large estate. But I can't accept the idea of you leaving here.'

Philippa lifted the napkin and reached for a slice of toast. She furrowed her brow. There was a small box of sorts beneath the piece she'd taken. 'What's this?' She took the square box out.

'Something I should have given you years ago. I had it with me the night of the Rutherfords' ball,' Valerian said quietly, motioning for her to open it.

She flipped the lid up to reveal a ring set with a tiny band of diamonds surrounding an emerald. 'It's beautiful.' She shot him a questioning look. 'What does this mean, Val?'

'It means I want to marry you. But there is something I need to tell you first so that you can make a fully informed decision about whether or not you want to marry me.'

The last bit took some sparkle off the proposal. It made her think of Lucien's letter. Was he going to confess to something terrible or was there a logical explanation behind it? Perhaps Lucien was just grasping at straws because he felt he'd been jilted.

Philippa set down her toast and folded her hands. 'More secrets, Val?' she tried to tease.

'Something like that.' Valerian looked pained as he took a moment to collect himself. Philippa's heart lurched. She wanted to comfort him and she feared the worst.

Valerian drew a deep breath and began. 'Lilya's father, Dimitri, was part of a rebel force that tried to throw off Turkish rule. They were successful at the start. The rebels were organised and the district of Negush was liberated from the Ottomans in 1822. That victory was followed by another in the Voden district, but the Ottoman army was too large for the rebels to stand against for long.

'The Turkish army sent delegates to speak to the rebels. The rebels were offered terms of surrender and a peaceful return to Ottoman rule. I was with the delegation that went to meet Dimitri's group. I had two years' experience in the field by then and was considered more than a junior aide. After the first few months in Vienna, my experience had been beyond the ballrooms, in the little villages where the real living took place. I was selected to go because I knew those men. I spoke their language. For their sakes and their families, I hoped they would be guided by my influence. They were not.

'The retribution the Ottoman army meted out to them was horrific. Villages were plundered, women and children were killed. The army finally advanced to Dimitri's village in Negush. He'd been taken prisoner earlier and I had seen him just once. He made me swear to look after his family. He knew what was coming and that he faced certain death.'

A sound at the door intruded. Philippa looked

away from Valerian, startled by the noise. Steves rushed forwards, a thousand apologies falling from his lips. 'My lord, they would not wait to be received. My lord…'

A large group of men flooded on to the terrace behind Steves, led by none other than Lucien Canton.

Valerian rose, placing himself as shield between Philippa and Lucien. His face was grim, set in threatening lines. But Philippa rose beside him, lacing her hand through his. Fear lanced through her. She wished she'd told Valerian about the letter. Lucien wasn't here to squabble over her. He was here for Valerian. 'I love you, Val,' Philippa whispered hastily. His hand tightened around hers in response and then he let it go.

'What is the meaning of this, Canton? You cannot just invade a man's home at will.' He crossed his arms, looking imposing and making the most of his two-inch height advantage over Lucien.

Canton thrust forwards a legal-looking document. 'I find anything is possible when one has a warrant for arrest,' Canton said icily. 'The rules no longer apply to you, St Just. You're under arrest for a crime of the highest order.'

Valerian managed to not look surprised. He merely raised his eyebrows and said, 'What would that be?'

Lucien met him with a level stare. 'That would be treason, my lord.'

Chapter Seventeen

'Treason? On what grounds?' Valerian responded in a tone that suggested he found the claims laughable.

Lucien was not appreciating the humour Valerian found in the situation. Philippa fought the urge to warn Valerian not to toy with Lucien's temper overmuch. Valerian might not be concerned, but Philippa was scared. This was her fault. She should have been more discreet when refusing Lucien's proposal. She should not have come to Roseland so soon after rejecting Lucien, giving him the impression she'd chosen Valerian over him. She should have told Valerian about the letter. He would have been prepared.

'I do not care for your naïve claims of innocence, St Just. You know exactly what you've done. And I know it too. You killed British allies at the Negush Uprising in 1822 for the express purpose of assisting the rebellion,' Lucien spat out.

Philippa felt Valerian stiffen beside her. 'How convenient it must be to label someone a traitor for unproved suppositions that occurred eight years and two thousand miles away,' Valerian snapped. 'I had no idea it was so easy to paint someone with the traitor's brush these days,' he mocked. 'Now, get out while you can. My footmen will not hesitate to use force.'

'And neither will we.' Lucien gestured to the men with him. 'I've brought a few of his Majesty's finest to ensure that you come with us in one way or another. Although you think the claims are flimsy, there are those in power who believe the claims are well substantiated,' Lucien said with a sneer.

'Did your father get you the warrant?' Valerian would not be cowed by the Lucien's assertion. Philippa would have laughed if the situation wasn't proving to be so dire.

One of the soldiers stepped forwards. 'I am sorry, milord, for the inconvenience. You will have to come with us and explain yourself to the justice system.' He held out cuffs. 'If you would please come peaceably.'

'Where are you taking him?' Philippa stepped around Valerian, cold horror knotting in her stomach.

'To London. It is where all good traitors are tried. And hung,' Lucien added.

'Stop this right now, Lucien. You've gone too far and you have no proof, only suppositions,' Philippa tried vainly to reason. She could not believe Lucien would do this. The wonderful, sunny morning was turning nightmarish.

For the first time since he'd intruded on to the

back terrace, Lucien seemed to notice her. Philippa did not drop her gaze from his intense stare. She was not certain what Lucien would do in regards to her. She expected he might rail at her in his jealousy. She thought he might bring up the damning letter he'd sent warning her. But Lucien did something worse than what she anticipated.

'Gentlemen, if you would excuse me. I would like a private word with the Duchess.' He was all politeness and manners. 'Perhaps we could step inside?' he suggested when she hesitated.

Valerian looked ready to tear Lucien to bits. 'If you harm her, I will see you dead.' Valerian's eyes flashed with menace as Lucien offered her his arm.

'Dig a little deeper, St Just,' Lucien snarled before raising his voice. 'Did you hear that, gentlemen? The viscount is threatening me with bodily harm.'

Once inside, Lucien faced Philippa with an inscrutable expression. 'Philippa, I am sorry you had to be here for this. I would have spared you if I could have. I did try to warn you.' Lucien was all sympathetic friend.

'Don't take him. You don't need to do this,' Philippa pleaded, hoping for a moment his guise as friend was sincere.

'I cannot forgo a clear duty to my country,' Lucien countered. 'In some way that would make me a traitor too, wouldn't it? A type of accessory to treason, I think. Dishonour comes in many forms in this world, Philippa. There are those who commit the acts and those who stand by and watch them without doing anything.' Lucien smiled and reached out a hand to touch her hair. 'You look lovely today. I've missed you.'

Philippa swallowed hard and fought the urge to flinch. How could she ever have thought this man was her dear friend? But Valerian needed her and she would gain him nothing if she lashed out at Lucien now. She did not miss the import of Lucien's message. He had not been talking about his obligations. He'd been talking about her. If he dared to come into a man's home and arrest him in front of friends, he would not hesitate to haul her off too.

She saw clearly the choices he was presenting her with. She could fight for Valerian and find herself facing scandal if not worse, or she could keep quiet.

'I will protect you, Philippa,' Lucien said, divining her thoughts. 'I won't tell St Just about the letter I sent you.'

'He knows about the letter,' Philippa snapped out, but it was a weak play and she knew it.

Lucien easily called her bluff. 'Yes? And the contents of the letter? Does he know those too?' He shook his head. 'I didn't think so. How do you think St Just would feel if he knew? Perhaps he would feel betrayed. Perhaps he'd even think you had a hand in this, that whatever feelings you professed to have were a lie simply to get close to him and steal a confession.' Lucien sighed heavily.

'This will not go down as the best day of his life. I almost pity the man. He's lost his freedom, his dignity—I am sorry about the cuffs, but they are necessary, my dear—and he's lost the woman he loves.'

Philippa's anger sparked. She'd never wanted to do violence to another person as much as she wanted to hit Lucien Canton at that moment. She was no fool. She saw all the implications of his subtle blackmail. She'd been right on the terrace. Lucien was doing this because of her. This was all her fault. But she could say nothing without ruining any hope she had of seeing Valerian safe again.

'I will protect you, Philippa,' Lucien repeated.

She wanted to scream out she didn't need his protection. She wanted to scream that she knew why he wanted to keep her separate from this travesty he was wrecking on Valerian. He wanted her mines and he couldn't have them without a legally binding commitment from her and Lucien Canton couldn't be associated with someone under the cloud of scandal. It would be bad for business. But she could say nothing.

The implicit devil's deal was struck and they returned to the terrace. Philippa was glad to see Beldon had made his way through the crowd and now stood with Valerian in soft conversation. Apparently, without Lucien to goad them, the men had been unwilling to forbid Valerian to speak with anyone.

Valerian caught sight of her immediately, his gaze roving her face, looking for something. But Philippa had nothing to show him. She kept her face as blank as possible. Her little part in all this was embarrassing. As for the rest of what had passed inside, Valerian didn't need to be told. He would be able to piece it all together soon enough. He'd been right from the start about Lucien's avaricious nature.

'Thank you, gentlemen. The lady is understandably overwrought,' Lucien explained glibly to the soldiers. 'Now, if Pendennys will step aside, we can get on with our unpleasant business. It's a long trip to London. I want to make the most of the daylight.'

'Lay out your proof, Canton.' Beldon spoke up this time. 'You cannot haul a man out of his home without a legitimate case.'

'I don't need to answer to you, Pendennys. I have already offered sufficient proof to those in power. I wouldn't have been granted the warrant otherwise.' He motioned to the men. 'Take him. I am done with all this stalling.'

A soldier stepped towards Valerian. Beldon threw a fist to the man's jaw, sending him reeling backwards. It was all the tension on the terrace needed to light the fuse. Beldon was in the thick of it with Valerian, swinging hard rounders. Footmen joined the fray. Philippa stepped backwards, removing herself from the fight. The last thing Beldon and Valerian needed was for her to get in the way. That was when she saw Lucien draw out a gun. There was no doubt who his target was.

She couldn't let it happen. She would not let Valerian die on his beautiful back terrace under his Chusan palm. Philippa screamed a warning. It was enough to halt the fray for an instant. 'He's got a gun!' The words rushed out in a hurry.

Valerian took a look at Lucien, immediately taking in the danger. But his fear was for her, not himself. Beldon started towards Lucien. Valerian shook his head. 'No, Beldon. I think I'd best go with them. I won't have you or Philippa hurt on my behalf.'

Philippa ran forwards, but Beldon grabbed her, whispering, 'No, Phil. We can't help him, not yet.'

Beldon was right, but it was a bitter task to stand by and watch Valerian roughly imprisoned in handcuffs and marched from his lovely home to be stuffed unceremoniously inside the dark coach that waited in the drive.

On the stairs in the hall, Lilya watched the scene, pale faced and frightened. 'His cloak,' she whispered as Beldon and Philippa followed the last of the soldiers outside, unwilling to let their friend out of their sight until the last possible moment. Philippa looked up blankly at the girl. Lilya nodded and thrust the cloak into her hands.

Beldon took it from her and went down the steps, having the forethought to lay it across Valerian's lap in the carriage. Philippa was glad for his quick thinking and for Lilya's. At least now he'd be warm. With any luck, the soldiers wouldn't think to search the cloak and perhaps Lilya had had enough time to put a few things in it.

As for herself, Philippa had to get her thoughts well in hand. She would be of no use to Valerian if she gave into the guilt and panic that threatened to swamp her. She watched the unmarked coach disappear on to the road, thinking of Valerian alone, surrounded by his enemies and no way to defend himself.

'Lucien means to see him dead in some fashion

or other.' The thought hit her all at once and it was all it took to galvanise her into action.

'We won't let it happen,' Beldon said staunchly beside her. But she noted he didn't bother to contradict her with soothing claims.

Lilya joined them on the front steps. 'Valerian is a strong man. He is resourceful.'

Philippa turned to the girl. 'I am sorry this happened. It's not much of a welcome for you. You did well to think of his cloak.'

Lilya shrugged and met Philippa's gaze meaningfully. 'In my country, this happens often. We are always ready.'

'You were with him that night in Negush,' Philippa said. It wasn't really a question. She was starting to see how the disaster had unfolded. 'Come inside and tell us about it. Perhaps there is something there that can help us.'

They rang for tea out of habit. None of them were particularly hungry, but it gave Cook something to do and the household a way to return to normal after the brawl on the back terrace. Everyone was anxious and Philippa knew the best way to beat anxiety was to keep busy.

'My father had been taken prisoner in earlier fighting. Valerian had been allowed to see him once. He promised my father he'd protect us. The army was coming. There was no way to escape it. I was nine, I think. Constantine was a baby, and my brother Alexei was twelve.' Lilya stopped here, struggling for composure.

Philippa shot Beldon a confused glance. She had

not heard of the older brother before. 'Did Alexei stay in the Balkans?' Perhaps the girl was homesick for her family.

'No.' Lilya said quietly, staring into her teacup. 'He and my Aunt Natasha were killed that night. We'd all have been killed if Valerian hadn't been there.' She went on with her story, telling of the fire and the fighting, how her Aunt Natasha had held off two Ottoman soldiers with a sword, how Valerian had arrived, slashing and killing like a berserker.

Valerian had got them to the relative safety of a copse, but the fighting had drawn too near and their hideaway had been invaded by Ottomans intent on blood. 'Natasha fell and Alexei picked up her sword. He fought back to back with Valerian. He fought well, but he was too young to fight with such a heavy weapon for long. Valerian killed several soldiers before the others fled the copse. Then he found our relatives who saw us to safety. He went back, though. The army was expecting him. I imagine he went back to the embassy shortly afterwards. His work was done on that mission.

'He didn't forget us. When he knew where we were, he sent clothes and food. He even came to visit us a few times when his work brought him into the area. On those visits, he gave us money. He kept us alive. Our circumstances had been greatly reduced after the uprising. We learned later that he had seen to a decent burial for Alexei and our aunt and that he was with my father at the last.'

After hearing Valerian's part of the story that morning, Philippa could accurately guess what the 'last' had been. Of course Valerian had done all that at personal risk and expense to himself. There was never a man more true to his friends than Valerian. He did not deserve to suffer for his kindnesses.

'But it is true, he killed Turks,' Beldon put in.

Lilya nodded. 'To save us.'

'The Turks aren't even our allies any more, which is what makes the situation so damnable,' Beldon huffed. 'There should be a statute of limitations on these sort of things the way alliances shift these days. After eight years of no one noticing, no one caring, it seems ridiculous that one good man should be brought to task for such a thing.'

'Lucien wouldn't care if it wasn't for me.' Philippa put in softly. 'He's doing this for spite.'

'More than spite, Phil. You can't take all the blame. Lucien believes Val stands in the way of his progress.'

'I think we have to go after Lucien,' Philippa said after a while. 'The charges of treason won't stick. Val has friends in the government who won't allow this to go very far once they hear of it. It's too bad his uncle is still abroad. But even so, there are people who can appeal once we're in town. No one is interested in calling a hero a traitor. Lilya will tell her story, we'll manage a few people in high places and the charges will go away accompanied by a nice public apology. Lucien must surely know this. The charges will stir up a short scandal but nothing more. In the end, they're only a red herring.'

Beldon nodded. 'I agree. Lucien does know all this. He is just buying time. A trial would be laughable. Perhaps he can manage a hearing, but he knows the charges are too frail for a full-blown trial. He means to see Valerian dead long before the charges are heard. Once Val is in prison, any number of unfortunate incidents can occur without anyone paying close attention to them.'

It was as she feared. Philippa felt her body grow cold. Her fingers became ice. Lucien meant to do murder. What could she do to stop him? To change his mind? She'd do anything, give anything to protect Valerian. She cast about in her mind for an offering. 'I will sell him the mines if needed.' It was all she could think of.

Beldon gave her a black look. 'While the sentiment is heartfelt, Phil, I dislike the idea of dishonour prospering. There's no guarantee that will stop Canton in the future. We don't want him to be able to blackmail you or Valerian in the future.'

'I have a plan, then, Beldon. You go to London and keep Valerian safe. I'll go to Truro and see if I can find anything that might be useful to pressure Lucien. I'll meet you in London after that.' It wasn't much of a plan, but it was a start.

'Agreed.' Beldon turned to Lilya. 'Will you be all right here?'

She was white-faced, her hands clenching the tea cup so tightly it was in jeopardy of shattering. 'I am coming with you. I will go to Truro with the Duchess. Valerian is my friend. He protected my family and now it is my turn to protect him.' Her voice was firm, but her gaze wavered in the direction of Constantine.

Philippa smiled approvingly. 'I will welcome

your company. The housekeeper will delight in looking after Constantine.'

'I will leave right away.' Beldon rose. 'On horseback, I can catch the coach by nightfall. No one can deny me the right to stay at an inn of my choice. So be it, if it happens to be the same one Lucien is at.'

'I'll send a note for you to give to Valerian. There are things he must know,' Philippa said quickly. 'Lilya, start packing our things. We'll leave after luncheon for Truro.'

An hour later, Beldon hugged them each goodbye in the drive and vaulted up on to the back of his hunter, a horse named Hercules, known for its endurance over long distances.

Philippa had no doubts about the horse's ability to catch up with the coach.

Beldon carried with him a valise strapped to the back of the saddle and a letter in his pocket that confessed the contents of Lucien's letter and one last secret.

Philippa raised her hand to wave as her brother clucked Hercules into motion, the sunlight dancing off the brilliant emerald she wore on her finger.

Chapter Eighteen

Valerian kept his gaze fixed on a spot on the carriage wall, his hands surreptitiously gripping the cloak Beldon had passed to him at the last moment. The day was mild, but come evening he'd be glad of the cloak's warmth. He had no reason to expect any courtesy from Lucien, who seemed committed to playing the righteous patriot to the hilt. The iron cuffs were an indignity that could have been done without, but Lucien was intent on making the experience as degrading as possible. He was meant to be put on display as a dangerous prisoner.

A man sat opposite him in the carriage, the other men and Lucien rode on horseback outside in the crisp spring air. Valerian ignored the man, keeping his gaze on the mark on the carriage wall, his thoughts fixed elsewhere, so that his mind was free although his body was trapped.

It was a trick Dimitri had told him about when he'd seen him that last time in prison before the exe-

cution. It seemed ironic that he was ostensibly facing
the same end as Dimitri and just days after Dimitri's
son and daughter had arrived.

For the first part of the journey, he allowed
himself to think about Philippa and the promising
start of the morning. He stored up images of her, of
Roseland, of Lilya and Constantine, and all the
things he loved. Night would assuredly come and
sleep would not. He did not dare let it, for fear of the
nightmare, for fear of giving Lucien some evidence
that could be twisted into incriminating proof. He
needed the peace of those memories to see him
through the night. He'd spent many lonely nights
practising that same technique in the Balkans.

They stopped briefly for a stretch around tea time,
then headed on, making the most of the daylight. For
the second part of the trip, Valerian thought about
Lucien's game, keeping his mind active by trying to
match wits with Canton. It was clear to him that
while Canton wouldn't mind seeing him tried as a
traitor, it was unlikely that anything would come of
it beyond an initial hearing. Canton probably wanted
to use the opportunity for something else.

It occurred to Valerian that Canton would have
ample time alone with him to carry out any das-
tardly plans. Canton would have plenty of chances
to kill him on this trip alone. Cuffed and confined,
Valerian was at the man's mercy. What he didn't
know was how much of a coward Canton was. Did
Canton have the temperament to kill a man outright?
Or was he the sort who favoured 'accidents', pre-

ferably those that were ordered by him, but carried—
out by others?

Accidental occurrences had certainly played a
lucky part in Lucien's life in recent years. The accidental appearance of Mandeville Danforth at
Lucien's home in Truro led directly to a seat on the
bank's board of directors. An accident at Cambourne's mines had offered him a direct connection
to the Cambourne inheritance and a chance to use
Philippa's friendship for his nefarious schemes.

That gave him pause. He'd seen all the angles
Canton had decided to play so far. But he'd not
looked past the present. How involved was Canton's
scheme? Had it incorporated the planning of Cambourne's death? Was this plot so detailed that he'd
been willing to invest three years in setting it up? To
wait until Philippa was out of mourning and able to
legitimately remarry? The potential depth expanded
the parameters of the situation. This was no longer
an opportunity to exploit a plum that had fallen into
Canton's lap on happenstance. It was much more
defined than that. If his suppositions were correct,
then Canton had known all along what he was doing.
It explained why Canton would be willing to go to
such lengths to remove him from the equation. He'd
unknowingly put the entire scheme at risk and
Philippa too.

He hoped Philippa was holding up. She'd looked
devastated after her discussion with Lucien and
she'd been pale after the fisticuffs. But she was tenacious and he had no doubt that she was planning
some way to assist him. He rather hoped he'd find a

way to resolve his situation before Philippa could leap into action. He didn't want her endangered and Lucien was a more perilous foe than she realised.

He fingered his cloak, taking comfort in the fact that someone had had the foresight to slip a few things into his cloak, probably Lilya. She would have been the only one able to do it. Beldon and Philippa had been on the terrace with him.

If he wasn't mistaken from the feel of things, there was a small knife, some money and a tiny vial. He could imagine Lilya racing to his room and seeing the vial on the bedside table. She'd probably grabbed it in hopes that if it was medicine he needed, he'd have it. If he lived long enough to see the inside of Newgate, the money would come in handy. He hoped he wouldn't have to use the knife. But he thanked Lilya silently for her efforts.

Dusk was falling when they stopped for the night at a wayside inn. An hour ago, they'd driven through a larger village. But Valerian could see now why Lucien had chosen to stop here. It was less likely to be frequented by travellers, less opportunity to call attention to their party. Such a choice supported Valerian's thoughts that Canton had other plans than a trial for treason in mind.

'My hands, please,' Valerian said as the coach rocked to a stop. He held them up to be unlocked.

The man riding with him shook his head. 'Sorry, I've got orders not to under any circumstances.'

'Very well. My cloak about my shoulders, then, if you don't mind,' Valerian ordered. 'The clasp is in front. Fasten it well, I don't want it sliding off in the dirt.'

Uncomfortably, the man did as Valerian asked, grumbling about being treated like a 'bleeding valet'. Valerian took some petty pleasure from the man's complaints. Perhaps the man would tell Canton he didn't sign on to be a 'bleeding valet' and get permission to remove his cuffs. It wasn't as if Valerian wanted to engineer a prison break, or in this case a coach break. Running away only enhanced the look of guilt. He simply wanted to stay alive long enough to reach London and put Lucien's case to rest.

The inn was rough, but empty of guests with the exception of a few locals. Lucien sneered at him as he clumsily took a seat at one of the benches. One of the men was allowed to remove his cuffs for eating. Dinner came shortly afterwards, greasy fare of lamb stew and overcooked carrots. But Valerian had eaten worse. Lucien apparently hadn't and pushed his plate away in disgust. He eyed Valerian malevolently over the plank table. 'Probably wise of you to eat what you can now. Can't say as how there'll be much food or opportunity to eat where you're going.'

Valerian met his gaze evenly and said nothing. He had no intention of saying a word to Canton. Lucien looked away, his attention drawn to the door and the newcomer. Lucien's eyes went hard.

'Pendennys, what a surprise to see you here,' Lucien drawled coldly.

'Ah, yes, who would have thought, out of all the

inns to choose from, we'd have the same taste?'
Beldon returned in a jovial tone, sounding as if he'd
just walked into the finest gentlemen's club on St
James's. 'St Just, I trust you're well?' Beldon came
over to the bench and sat beside him.

Valerian stifled a laugh. 'Whatever are you
doing here?'

'I'm journeying to London on business, much
the same as you, I am guessing,' Beldon said off-
handedly. 'Is the ale here any good?'

Lucien stalked outside in anger, barking an order
to keep a close eye on the prisoner.

'We're going nowhere,' Beldon said cheerily,
lifting his tankard in a salute. 'At ease, gentlemen, I
am simply here to keep an old friend company.
There's no crime about that in your law books, is
there? Here...' Beldon slapped down two coins on
the table '...innkeeper, ale for everyone and keep it
coming. These boys have had a long day.'

Valerian shot Beldon a quick look. He was up to
something. Surely he realised 'rescue' or 'escape'
was out of the question? Beldon merely smiled.

After the first round, the men had gathered around
the table where they sat. After the second, they were
comparing battle scars from the morning's fisticuffs,
more like comrades instead of enemies who had been
on opposite sides of the fray. When the third round
arrived, Beldon asked congenially, 'So, how much
does it pay to take a facer from a viscount these days?'

'Enough,' one of the men replied. 'Double what
we'd earn in a week on half-pay.'

'I'm not sure the wages are enough, considering

the beating we took from you and the viscount today.' A man called Johnny gingerly touched his black eye, courtesy of Beldon's fist.

Beldon nodded in empathy. 'Sorry about that.'

'You and the viscount don't fight like sissified dandies,' Johnny put in.

'We're old friends,' Beldon said, throwing an arm around Valerian. 'We go way back. We've been in more than one scrape.'

For the next half-hour, Valerian sat back and watched Beldon charm the group of rough soldiers He saw his friend's ploy. Beldon too realised that escape was moot. But there were benefits to having one's captors on one's side. Valerian wouldn't be surprised if he'd be allowed to remain uncuffed during the ride tomorrow or if Beldon would be allowed to sit with him in the carriage. Little pleasures meant a lot in these situations. And perhaps, too, Beldon was trying to establish an ally to use once they got to London, someone who would prove to be sympathetic to their cause.

Eventually it was time to bed down. Lucien had arranged for a private room upstairs for himself. The others were expected to bed down in the common room on pallets, Valerian included. Men were appointed to stand watch in shifts in case Valerian tried anything foolish.

It was an immense relief to have Beldon with him. 'You sleep first,' Beldon said quietly, gesturing to a pallet. 'I'll stand watch for us.'

Valerian nodded. Beldon implicitly understood

his concern that Canton would not be beyond murdering someone in his sleep.

'How is Philippa?' Valerian asked in low tones.

'She is well.' Beldon looked around him at the room of men. 'Tomorrow in the carriage, I'll tell you more. Not now. I have a letter from her.'

A man shouted over at them to stop talking. Beldon raised his hand in acknowledgement. 'Sorry to disturb you.' But both of them knew the ale had paid off. They shouldn't have been allowed to exchange even those few sentences. The shout had been for good form alone to keep up appearances.

Valerian lay down with his cloak about him, his hand closing over the handle of the small knife. The setting reminded him of many evenings spent in uncertain circumstances in the Balkans—the only difference was that he'd been alone then. Valerian glanced over at Beldon, who was already deep in a chess game with the soldier appointed to the first watch. It had been more than he'd expected to see Beldon come through the inn door. Beldon's presence was a good sign, too, that Philippa had not been revolted by the charges laid at his feet. For the first time since Canton had dragged him from Roseland, Valerian felt the foreboding recede.

Philippa could not quell the sense of foreboding that infiltrated her thoughts. The carriage ride to Truro had been interminable, although Lilya had done her best to keep up a stream of conversation in the hope of taking her mind off the circumstances.

Philippa only followed the stream of chatter in

snatches, her mind fully riveted on Valerian. Was he safe? Had Beldon reached him in time? She worried for her brother too. Perhaps it had been a fool's madness to throw her brother after Canton. She'd never forgive herself if anything happened to Beldon.

But Beldon was adept in the art of protecting himself. She'd seen him box and handle a sword on occasion. It was quite telling to think of Lucien as someone who was capable of harming another. But Beldon had gone after Valerian because he agreed with her that Lucien wanted Valerian dead. Beldon's presence might act as a shield, at least until they got to London. She desperately hoped by then she'd have something else to act as a shield, some proof of Lucien's unethical behaviour. But it would be difficult. Valerian had technically committed treason. Technically, Lucien had done nothing wrong. How did one prove nefarious motives?

Philippa grappled with the conundrum throughout the afternoon until the carriage finally rocked to a halt in front of a respectable inn in Truro. It was too late to do anything tonight, but in the morning she and Lilya would pay a visit to Lucien's Truro manor. She hoped she could gain entrance based on the servants' familiarity with her, but if not she was prepared to use force and intimidation.

In the morning, she dressed in her best day gown. Lilya dressed as her maid. They went straight to the manor. The butler recognised her immediately.

'Your Grace, milord isn't home,' the butler said,

flustered by her sudden arrival. 'Surely you knew of his plans?'

'That's why I'm here,' Philippa said, quickly moving into the story she and Lilya had concocted. 'Mr Canton has forgotten some items he needs. He asked me to come back for them. It's quite desperate. He fears his new contracts can't be signed without them.' Philippa wrung her hands for good measure.

'Do you know where he left them?'

'He thought they were in his office or maybe in his bedchamber,' Philippa said.

'I'll help you look,' the butler offered.

Philippa declined the offer, gesturing to Lilya. 'I brought my maid, so as not to bother you. I know you have responsibilities.' She swept into the hall and began making her way up the stairs to the room Lucien used as his office before the butler could muster up any other concerns.

'What are we looking for?' Lilya whispered once she'd closed the office door behind them.

'Anything incriminating. I don't know beyond that. There might not be anything here at all,' Philippa said. It had been something of a victory to get into his house. They would have to be quick. She had no idea how long it would be before the servants began to suspect something was wrong. How much time they had would depend on how much Lucien had told the staff about their estrangement. She hoped Lucien had remained true to his arrogant character and not lowered himself to share their relationship with the staff.

Their luck held in terms of discovery. No one

bothered them beyond an occasional inquiry. But luck was against them in unearthing anything of merit that might indicate Lucien was capable of such deceitful conniving.

'We'd better try somewhere else. I don't think anything is here,' Philippa said when they'd exhausted the office.

'I'll check his bedroom,' Lilya offered.

'I'll check the library.'

In the library, Philippa gazed at the walls of bookshelves. She'd never be able to check each of those books in a reasonable amount of time. Even if she had time, it would take more than a day to check them. She supposed it would not be beyond the realm of possibility that a book was hollowed out or that the cover masked the book's true contents. But she didn't have time to make that check. She also thought it would draw undue suspicion from the staff if they found her looking through books.

Philippa checked the small desk that sat in the corner, but it was virtually empty. Flummoxed, she sank down on the sofa. It was hard to believe a few months ago she'd received a marriage proposal in this very room from someone she had believed to be her friend. She remembered the incident quite clearly. The room had felt awkward, as if she were being watched.

She stood up and started to pace in front of the fireplace. Given all that had happened in the past months, she was starting to feel that it was not unbelievable that she had been watched. Perhaps there was a hidden panel somewhere.

Philippa shot a furtive glance at the doorway, then back at the fireplace. The portrait above the fireplace had given her a strange feeling the night Lucien had proposed. Perhaps there was a switch in the fireplace that led to a secret room.

She didn't have to feel for long before her hand felt a knob in a place no fireplace typically had one. Philippa held her breath and pressed. A panel slid open. Elation coursed through her. She'd found a secret room! She cautioned herself. A secret room didn't mean anything was in it. Lots of houses had such rooms left over from the Civil War, and further back in time.

Philippa stooped and stepped inside. The room was far larger than she'd anticipated. A table and chair sat against one wall with a few books stacked on the table. A rug was on the floor. A small spiral stairway led to a little alcove big enough for a person to stand in. Philippa grimaced. She'd bet there were peepholes through the queer portrait.

She went to the desk and picked up one of the books. Her hand stopped. There were crumbs on the desk. This room had been used recently. Hurriedly, she sat down at the desk and opened the drawers. They weren't locked. She supposed there was no need to lock drawers when they were in secret rooms.

Her heart raced a bit faster. Her letter to Lucien, rejecting his proposal, was there in the top drawer. It was proof Lucien used this room. But not any proof that would do Valerian good.

In the last drawer, she found a set of three diaries dating from the last three years. Philippa leafed through the first one, noting the date. The diary had been begun a few months before Cambourne's death. In fact, the diary seemed focused on his relationship with Cambourne to the exclusion of all else. No other events were recorded, no mention of any of the mundane issues that usually made up diaries.

Philippa flipped faster through the pages. She stared in horror at an entry one month before Cambourne's death.

> I believe I have the duke's trust and his wife's too, after two months in their social circle. It is time to set the scheme in motion.

Philippa stifled a gasp at the entry written on the day Cambourne had been injured. It had been no accident that the Duke had been caught in the shaft. The accident had been planned. Lucien had deliberately seen to John's murder.

Philippa steadied herself and forced herself to glance through the other two diaries. They were even worse. In them, Lucien outlined his plan and subsequent progress in currying her friendship. At the sight of one entry, Philippa felt physically ill.

> After a year or so of marriage, a horrible death will claim my dear beloved, leaving me a wealthy widower and next of kin when it comes to dividing up her estate.

Shock threatened to claim her. Her hands shook as she stared at the pages. Lucien had fooled her entirely. Never once had it occurred to her that Lucien was contemplating premeditated murder. She'd never suspected he'd been connected to the mine incident or Cambourne's death in anyway. *She had nearly married a murderer.*

She had to get out of the house. There was no telling how much the servants knew. Philippa forced herself to stand and gather up the books and carefully re-enter the library. Her legs trembled beneath her skirts. She gathered her strength. She had to look normal! She went back to the study and stuffed some paper in a random folder to create a decoy. If anyone asked if she'd found anything, she could show them the folder. Lilya was coming down the stairs, shaking her head in disappointment.

Philippa gave her a little smile as the butler came into the hall.

'There you are, your Grace. I've been looking for you. Did you find what you needed?'

Philippa held up her hastily assembled folder. 'Yes, we'll be on our way. Lucien will be anxious for us to catch him up.'

'You've found something!' Lilya exclaimed as they settled in the carriage.

'Yes,' Philippa said grimly, waiting for her racing pulse to slow. The discovery had shaken her and it had been all she could do to get them out of the house without acting suspiciously.

She handed Lilya one of the diaries. 'Once we get to London, we'll have something to bargain with. In his arrogance, Lucien has given us enough rope to hang him.'

Chapter Nineteen

After the long coach journey with far too much time to ponder the desperate situation she faced, Philippa was glad to see London. London meant Valerian and London meant action. She'd been idle for too long. A day out of Truro, the weather had conspired against them with a fierce deluge that managed to flood the roads and wipe out a bridge. They'd had to cool their heels at an inn, waiting for the roads to dry out. When it was possible to travel, they'd had to detour quite a way in order to find a serviceable bridge.

The three-day journey had turned into a long week. Now they were here. At last, she could do something.

She directed the driver to take her straight to Pendennys House instead of the Cambourne townhouse. She and Lilya would stay with Beldon. There would be safety in numbers and comfort too.

Night was falling and lights already burned their welcome from the Pendennys's window when the coachman opened the door and helped her down. Lilya followed her out, gazing about, wide-eyed at the magnificent homes lining the street. Philippa linked her arm through Lilya's. 'You'll come to know London as your own city. By next year, these houses will be well known to you.'

'I can hardly believe that. I never expected to be surrounded by mansions,' she breathed in awe, letting Philippa guide her up the steps while she stared.

Beldon was at home. At the knock, he came to the door himself. 'I thought it might be you. I've been on the lookout since yesterday,' Beldon said, wrapping Philippa in a genuine embrace. 'Are you well?'

'Yes, just tired. Lilya has been a great support. How is Valerian? Where is he? Did you petition for a house arrest?' Philippa stepped back, the questions that had occupied her mind during the slow journey tumbling out of her mouth.

'Come and sit. I'll ring for tea and tell you all the news if you're up to it. Are you sure you don't want to change first?'

Philippa shook her head. 'I've thought of nothing but Valerian for days now. I must have some news.'

Beldon led them to the music room and the three settled on the cluster of chairs near the fireplace. The room was warm and intimate. It eased Philippa's nerves simply to be there in a room full of long-ago memories of time spent here with her family, with Valerian.

'How was the journey?' Philippa asked the moment she was settled to Beldon's satisfaction.

'As good as it could be. He and I took turns keeping watch in the night. I bought kegs of ale to keep the guards affable. During the day I rode in the carriage with him. I didn't leave his side for a second out of worry that Lucien would take any opportunity.'

'I wish I could see him now,' Philippa whispered, staring at the pianoforte in the far corner. Valerian had spent hours at the instrument, playing for them after family dinners.

'No, Philippa,' Beldon said sharply. 'Valerian insists you don't visit.'

'I can't support that,' Philippa said. 'I want to see him. I cannot sit around in the house all day doing nothing.'

'You can send a letter. I'll take it when I go. Newgate is a filthy place even with my blunt greasing every step of the way.' Beldon was firm on this.

'Newgate!' Philippa exclaimed, horrified. She hadn't known. She supposed in her mind she'd speculated about the possibilities of where Lucien would take him, but she hadn't allowed her mind to grasp the full import of those speculations. Of course Lucien would push for Newgate. It was lawless and all the better suited for an accidental death, a stabbing, a poisoning. The guards would hardly care if there was enough money to blind them with.

'Yes,' Beldon said quietly. 'I've done everything I can, bought him every convenience they'd sell. He has his own small chamber. He has food from this house every day that I personally deliver myself.

Cooky fixes all his favourites. I've taken him clean clothes.'

Philippa studied her brother, seeing the signs of strain around his mouth and his eyes. Beldon had only been in London a week ahead of her, but it seemed an eternity separated them. In that time Beldon had been immersed in a dark world of experiences neither of them had ever thought to endure. She heard the unspoken 'but' at the end of his litany of activities. 'What is it?'

'There's an initial hearing scheduled for tomorrow to determine if there's any substance to the charges. Valerian's friends in the government are outraged. At least they've managed to make it a very quiet affair. It'll be at Whitehall. Lucien's father is on the committee.'

Lilya gasped beside her. Beldon reached across to place a comforting hand on the girl's arm. 'We will be vigilant, Miss Stefanov. Valerian has a friend on the committee as well.'

'We haven't come this far to be thwarted now. I have faith in English justice,' Philippa assured her. She better understood Lilya's life after spending so much time with her on the road. She understood Lilya's reaction. In the girl's country, it was unlikely someone survived prison or hearings or trials. They were all slow precursors to the gallows.

Philippa wished she felt as confident as her brave words. She grasped the full import of Beldon's news. A hearing would bring everything to a head. If the committee dismissed the charges, Lucien would have to act quickly if he meant to have Valerian fall victim to an accident while in Newgate. If the charges stuck, then there was a very real chance Valerian would stand trial.

'Can we attend the hearing?'

'I might be able to arrange it,' Beldon said.

'How is Valerian taking all this?' Philippa asked. It was the question she wanted answered most, but the one she wanted to ask least. How had he taken the letter? Did he blame her?

'He is doing as well as can be expected. He stays on guard constantly. He knows what the real danger is at this point. But it is wearing on him. I stay as long as I can each day so that he can sleep. Sometimes we play chess, we talk. I've engaged a discreet, highly recommended barrister and he's come to meet Valerian several times in case he's needed. But at night, I have to leave. He doesn't sleep at night for fear Lucien will send his assassins in the dark. I can't say the fear is unfounded. And I think, too, that he fears what he may dream.'

'I wish I could help him.' Philippa felt tears fill her eyes. It was dark now outside and she wanted to be with Valerian, to throw her arms about him and take his worries away. Right now, across town, he was beginning his long, lonely night vigil, wondering if this would be the night he had to fight for his life.

'You do help him, Phil. He was appreciative of your letter,' Beldon said cryptically.

Lilya took the cue. 'I think I'll go on up and unpack. I'll find someone to show me my room. You go ahead and talk to your brother, Philippa. I'll be fine.'

'A baby, Phil? Are you sure?' Beldon whispered fiercely as the door shut behind Lilya.

Philippa nodded. 'I didn't want to wait to tell him in case I waited too long. It seems Valerian and I have an unfortunate habit of holding off on sharing until it's too late.'

'Valerian was thrilled, but anxious,' Beldon said honestly. 'He doesn't want his child born under the banner of such nasty events.'

Philippa's hand went to her flat stomach. 'These events will be long past when this child arrives.'

'Let's hope so. Did you find anything in Truro?'

'More than I wanted to find, I think,' Philippa said sombrely. 'I have diaries Lucien kept about Cambourne, and about me. He's schemed to get control of the Cambourne mines for years and he's willing to stop at nothing to get them.'

Beldon nodded grimly. 'Then we have something to bargain with when the time comes.'

Philippa dressed carefully the next morning in a dress of flowered blue delaine. True to his word, Beldon had secured the right for them to be present at the hearing. She wasn't sure how he'd done it. But she'd heard him leave last night to go 'out' and he hadn't been home when she'd retired at midnight.

The carriage ride to Whitehall took twenty minutes. They were expected and an escort hurried them inside into a basement room hidden deep in the building. Philippa doubted she could find her way out on her own. She and Beldon were given chairs at the back of the room and told to remain silent. They were in no way to interrupt the proceedings.

The committee came in and took their places. Three of them were ministers from various departments of the Foreign Office. Philippa recognised Lucien's father, Viscount Montfort, among them, an older, chiselled rendition of Lucien at sixty. She didn't know the other two members, but Beldon whispered they were from the Home Office, one of them a particular friend of Val's. Valerian's barrister was there as well. Even though it wasn't technically a legal proceeding, Beldon had insisted.

Valerian was brought in at five minutes past the hour and Philippa's heart was in her throat at the sight of him. He was dressed well for a man who'd had to dress without his valet. His clothes were clean, and his hair was well ordered. But his features were haggard, his skin pale. For a man who loved the outdoors, she was starting to realise just what an agony the week in Newgate had been.

But his eyes were sharp as they swept the room, assessing the committee, taking the measure of each man present. His roving gaze fell on her in the back of the dim room. Philippa sat up straighter, fighting the urge to acknowledge him in some way. She didn't dare call out for fear of being dismissed. But she did hazard a wave of her hand in hopes that he would see that she wore the ring he'd given her. In fact, she hadn't taken it off since Lucien had come to take him away. She thought she saw the minutest of smiles pass across his lips.

* * *

Philippa was here. Her presence shocked him utterly. Valerian had not expected it. Indeed, he was beleaguered by conflicting emotions at the very sight of her. He'd hungered for her steady presence all week, filling his lonely night-vigils with the mental pictures he had of her and the new ones he conjured up of her growing big with their child. That news had overwhelmed him with joy in spite of the darkness he faced.

This morning, he thrilled to the sight of her serene beauty lighting up the back of the room, knowing that such loveliness was a mere foil for the intelligence and temper that lay beneath the surface. The sight of his ring on her finger meant more to him in that moment than she could probably guess or understand.

But now that she was here, he'd rather she not be subjected to what the hearing would reveal. She would leave here firm in the knowledge that he was a tarnished hero, if a hero at all. He'd done his country's bidding, but it had often been grim work. He hoped it had been worth it, that his services in all their forms would be enough to offset the death of Turkish soldiers by his hand.

Valerian knew how important it was that he fight these charges with everything at his disposal. The longer he remained in Newgate, the longer Lucien held the upper hand. He didn't worry so much for himself. In a fair fight, he could manage Lucien's henchmen. It was Philippa for whom he had the most concern. The longer he was imprisoned, the longer she was unguarded. Of course, she had

Beldon, but Beldon could not be in two places at once. Beldon could not watch them both.

He sat straight in his chair, refusing to look ashamed of the charges as they were read.

'What do you have to say to these charges?' the chairman of the committee asked, setting down the papers.

Valerian speared him with a sharp glance. 'I rescued two innocent children from certain death, one of them a babe only a few months old. Since when is it England's policy to make war on women and children who have no say in the politics and treaties of men?

'I for one could not countenance such wanton and unnecessary violence. They were of no threat to us or our ambitions in the region. Yet the Turks were allowed to destroy their homes and take their lives. I do not believe any of you gentlemen would stand by and watch that type of slaughter take place if you had the means to stop it.' Valerian looked each of them in the eye. 'Am I wrong? Has English chivalry been bought for gold and trade routes?'

The men shifted uncomfortably in their seats. He'd hit a mark with them. No one would want to be branded a coward and they'd certainly appear less than saintly if they argued it was acceptable to slay women and children, all for the sake of a passage to India.

Viscount Montfort blazed at the insinuations. 'You paint the truth too lightly, St Just. You didn't save random children on a battlefield. The children you saved were the get of rebel leader Dimitri

Stefanov. He worked hand in glove with the secret society, Filiki Eteria, to fight against the Turks. You befriended Stefanov's family and remained in contact with them after British negotiations with the Phanariots ceased.' Montfort pointed an accusing finger at him. 'You were the last visitor to see Stefanov alive before his execution. You stand as guardian to his surviving children.'

'I was,' Valerian answered smoothly. 'Children are children, it hardly matters who their fathers are. They are all worthy of our protection.'

The chairman glared at Montfort. 'These proceedings must be managed in an orderly fashion. We will get to everything in time, but we must not resort to outbursts.'

Valerian's barrister intervened. 'Viscount St Just has an exemplary record of loyal service to England in the discharge of his duties abroad.' The man skillfully began laying out Valerian's career. 'He was responsible for critical negotiations in Morea that mitigated the civil war there…'

The list was long and Valerian was well familiar with it. From his work in Port Navarino to prevent an Egyptian invasion of Morea, to the sinking of the Egyptian navy, which ended Egypt's bid for power in the area, to the Phanariot issue and ultimately his latest participation in the London Protocols, he'd participated deeply in what had once seemed to him a noble calling.

Even after the harsh realities of his work had become apparent to him, he'd stayed involved, no longer for the sake of lofty philosophical principles, but in the hopes that he could do something practical. He no longer ascribed to the battle cry of 'make the world England' but to his own heartfelt calling— make the world better.

The barrister had set down his list. 'I submit to the committee that this is a man who hasn't a dishonourable bone in his body, who has spent his life serving England most nobly. To even suggest that what happened on the battlefield in Negush is akin to treason is an absurdity and waste of our time.'

Valerian watched the group for a reaction. Beldon had found a deuce fine barrister. He almost believed his work had been useful once the man had finished with the list. The group seemed to think that, too, except for Montfort.

'We are splitting hairs over an issue that can only be black and white. We cannot start forming grey areas where national security is concerned,' Montfort began. 'We cannot begin establishing different standards for different situations. He killed allies who were acting in British interests. He did it deliberately in an attempt to protect the enemy. By doing so, he put a rebel's concern above the needs of his country. If he'd killed Englishmen to save the children of rebels, I think you'd feel quite differently about where the line is drawn in the sand. Our sands cannot shift.'

One of the ministers nodded his head slightly and Valerian began to wonder how many of these men Montfort had in his pocket. Montfort meant to take the high ground and argue from a philosophical standpoint. It would come down to philosophies against practicalities. Reality against theory. Honour against dishonour, and what constituted either.

'If that is all, the committee will deliberate,' the chairman said. 'Viscount St Just, you'll be informed of our decision as soon as it is made. It could be hours, or days.'

Valerian rose and nodded to the group. 'I thank you for your time, gentlemen.'

A guard came forwards to escort him from the room. He fought back his disappointment. He couldn't allow himself to think of going back to the tiny room. If he dwelled on it, he thought he might go mad. The precarious nature of his safety while at Newgate made it impossible to wander about the yards. Even with Beldon's presence, he felt it was too dangerous to risk his friend. It would be all too easy for one or both of them to fall prey to a subtle knife as they walked passed. He wouldn't allow the committee, most of all Montfort, to see how the thought of going back affected him. He didn't dare look back at Philippa and Beldon. He didn't have the mental fortitude left to manage that as well. More than he wanted daylight and sun and clean air, he wanted Philippa.

In the hall, there was a patter of heels purposefully clicking on the flagstones. Philippa's voice called out in its most imperious tone. 'Guard, I'll need a minute with the viscount.'

'I'm afraid I can't allow that. I have orders...' the guard stammered, clearly weighing the haughty woman in front of him against the orders of his supervisor at Newgate who was across town, tucked away in his office fleecing bribe money from unfortunate patrons.

'There's a room right here. I just want a moment,' Philippa said, gesturing to the small room off to her left. She didn't wait for the guard's approval. Instead, she took Valerian's hand and marched into the room. She slammed the door in the guard's face, hearing him protest and then Beldon's smooth tones reassuring him all would be well.

Philippa threw herself into his arms, her own arms going about his neck, and kissed him with all the emotion she owned. He met the kiss with his own intensity, his mouth pressing hard against hers, hungry and desperate, and yet somewhere in its depths was reassurance. In spite of all that had happened, their love still stood.

'Val, I've missed you,' Philippa gasped, touching his face as they drew apart, tracing the lines of his worry with her hands.

'You're well? And the baby?' His hand dropped to her waist, framing her stomach with his fingers as if he could feel the baby already.

'We're well. There won't be anything to see for a few months yet.' Philippa gave a tremulous laugh.

'I am so happy about it,' Valerian whispered. 'Promise me, you'll keep the child safe. Don't do anything foolish, Philippa, promise me.' His voice was urgent, desperate to wring a vow from her.

'I won't need to. You'll be free as soon as the committee makes their decision,' Philippa said brightly.

Valerian shook his head. 'I think Montfort will buy a trial.'

'Then I will go to Lucien. I have enough to sway him, I think,' Philippa said, trying to be confident against Valerian's dire words. She rapidly explained what she'd uncovered in the diaries.

Valerian's eyes filled with concern. 'Philippa, you cannot toy with Lucien Canton. If you threaten him, it will be open war. Do not confront him alone. Take Beldon with you and the Watch if you must.'

The guard banged on the door, Beldon's charm having finally worn out. Philippa kissed him hard one last time. 'I love you, Val. Nothing will change that.'

Philippa clenched her fists in the folds of her skirt, using all her willpower not to chase after him or cry as the guard led him away. A terrible foreboding filled her as she watched Valerian stoically accept the handcuffs and was ushered down one of Whitehall's many secret hallways. If he didn't get out of Newgate tonight, he might not get out at all, at least not alive. It was time to act. In fact, she felt that she had little time to lose.

Chapter Twenty

Heavy booted footsteps pounded up the stone corridor of Newgate. Valerian heard them and was instantly on alert. It had only been four hours since the hearing. Surely they hadn't made a decision already? He rose from the cot, tense and ready. It was too soon for a decision and slightly too early for Beldon to come with a supper basket. But the footsteps were definitely for him. They came to a stop outside his heavy, barred door. The jangle of keys sounded and then a thick metal key clunked in the lock.

Valerian sprang behind the door. If Lucien had sent an assassin with a gun, he wouldn't get a clear shot. That was Valerian's greatest concern, that the assassin would come with a gun and he wouldn't have a chance to fight for himself. The door would open, a shot would be fired before he even knew who was there.

The door opened. A man dressed as a guard

entered the room. Valerian didn't recognise him. He was not one of the usual men who watched his room. 'What do you want?' Valerian growled. The man was burly with a barrel chest and nose that looked as if it was used to being broken. He looked a menace.

'You're free to go. Your release is in my pocket if you're man enough to take it from me.' A blade flashed in his hand from a concealed sheath in his sleeve. The sharp edge glinted dangerously.

Valerian assessed the situation in an instant. The committee must have decided before Montfort could stand against them in full force. He was free, but Lucien couldn't allow that to happen so this man had been sent to silence him once and for all. His small knife was hidden in his pallet, so he had no weapon to counter the knife, except his own brute strength. The man clearly looked to outweigh him. His best defence would be to disarm the man and seize control of the weapon.

Valerian tensed into a fighter's position, ready to take the impact of the man's lunge. If the man wanted to fight, he'd have to make the first move. Valerian was not going to risk serious injury by launching himself at an armed combatant.

They circled each other in half-crouches, the man making jabbing feints with the blade, emphasising just how small the room was. 'I can walk all day,' Valerian taunted as they completed another circle of each other. 'Why don't you come and do what you've been paid to do? What's the going rate on killing viscounts these days? I hope it will be enough to start over in exile. Once Baron Pendennys arrives, you'll be caught.'

The man snarled, 'Then I better make short work of you.' He lunged, the knife making a downward slashing motion intended to catch Valerian in the shoulder. Valerian was ready for it, his arm going up in instant reflex and his hand gripping the wrist of the knife hand with the full force of his strength. Valerian grunted and used his power to push the man back to the wall, banging the knife hand against the stone, in hopes of shaking the knife free from his grip.

The man kicked out, catching Valerian in the shins, but the kick had very little impact since they were locked so closely together. Valerian gave a final pound and the knife clattered to the floor. He landed a jab to the man's stomach and dived for the blade.

His assailant was faster than he'd anticipated. He'd no sooner got his hand around the knife handle than the man jumped him from behind. He had no time to roll over and slash with the knife. He was effectively imprisoned underneath. A kidney punch caused him to cry out, followed by another. He could not lie there and do nothing.

The man's weight was formidable, but Valerian found the strength to heave himself up to his knees, slashing blindly with the knife to distract the man. He had some luck. The blade met with muscle and his attacker cried out, loosening his hold on Valerian long enough for Valerian to fling him off and regain his feet. He came up fast, ready to fight, ready to kill. The man rushed him, sensing his chance for victory slipping away.

Valerian felt a stinging sensation travel down his arm, cloth ripped. A red stain spread on the material. The bastard had another knife! He could see blood on the other man now, at his thigh where his blade had made contact. The man slashed at his face, Valerian reached out and grabbed the knife hand with his left. In the moment he held the assassin's blade at bay, he drove his own blade home. The man gasped and collapsed, hatred and disbelief frozen on his fading features. The fight was over.

'I guess I was man enough,' Valerian snarled, the rage of the fight starting to ebb from him. He straddled the man's form and rooted in his pocket for the release. He found it sealed and tied with a red ribbon. He tore it open, hardly daring to believe it was over.

'Val!' Beldon rushed into the room, dropping the dinner basket he carried. 'What's happened?'

'I'm free.' Valerian felt himself shudder from the shock. 'Now we can deal with Canton. He sent his man with the message. I wasn't supposed to leave here.' He drew a deep breath. 'Philippa won't have to do anything foolish.'

'I am afraid it's too late for that,' Beldon said, realisation starting to dawn. 'She doesn't know you're free. She's gone to see Canton, to bargain with him.'

Philippa faced Lucien Canton over the walnut desk in his town-house study. 'Lucien, I have come to bargain with you for Valerian's freedom.'

Lucien's mouth twisted into a sneer. 'Bargain or beg, my dear? I can't imagine what you have to bargain with. Your body, perhaps?' His gaze raked her form in a slow, deliberate perusal. 'If so, I am not interested in used goods.'

Philippa refused to be cowed by coarse innuendo. 'I have something better, I think. An even exchange. Your freedom for his.'

Lucien's eyes narrowed. 'Whatever are you talking about?' His voice protested innocence, but his narrow gaze suggested he was concerned.

Philippa took her courage in both hands. 'I am talking about how you plotted to kill Cambourne. There was no real accident in the mine. It was deliberately sabotaged and you planned it, right down to outlining it in your personal diary.'

'Do you have the books, then? It's quite intrepid of you to break into my home and steal from me, but anything for love, eh, Philippa?' Lucien said coldly. 'Still, your threat is empty and your bravado is desperate. St Just got in my way. I will not tolerate his interference. He is going to pay. It's too late to change that. I expect any minute my hired assassin will be paying him a visit, if he hasn't already. The man's formidable. St Just doesn't stand a chance. The irony is that the committee dropped the charges. St Just's release is in my man's pocket. He may be dead already.' Lucien sighed with mock pity. 'But you, Philippa, I could still save and we can forget about your little foray into thievery.'

Lucien reached into the top drawer of his desk and drew out a sheaf of papers. 'This is from when I had a more optimistic outlook on our relationship. Perhaps I became cynical too soon? Now, I have a deal for you. This is a marriage contract. Marry me,

sign over the mines and save your social re-
spectability and your social standing. You will not be
dragged down by Valerian's scandal. I doubt anyone
will much care to have the political backing of a suspected traitor's wife. It would be a shame to see all
your hard work with mining schools and mining
reform fall into ignominy simply because you made
a poor decision in marriage. We were friends once—
I am confident we can be again.'

Philippa picked up the contract. 'You were never
my friend.' She tore the contract in half and threw it
on the desk. 'I would rather be dead than see myself
married to the likes of you, since that's what you had
planned all along.'

The rashness of her words was punctuated by the
ominous click of a pistol's cocking motion. 'That
can be arranged. Since you know about that little
addendum to my plan, I am left with no choices,
Philippa.' Lucien raised a small silver pistol from
behind the desk. It was pointed at her. 'I had rather
hoped this would come later instead of sooner.'

Philippa forced herself to breathe deeply and to stay
calm. She couldn't think about the baby, about
Valerian, or about Valerian's warning that she not
confront Lucien alone. She could only allow herself to
think about Lucien and what she could do to stay alive.

She managed a believable laugh. 'Are you going
to shoot a woman in your town house and expect to
get away with it? It's still daylight. You're usually
cleverer than that. Besides, if I die, you can't find the
diaries. Only I and one other know where they are.'

'I don't have to shoot you. I'd rather not. Murder

is rather drastic.' Lucien waved the pistol towards a chair. 'Have a seat. I have another contract here. This one is a bill of sale between you and me. It's for the mines. The price is fair, at least for the record. You and I know what the real price is. That money will never show up in your bank account, but I will let you walk out of here.'

Philippa stared at the documents. She'd not thought to bring a weapon. She'd thought her threat would be enough.

'Here's a pen.' Lucien handed her the instrument, towering over her. 'I've been generous with you out of a sense of misplaced affection.'

Philippa's eyes narrowed. 'Your affection has never been misplaced.' Perhaps she ought to take the deal and live to fight another day. But then she thought of Beldon's words the time she'd suggested giving Lucien the mines. She thought of Valerian's honour and all that he'd risked over the years to live by his code. It gave her the strength to stand up, toe to toe with Lucien Canton.

'I won't sign the bill of sale. I won't give you permission to take what isn't yours. Nor will I give you permission to start a career of blackmail. This won't end until you possess every mining asset Cambourne ever owned. I see your game and I won't play.'

'You're beautiful in a temper, my dear. Perhaps there's another game you'd play to save your mortal soul?' Lucien whispered, his eyes going to her lips. 'I'd play that game with you.'

Philippa lowered her eyelids to hide her thoughts, trying not to flinch at Lucien's hands on her waist, trying not to think about the gun he held laxly in one hand as he began a lazy seduction. This was her chance, a chance to grab the gun, a chance to flee out of the door and into the street. If only she could make Lucien believe.

'Open your mouth, darling.' Lucien whispered, but they were not love words, they were commands. She did, trying to guess what he wanted. His kiss was rough, bruising against her mouth. Reflexively, her body tensed in resistance at the hard pressure of his member against her. He held her tightly, aroused by her instinctive struggle.

'Oh, yes, don't make it too easy,' he moaned, his eyes dangerous glints of malicious desire. 'I like a challenge.'

He had her against the edge of the desk, the hard wood biting into her back. Her resistance was real and it seemed to inflame him further. With one arm, he swept the desk clear of ledgers, laying the gun on the corner of the desk to force her on to the surface. Philippa saw it out of the corner of her eye, not daring to look at it fully lest she give away her intentions. She let him lay her back on the surface. The gun was closer now, her fingers could almost stretch out and claim it. She wriggled, hoping to inch closer to it.

Lucien's hips pressed into hers, grinding out his rising desire. She fought back the urge to give into tears. She'd been so foolish to think a man capable of Lucien's evil could be stopped by the threat of blackmail. That was his speciality, not hers.

His lips were on hers, hard and unrelenting, his

body stretched over her, his hands in her hair, painfully pulling it free. She reached out her hand and found success. Philippa closed her hand over the gun and brought it up with a sickening thud against Lucien's head.

He jerked back howling, dizzy with surprise and pain. 'What the hell!' Philippa shoved with all her might, sending him toppling to the floor. She sprang up from the desk and ran for the door. But Lucien was not done.

He grabbed a handful of her skirt as she sprinted past. She tripped, half-falling, then half-running to put the sofa between them as a barrier. Lucien grabbed up a vase and threw it at her. Philippa screamed, ducking as crystal shattered against the wall.

Like a miracle, she heard someone call her name. She screamed again. This time the door burst open, cracking against the wall so hard it fell off its hinges. Valerian was there, followed by a half dozen members of the Watch, and Beldon.

'Stop where you are, sir!' the captain yelled. 'Is that the man?' He turned to Valerian for identification, who nodded. 'Mr Canton, you are under arrest for the murder of the Duke of Cambourne and for attempted blackmail.'

Lucien went rabid. 'You have no proof. Those are not easy accusations.'

'We have diaries, supplied by the Dowager Duchess of Cambourne, that are written in your hand, outlining your premeditation of the crime and your intention to swindle the Duchess out of her holdings, either through marriage or blackmail, and also including over-exaggerating charges of treason against Viscount St Just.'

Lucien paled. Then he roared and lunged for Philippa over the sofa. 'Bitch!' She was no match for his angry strength and she went down beneath him, the gun sliding out of her hand and beyond her reach.

She heard Valerian yelling, 'Get off her!' And then Lucien's crushing weight was lifted from her. Valerian and Lucien fell to the ground, wrestling, punching. They were too closely engaged for anyone to intervene. Valerian had the advantage, landing punch after punch, but, in one desperate move, Lucien had the gun.

Philippa screamed a warning. Valerian's arm reached out with lightning speed and grappled with the gun hand. But the gun was cocked and volatile. It fired and both men lay unmoving. 'Help me! Someone help me!' Philippa was down next to Valerian in an instant, shoving him away from Lucien's body. 'No, no, no, no.' There was blood everywhere, on his shirt, his face—she couldn't be sure it was not all his. 'Val, please wake up.'

'I'm awake,' Valerian groaned.

'Are you hurt?' She started searching his body through his clothes, frantic over what she might find.

'Miss, it's the other one,' the captain said quietly, motioning for men to join him at Lucien's still form. 'He took the bullet.' The captain shook his head. 'He's gone.'

Valerian struggled to sit up. 'Are you all right, Philippa?'

'Yes. Yes, we're both all right,' she said but she

was shaking and she couldn't hold back her tears. It was all suddenly too much. Lucien had died in front of her. One moment, he'd been living among them; the next, he'd simply ceased to be. It could just have easily been Valerian. Valerian's arms were about her and he cradled her to him, murmuring reassurances.

The captain was efficient, but it still took the better part of the evening to wrap up loose ends and make statements. At nine o'clock the captain shut his notebook. 'We have all we need, my lord. Thank you for your patience. You may all go home. I'm sure it's been a very trying day. We will let you know if anything further is required.'

Philippa let Valerian lead her to his coach, which had stood waiting for them. The afternoon and early evening had been a blur of repeating stories and events. She was only just now able to shut out the horrors and appreciate the joys of the day. Valerian was free. The last threat that had stood in the way of their happiness had been removed.

She snuggled against Valerian's shoulder. 'What shall we do now? After all this excitement?'

Valerian looked down at her, a smile starting in his green eyes. 'We go home.'

'I've waited a long time to hear that.'

'Just as long as I've waited to say it, my love.' Valerian pressed a kiss to the top of her head and held her close. They might be days from Roseland, but Philippa knew she was home already.

Epilogue

1 January 1831

Valerian Inglemoore, the Viscount St Just, had a secret, a joyful secret that caused him to smile unceasingly as he stood with his wife and four-week-old son in front of the assembled congregation of St Justus's for the baptism of his child. He was desperately in love with his wife and she was in love with him.

That wasn't the secret. He doubted he could have kept his bliss hidden from anyone for long. He was all too aware that he wore his heart on his sleeve when it came to Philippa and his new family. Valerian's eyes flicked to the front row where Lilya and Constantine sat. In the span of a year, he'd become a husband and a father to two boys and one beautiful young woman preparing to take on London in the spring.

His life was full. But that wasn't the secret either. A year ago on New Year's Eve, he'd silently vowed to court Philippa and win back her trust in him so that his life could be complete. That was his secret.

His resolution had been fulfilled, although not with ease. He and Philippa had done battle with the past and the present for the sake of their love. Now, there were no more secrets between them.

Philippa passed the baby to him, all blankets and dark hair in his arms. He passed the baby to Beldon, who stood as godfather to little Aidan Alexei. Beldon said the words easily and the ceremony was over.

There was mingling afterwards, everyone crowding the altar to get a good look at Roseland's new heir. Valerian watched Lilya and Beldon exchange a quiet look apart from the crowd, a knowing smile spreading across his face.

Philippa elbowed him gently. 'What are you thinking with that wicked grin on your face?'

'I am thinking that everyone deserves to be as happy we are.'

* * * * *

'I've found her.'

Max froze.

It was what he'd been waiting for since June, but now—now he was almost afraid to voice the question. His heart stalling, he leaned slowly back in his chair and scoured the investigator's face for clues. 'Where?' he asked, and his voice sounded rough and unused, like a rusty hinge.

'In Suffolk. She's living in a cottage.'

Living. His heart crashed back to life, and he sucked in a long, slow breath. All these months he'd feared—

'Is she well?'

'Yes, she's well.'

He had to force himself to ask the next question. 'Alone?'

The man paused. 'No. The cottage belongs to a man called John Blake. He's working away at the moment, but he comes and goes.'

God. He felt sick. So sick he hardly registered the next few words, but then gradually they sank in. 'She's got *what?*'

'Babies. Twin girls. They're eight months old.'

'Eight—?' he echoed under his breath. 'They must be his.'

He was thinking out loud, but the P.I. heard and corrected him.

'Apparently not. I gather they're hers. She's been there since mid-January last year, and they were born during the summer—June, the woman in the post office thought. She was more than helpful. I think there's been a certain amount of speculation about their relationship.'

He'd just bet there had. God, he was going to kill her. Or Blake. Maybe both of them.

'Of course, looking at the dates, she was presumably pregnant when she left you, so they could be yours, or she could have been having an affair with this Blake character before…'

He glared at the unfortunate P.I. 'Just stick to your job. I can do the math,' he snapped, swallowing the unpalatable possibility that she'd been unfaithful to him before she'd left. 'Where is she? I want the address.'

'It's all in here,' the man said, sliding a large envelope across the desk to him. 'With my invoice.'

'I'll get it seen to. Thank you.'

'If there's anything else you need, Mr Gallagher, any further information—'

'I'll be in touch.'

'The woman in the post office told me Blake was away at the moment, if that helps,' he added quietly, and opened the door.

Max stared down at the envelope, hardly daring to open it, but when the door clicked softly shut behind the P.I., he eased up the flap, tipped it and felt his breath jam in his throat as the photos spilled out over the desk.

Oh, lord, she looked gorgeous. Different, though. It took him a moment to recognise her, because she'd grown her hair, and it was tied back in a ponytail, making her look younger and somehow freer. The blond highlights were gone, and it was back to its natural soft golden-brown, with a little curl in the end of the ponytail that he wanted to thread his finger through and tug, just gently, to draw her back to him.

Crazy. She'd put on a little weight, but it suited her. She looked well and happy and beautiful, but oddly, considering how desperate he'd been for news of her for the past year—one year, three weeks and two days, to be exact—it wasn't only Julia who held his attention after the initial shock. It was the babies sitting side by side in a supermarket trolley. Two identical and absolutely beautiful little girls.

* * * * *

When Max Gallagher hires a P.I. to find his estranged wife, Julia, he discovers she's not alone—she has twin baby girls, and they might be his. Now workaholic Max has just two weeks to prove that he can be a wonderful husband and father to the family he wants to treasure.

Look for TWO LITTLE MIRACLES
by Caroline Anderson, available February 2009
from Harlequin Romance®.

CELEBRATE
60 YEARS
OF PURE READING PLEASURE
WITH **HARLEQUIN®**!

We'll be spotlighting a different series
every month throughout 2009
to celebrate our 60th anniversary.

Look for Harlequin® Romance in February!

**Harlequin® Romance is celebrating by showering
you with Diamond Brides in February 2009.**

Six stories that promise to bring a touch of sparkle to
your life, with diamond proposals and dazzling weddings,
sparkling brides and gorgeous grooms!

Collect all six books in February 2009,
featuring *Two Little Miracles* by Caroline Anderson.

*Look for the Diamond Brides miniseries
in February 2009!*

www.eHarlequin.com   HRBRIDES09

HARLEQUIN® Romance®

This February the Harlequin® Romance series
will feature six Diamond Brides stories featuring
diamond proposals and gorgeous grooms.

Share your dream wedding proposal and you could WIN!

The most romantic entry will win a diamond
necklace and will inspire a proposal in one of
our upcoming Diamond Grooms books in 2010.

In 100 words or less, tell us the most romantic
way that you dream of being proposed to.

For more information, and to enter
the Diamond Brides Proposal contest, please visit
www.DiamondBridesProposal.com

Or mail your entry to us at:
IN THE U.S.: 3010 Walden Ave., P.O. Box 9069, Buffalo, NY 14269-9069
IN CANADA: 225 Duncan Mill Road, Don Mills, ON M3B 3K9

REQUEST YOUR FREE BOOKS!

Harlequin® Historical
Historical Romantic Adventure!

2 FREE NOVELS PLUS 2 **FREE GIFTS!**

YES! Please send me 2 FREE Harlequin® Historical novels and my 2 FREE gifts (gifts are worth about $10). After receiving them, if I don't wish to receive any more books, I can return the shipping statement marked "cancel". If I don't cancel, I will receive 6 brand-new novels every month and be billed just $4.94 per book in the U.S. or $5.49 per book in Canada, plus 25¢ shipping and handling per book and applicable taxes, if any*. That's a savings of 20% off the cover price! I understand that accepting the 2 free books and gifts places me under no obligation to buy anything. I can always return a shipment and cancel at any time. Even if I never buy another book, the two free books and gifts are mine to keep forever.

246 HDN ERUM   349 HDN ERUA

Name	(PLEASE PRINT)	
Address		Apt. #
City	State/Prov.	Zip/Postal Code

Signature (if under 18, a parent or guardian must sign)

Mail to the **Harlequin Reader Service:**
IN U.S.A.: P.O. Box 1867, Buffalo, NY 14240-1867
IN CANADA: P.O. Box 609, Fort Erie, Ontario L2A 5X3

Not valid to current subscribers of Harlequin Historical books.

Want to try two free books from another line?
Call 1-800-873-8635 or visit www.morefreebooks.com.

* Terms and prices subject to change without notice. N.Y. residents add applicable sales tax. Canadian residents will be charged applicable provincial taxes and GST. Offer not valid in Quebec. This offer is limited to one order per household. All orders subject to approval. Credit or debit balances in a customer's account(s) may be offset by any other outstanding balance owed by or to the customer. Please allow 4 to 6 weeks for delivery. Offer available while quantities last.

Your Privacy: Harlequin Books is committed to protecting your privacy. Our Privacy Policy is available online at www.eHarlequin.com or upon request from the Reader Service. From time to time we make our lists of customers available to reputable third parties who may have a product or service of interest to you. If you would prefer we not share your name and address, please check here. ☐

HH08R

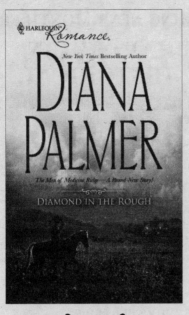

DIAMOND IN THE ROUGH

John Callister is a millionaire rancher, yet when he meets
lovely Sassy Peale and she thinks he's a cowboy, he goes along
with her misconception. He's had enough of gold diggers,
and this is a chance to be valued for himself, not his money.
But when Sassy finds out the truth, she feels John was merely
playing with her. John will have to convince her that he's truly
the man she fell in love with—a diamond in the rough.

**THE MEN OF MEDICINE RIDGE—a brand-new miniseries
set in the wilds of Montana!**

Available April 2009 wherever you buy books.

COMING NEXT MONTH FROM

HARLEQUIN®
HISTORICAL

- **WANTED IN ALASKA**
by **Kate Bridges**
(Western)
Outlaw Quinn Rowlan kidnaps a nurse—only to discover he's got
the wrong woman! Desperate to feel proud about his life once
again, he needs Autumn MacNeil's help to clear his name in town.
But Quinn had never expected a curvy, blond, ambitious singer to make
him feel so whole again....

- **THE RAKE'S UNCONVENTIONAL MISTRESS**
by **Juliet Landon**
(Regency)
Miss Letitia Boyce didn't begrudge her sisters the pick of London's
available bachelors. She'd chosen her own path, and book learning and
marriage rarely mixed. Notorious rakehell Lord Seton Rayne had every
heiress hurling herself at him. So his sudden kissing of unconventional
Letitia took them both by surprise....

- **THE EARL'S UNTOUCHED BRIDE**
by **Annie Burrows**
(Regency)
Charles Fawley, Earl of Walton, never thought he'd fall for plain
Heloise Bergeron in Paris, the city of romance! But Heloise needed
to escape a vile betrothal, so they married quickly. And then Charles
discovered just how untouched his French bride really was....

- **THE VIKING'S DEFIANT BRIDE**
by **Joanna Fulford**
(Viking)
Since her father's death, Elgiva needs protection more than ever.
When a brooding dark-haired Viking warrior rescues her young nephew,
he looks at her and her fate is sealed.... Earl Wulfrum
has come to conquer, and he takes the beautiful, spirited woman
as his bride—but now he must break down the walls of his defiant
bride's heart!